To Lesley
Happy Reading.
Emily Royal
x

RODERICK'S WIDOW

London Libertines, Book Three

by Emily Royal

ARE YOU SIGNED UP FOR DRAGONBLADE'S BLOG?

You'll get the latest news and information on exclusive giveaways, exclusive excerpts, coming releases, sales, free books, cover reveals and more.

Check out our complete list of authors, too!

No spam, no junk. That's a promise!

Sign Up Here

www.dragonbladepublishing.com

Dearest Reader;

Thank you for your support of a small press. At Dragonblade Publishing, we strive to bring you the highest quality Historical Romance from the some of the best authors in the business. Without your support, there is no 'us', so we sincerely hope you adore these stories and find some new favorite authors along the way.

Happy Reading!

CEO, Dragonblade Publishing

Additional Dragonblade books by Author Emily Royal

London Libertines
Henry's Bride, Book 1
Hawthorne's Wife, Book 2
Roderick's Widow, Book 3

★★★ Please visit Dragonblade's website for a full list of books and authors. Sign up for Dragonblade's blog for sneak peeks, interviews, and more: ★★★
www.dragonbladepublishing.com

PROLOGUE

Sussex Gardens, London
July 1814

"NO, ALICE, I refuse to believe it. You love me. I know you do!"

"I'm sorry, Ross." Alice turned her head to conceal her expression. "I've reflected upon my error in judgement."

"Your *error in judgement?*"

Alice bit her lip, letting the sharp sting conquer the ache in her heart. The silence stretched, punctuated by wind in the trees, whispers to admonish her.

At length, he issued a sharp sigh. "Have the decency, madam, to look at me while you break our engagement."

Her chest tightened at the hard edge to his voice, and she turned to face the darkness in his gray eyes.

"I take it I have a rival," he said. "My lack of a title renders me unworthy of Viscount de Grecy's daughter."

Her skin prickled at Papa's name. The bruises hidden by the uncomfortably long sleeves of her dress were still fresh from his education on how to be a dutiful daughter.

"Is it Roderick Markham?"

She remained silent.

He narrowed his eyes. "You are to be congratulated in securing the heir to a dukedom. Forgive my folly in believing the Honorable Alice de Grecy was more than an insipid, soulless, little hunter of titles."

Insipid. Soulless...

Had he added *weak* to her catalogue of faults, he might have penetrated the hard shell she'd erected around herself to prepare for this interview. Weakness had driven her to this—her weakness to withstand Papa.

In her dreams, she'd imagined Ross sweeping her into his arms and carrying her off to Gretna Green. But such action went hand in hand with scandal. As a tradesman, however rich, Ross had struggled to secure a footing in society to further his business interests. She could not ask him to do anything to risk his livelihood.

Or could she?

Could she make one last bid for life, as a drowning man reaches out before the water engulfs him?

"Ross, I..."

"I believe the correct address is Mr. Trelawney," he said. "Save your familiarities for your fiancé. I trust they will earn you a satisfactory number of trinkets."

Alice fingered the object in her hands—the gift Ross had handed to her not five minutes before. A perfect orange. She dug her fingernails into the skin and released the tangy aroma.

Such a simple offering, unlike the hothouse bouquets with all the character bred out of them, which all suitors in London used to secure a lady's heart and hand.

All except the suitor standing before her now. The Cornishman who smelled of the sea. The man who'd captured her heart months before with the offering of a simple orange.

"Give me your hand, Ross," she said.

He held out his hand, and she dropped the orange into his palm. His eyes hardened, and he turned his hand sideways, letting his offering fall into the soft mud.

"Don't hate me, Ross."

"I could never hate you, Alice," he said. "Hate is not love's enemy.

Hate is love's cousin. Strip away the dark hues of hate and often love remains, a softer shade on the palette."

He stepped toward her until the shadow of his firm, athletic body touched her.

"I don't hate you, Alice. I have no feelings for you at all. I hope you and Markham enjoy a long and prosperous marriage."

He turned his back on her and strode out of the garden, his feet grinding the orange deeper into the mud as he walked out of her life.

CHAPTER ONE

Hyde Park, London
September 1821

"THE PROBLEM WITH a madwoman is her inability to understand the world."

Alice watched the couple walk past, quickening their pace as they recognized her.

The man had echoed the words her doctors had said. Their justification for her incarceration.

Every night for two years, they had strapped her onto the bed, then poured laudanum down her throat, the cold liquid seeping into her bones until blackness engulfed her. At first, the blackness had become a comfort to shield her from the nightmare that had been her life.

It was a nightmare of her own doing. She deserved to be punished. That's what they'd said, the voices in her head, whispering to her at every waking moment.

The voices in her mind had faded, now the threat of a lifetime in Bedlam had driven them away. But the real voices remained. Human voices.

Mad Alice. The deranged duchess.

She picked up a leaf which had fluttered onto the bench beside her and held it against the sunlight. An ordinary object, fated to spend the remainder of its life rotting on the ground, trampled underfoot and ignored by society. But a thing of beauty, nonetheless. The lush green of the summer had almost faded. But at the center was a vivid red, morphing into orange, then yellow, before the green gave its last gasp, skirting round the leaf's edges.

Alice smiled to herself. She'd once had a friend who talked like that. A woman with an artist's eye, who always explained how difficult it was to replicate a precise shade of green in paint because it wasn't a simple exercise of mixing blue and yellow.

Frederica Stanford, now Countess Stiles.

The woman Roderick had almost destroyed.

Roderick...

The cold air rippled through Alice. Her late husband's violent death still haunted her dreams. Though it had been an accident, society whispered it had been Alice's doing. And why shouldn't they? She'd been carted off to Bedlam within hours of the events which had killed Roderick and almost brought about the death of Frederica's husband. A salacious story which had kept the gossips entertained for weeks.

After all, it wasn't every day a duchess was publicly declared a madwoman.

She released the leaf, and it swirled upward, taking flight in a gust of wind. Then it spiraled downward, weighted, as all things are, toward the ground, unable to conquer the solid earth.

The small bundle of fur in her lap stirred and she picked him up, cradling his rotund little body. He gave a grunt of satisfaction, yawned, and licked his front paws. She ran her hand along his back, the fur smooth and silky against her fingertips.

"Are you hungry, Monty?"

The pug's tail twirled in excitement at his mistress's voice, and she leaned forward and kissed the top of his head, breathing in the scent of sandalwood. She reached for the four roses on her lap and closed her eyes.

Monty might be just an animal, but he was the only creature in the world who posed no threat to her.

And he was the closest she would come to having a child.

Clutching the roses, she whispered a silent prayer.

Sarah, Anna, Thomas, Ross…

At that last name, the familiar pull at her heart constricted her chest. Like the doctors had taught her, she drew in a deep breath through her nostrils and exhaled through her mouth.

Ross.

What greater sin can a woman commit than to break the heart of the man who'd bared his soul to her? Her reward had been to watch him court and marry another while she had sold herself for a title.

She closed her eyes, the memory of his voice resonating through her—a rich baritone softened with the warmth of a Cornish burr.

Alice. My Alice…

When he spoke her name, his voice would deepen, and his eyes pulsed with love. They were the grayest eyes she'd ever seen. She had clung to the memory of the love which had once resided in their thoughtful expression, and the touch of his hand which had sent shivers of desire through her, whispering of what was to come, the anticipation of unawakened pleasure.

The last time she'd seen those eyes was the day Roderick had died. Corroded with contempt, they had watched while she was carried away to her fate, her mind broken.

She stood and sighed. There was no use regretting the past. She was an outcast, laughed at by the cruel and pitied by the good. But she had much to be thankful for. Had Papa not agreed to resume responsibility for her after her release, she'd have lived out her days incarcerated. A lifetime under Papa's authority was marginally better than a lifetime locked in a cell.

At least Papa gave her liberty to visit the park and breathe the fresh air again, even if he would never give her parental love.

She shook her head to dispel the memory and continued along the path. A couple stood near the entrance to the park, arm in arm, their backs to her. The gentleman was tall, broad-shouldered, his dark, green coat fitting his form perfectly. His companion was more brightly colored, her dress a rich, pink silk with red trim, the tell-tale style of Madame Dupont's work, the color all the brighter for Alice's months of depravation with only gray walls for company. Her hair was piled on top of her head in fashionable curls, and her statuesque frame almost met the height of her companion.

She was a courtesan. One might feel sympathy for such a creature, having to devote her time to maintaining the interest of her patron, relying on her youth and beauty which would inevitably fade with time. But power exuded from this woman. The air surrounding her shimmered with it.

As if she knew she was being observed, she turned and saw Alice. Her smile of greeting turned into the look of scorn which adorned the face of every member of society Alice came into contact with.

Alice could almost read her thoughts.

The deranged duchess.

The newspapers had done their job. Society's hunger for gossip had increased over the summer when the queen died after a short illness, following a public outcry when she'd been refused admission to the king's coronation. Drawing rooms echoed with whispers that, after failing to secure a divorce, the king had disposed of his wife in a more permanent manner. Wives, after all, were expendable. But society had now turned its attention to a new tale—her release.

The woman tugged at her companion's sleeve.

The man turned to face Alice, and the smile in his eyes died.

His nostrils flared, and he clamped his lips together in a thin, unforgiving line. Creases formed around his mouth, the strong mouth which had brushed against her lips the day he'd made her the happiest of women.

Monty whimpered, and she tightened her grip on him.

He tilted his head and gave her a slight bow, enough to demonstrate acknowledgement of her presence but insufficient to show civility. One might have almost believed it was calculated at such an angle as to cause the most insult.

"Duchess."

She inclined her head.

"Mr. Trelawney."

For a moment, the world around her blended into an amorphous blur of noise, the colors fading into gray.

A shape moved in front of her, its vibrant hues snapping her back into reality.

"Ross, darling, aren't you going to introduce us?"

The woman smiled at Alice, but her lips curled into a sneer, her pale, blue eyes as hard as steel. She tightened her grip on his arm in a gesture of possession, and he narrowed his eyes.

"Of course," he said. "Duchess, may I present Catherine, Mrs. Bonneville. Kitty, my dear, this is Alice, Duchess Markham."

"What a pleasure," the woman said, the musical tones of her voice reminding Alice of a bird of paradise. "I rather wonder at not having seen you hereabouts before."

The veneer of civility could not mask the hostility in her tone.

Alice returned the smile. "I understand Miss—forgive me, *Mrs.* Bonneville," she said, the lightness of tone masking her unease. "A woman engaged in your style of employment would find little opportunity to acquaint herself with society."

"Quite so," the woman replied. "Your very particular corner of society is thinly populated, is it not? Tell me, how easy is it for the Deranged Duchess to find like-minded souls in Hyde Park?"

Her smile remained fixed, as if in challenge. Swallowing her pain at the insult, Alice set her mouth into a hard line.

"There are plenty of companions to be found if one looks hard enough," she said. "But I admire *your* fortitude, Mrs. Bonneville. Your efforts need to be doubly vigorous. Society is an unforgiving animal at the best of times. There are madmen aplenty to be found within its population. Harlots, however, are rarely to be seen. I applaud your tenacity."

The woman recoiled and cast a sideways glance at her companion. Then she shook her head and let out a long, plaintive sigh and stumbled into his arms.

"Oh Ross…"

He pulled her close and turned to Alice, his eyes black with anger.

"How dare you insult Mrs. Bonneville!"

"As she insulted me? I merely stated what she is."

"As did she," he said. "Tell me, madam, which is worse, a woman who devotes her life to making a respectable man happy, or the plaything of a beast who ruined the lives of many?"

For a moment, she thought she saw a flash of regret in his eyes, but he blinked, and the cold expression returned.

She lifted her chin and forced her expression into a cold smile.

"It was such a pleasure to speak to you again," she said. "Please, excuse me."

Clutching her little dog in her arms, she hurried past them and out onto the street. Only then did she slow her pace and allow herself to breathe.

She could withstand loathing and censure from members of society, in fact, by now, she expected it. But not from him. Deep down, she'd always hoped a part of him still cared about her.

But it wasn't the calling of his heart that gave rise to the pain threatening to crush her. It was the calling of hers.

Ross Trelawney might harbor irrevocable hatred for her, but Alice still loved him.

CHAPTER TWO

"**I** NEVER EXPECTED to see *her* out in public so soon after her release. But I suppose her father must tire of her plaguing him with her insanity about the house."

Ross didn't respond. Kitty's allure was matched only by her cruelty.

"My love, would you not agree?" Kitty's voice took on a hard edge.

She curled her lush mouth into a sneer, her beautiful face turning quite ugly for a moment. Her eyes glittered with spite. They were such an extraordinary shade of blue, Ross had once thought he could dive into them and forget past loves won and lost. But gratification in bed only partially numbed the pain. As all rational creatures knew, pain relief was an illusion which alleviated only the symptoms. In order to truly heal, a man needed to address the origin of his suffering.

The origin which had invaded his senses so rudely in Hyde Park today.

Were Kitty any other woman, he might have believed she was attempting to ease his pain. But he knew her too well. An accomplished courtesan, she'd lasted longer than most in her profession, using her predatory sexuality to secure the bodies and hearts of many. Rumor had it, she'd amassed a fortune. Her talents as a businesswoman almost surpassed her talents in the bedchamber.

Purring with sensuality, she caressed the lapels of his coat, brushing the skin of his neck, almost as if by accident.

But Kitty's actions were always deliberate, planned with precision to get what she wanted. She traced the outline of his mouth, then leaned forward. Full lips brushed against his, and she swept her tongue along the seam of his lips, probing, demanding entrance. He remained motionless, and a frown rippled across her forehead.

Hard, insistent little fingers fumbled at the buttons of his breeches, and a hand slipped inside. His groin twitched in response, and she gave a little mew of victory as she circled his girth and rubbed the base with her thumb, using her knowledge of his body to render him powerless in her hands. He gasped as he hardened almost instantly. She seized the moment and plunged her tongue inside his mouth, claiming him in triumph. Teeth grazed against his bottom lip, and a spike of pain shot through him as she bit down, and he tasted the metallic tang of his blood.

Punishment for his earlier reluctance.

He grasped her shoulders and pushed her back. "Enough."

Ignoring him, she tightened her grip, but this time his body failed to react. The memory of another woman doused his pleasure as if ice-cold water had been poured down his front, and his manhood softened. Undeterred, Kitty undid the rest of his buttons, slid to her knees, and pulled him free from the restraint of his breeches. He fisted his hands in her hair as if to pull her away, but she forced herself forward, and a groan bubbled in his chest as her warm, wet mouth enclosed him. He closed his eyes, and the image of a face swam before his mind's eye. Not the perfectly painted face of a woman bent on seduction, but another face.

A face most deemed insipid. Fine porcelain skin, a bone structure so delicate, he'd once thought she might snap in two if he held her too tight. Eyes which, though blue like Kitty's, held a more benign shade. Not as vivid as that of a seductress who used her vitality to ensnare the men in her path, but a clearer shade, like that of a freshwater lake.

But those eyes had deceived. Ignoring the counsel of all his friends Ross had given her his heart, and she'd drawn him closer, like a siren, before dealing the blow which shattered his heart.

And now she had returned the Deranged Duchess.

A cruel title, but she'd earned it. The scandal surrounding her husband's death had kept the journalists busy for weeks.

Ross hated Alice for what she'd done. Why, then, did she plague his waking thoughts? Why did he look at the woman at his feet now, pleasuring him, and wish it were another?

Alice...

A murmur of pleasure vibrated through him as the woman kneeling at his feet took him deeper into her mouth.

"Mmm, my love," she murmured. "I'll soon drive all thoughts of the Deranged Duchess from your mind..."

Kitty's words broke the spell, and he pushed her away and buttoned his breeches.

She rose to her feet and wiped her mouth. "Are you unwell, my love?"

"Jealousy doesn't become you, Kitty."

"I know not what you speak of."

He almost laughed. "You may be skilled in maintaining the demeanor of the goddess who rises above human weakness, but you cannot conceal your emotions from me. My years at the card tables have taught me much."

She began to unlace her corset. But his ardor had cooled, frozen by the memory of the only woman he had given his heart to.

"You speak nonsense, Ross, my love."

"Do I?" he asked. "A gamester conceals his emotions in much the same manner when he has no wish for his opponent to recognize when he has a losing hand. I first noticed it in you, my dear, while we were negotiating out arrangement."

"If I recall," Kitty said, "you did not view me as a player with a losing hand. In fact, you were eager to gain possession of all the cards I held."

"All except the one bearing your offer for exclusivity in exchange for an increase in my stake."

"It was your choice to reject exclusivity of my hand, Ross, not mine."

"And a wise choice it was, my dear. Do you think I was foolish enough to place a bet when I knew the horse would never run? Your reputation preceded you. Not only the reputation for pleasuring a man—one which, I might add, is richly deserved—but your reputation for stamina and the ability to deliver your wares to all corners of the market."

"And now you wish to enter into the same game as I," she said. "Having grown tired of the goddess, you seek to seduce a demon?" She pulled at her corset and let it fall to the ground. Her breasts spilled over the lace trim of her chemise, deep, red nipples poking through the delicate pattern.

The demon. The Deranged Duchess. Derided and ridiculed, even behind closed doors. She deserved to be punished for having allied herself to that monster, Roderick Markham.

But to see the derision of others so close at hand, others who had no reason to attack her other than for gratification and entertainment...

Kitty ran a fingertip across the front of her gown, dipping it between her breasts.

"I understand there was a time when you were partial to her yourself." She traced a line across one breast until she reached the nipple. Her nostrils flared as she pinched it, and she let out a little gasp of pleasure.

But the pleasure was false. Kitty was a fool if she thought he believed she took equal pleasure from the men she serviced. Courtesans were accomplished actresses, playing the part of the loving, walking companion, the well-pleasured bedmate...

But it was all an act in order to garner a living.

Cold, hard cash. The men who fell for Kitty's charms were darned fools. Ross would never be fooled by a woman—any woman—again.

"I am partial to no woman, my love," he said. "I never have been. I value my soul too much. Once your heart is given to another, your soul follows. You, of all people, should understand that."

She pouted in mock disappointment. "Surely you must have loved your late wife?"

Caroline...

Guilt twitched at him, and he ground his teeth to drive it out. The memory of her sweet face still plagued him. Mild-mannered, curvaceous with thick, dark locks, she had been the perfect diversion for a man with a broken heart. She was in her fifth season when he'd offered for her, and he had basked in her family's gratitude. A sweet, biddable companion, Caroline had possessed every quality he desired, save one.

She was not Alice.

His relish at her sweet-tempered obedience had soon turned to dust, eroded by guilt as he tried—and failed—to feel anything but bland affection for her. Even when she entered her confinement, heavy with his child, he had failed to nurture anything akin to passion.

And Caroline had known. The last time he saw her, she'd taken his hand, uttering the words of forgiveness he could not begin to deserve. As if she'd known the end was near, she had made him swear an oath. The prospect of an heir had driven away any sense of foreboding, and he'd complied.

Promise me, Ross. If I die, you must promise never to marry another unless you love her to the exclusion of all others. I will rest easy if I know you have spared yourself the pain of loving without any hope of having that love returned.

The casual laugh he'd uttered as he made his promise still tortured his dreams. How easily he'd dismissed her, not once believing the birth of their child could take her from him. He'd only looked forward to the days when he could atone for not loving his wife by being the best father to their child.

But little Amelia's entry into the world had killed her mother. Try as he might, each time he looked into his daughter's eyes, Ross failed to shake off the image of Caroline's gentle plea. It was as if her mother constantly stared back at him, reproachfully, from the grave.

He shook his head to dispel the memory.

"My wife is no concern of yours," he said roughly.

"Come, Ross!" Kitty laughed. "Death does wonders for one's career as a lover. It places you on a pedestal, to be remembered with reverence and love. Nobody speaks ill of the dead." Her eyes glittered with renewed spite. "I'll bet the Deranged Duchess mourns her late husband daily. She's had two years in a madhouse to think of little else."

Ross curled his fingers and dug them into his palms. The sting of pain diverted him from the need to wrap his hands around Kitty's throat and choke the evil words from her.

He'd seen Kitty's behavior in the park, her attempt to convince him Alice's retorts had caused her pain. But the only pain Kitty ever felt was physical, and she took pleasure from it, squirming with delight every time he brought his hand down on her thigh, her skin reddening with lust as she bared herself to him and begged him to punish her.

Real pain could not be faked. Like it or not, he saw it in Alice in the park. Her expression, the tremor of her body and the way she clung to that small dog in her arms. Her pain should elicit pity, not scorn.

He sighed and reached for his coat.

"Ross, you're not *leaving*?" Kitty asked.

He drew out a sheaf of notes and placed them in the usual bowl on the table beside her bed.

"Here," he said. "Buy yourself something pretty."

Her fingers reached for the money with the practiced movement of the seasoned courtesan. Her eyes widened as she counted them, taking on the air of greed, before she lifted her gaze to him, and an expression of concern raked across her brow.

"Consider the extra amount as a parting gift, in addition to my usual contribution to your lifestyle."

"A parting gift?" The undertones of fear in her voice spoke of desperation. He might have felt sorry for her, had she not revealed her relish in taunting a weaker soul.

"I'm sure a woman of your talents will soon find solace in another's arms," he said. "But take heed, my dear. Fucking can only get you so far in this life."

"It's served me well to date," she said, "and you've never complained. When you screamed my name and ordered me to spread my legs for you, were you thinking of your precious Alice? Or your dead wife?"

Anger swelled within him. If a man had said as much, he'd have called him out—bloodied him with his sword. But real man did not hurt a woman, no matter how much the provocation.

"You'll find another benefactor," he said. "I'll wager in a matter of hours your dance card will be filled again. Try Dominic Hartford. He's just returned from France and, I'm sure, is eager to find a companion able to match the prowess of Parisian whores. I'd be glad to give you a reference."

He moved to the door and opened it, then stopped, turning to look at her one last time.

"Who knows," he said. "He may even be able to teach *you* a thing or two. Consider it an opportunity to increase your repertoire of talents."

He closed the door, straightened his cravat, and slipped outside.

The cold night air caught him, and he hunched his shoulders and increased the pace. The long walk to his own townhouse would serve to cool his discomfort brought about by the renewal of his memories of her.

Alice.

A pitiful creature she'd looked when he saw her two years ago, sobbing over the corpse of her husband, her skin a sickly gray color, her frame nothing more than skin and bones. She'd put on weight during her incarceration, but the haunted look still lived in her eyes.

He would never forgive her, but at least he could bring himself to pity her.

His daughter claimed what little love he had remaining. As for Alice, pity was the only emotion he had left.

CHAPTER THREE

As Alice entered Hyde Park, she turned left, rather than right. With luck, in another part of the park, she'd be spared another confrontation with *him*.

"Come along, Monty."

The sharp wind rippled through her dog's fur. A light dusting of frost covered the path, punctuated by footprints—some solitary, most in pairs.

Why was it that a person could only be satisfied if they were part of a pair? Society pitied a lone creature, more so if she was a woman. But did submission to a husband, or protector, improve the woman's quality of life? One thing Alice's marriage had taught her was the ability to observe, to perceive the human soul beneath the veneer of respectability. As Alice passed couples on the path, she studied each woman's expression. Did the benign smiles hide a life of pain? Once away from the eyes of the public, did the gallant husband's true nature emerge? A wife was her husband's property, for him to treat as he saw fit.

Of course, a single man was never to be pitied. He found solace in the arms of others, purchased either with promises of more or with coin.

Is that what Ross had done after Alice had rejected him, found comfort in the arms of a wife who'd lasted barely a year, and then a line of mistresses?

To Alice, the notion of a life in the power of another creature was infinitely more repugnant than the prospect of solitude. Yet Papa, over breakfast, had lectured her once more on the need to secure herself a second husband.

A husband...

Only last night, Roderick had entered her dreams, smashing through her consciousness. The image of his cold, blue eyes, the snarls of lust, the roars of anger, and finally the pain as the life left her body. The cycle would resume: fear, pain, despair, and grief. She may have grown immune to the physical pain, but the loss of each child destroyed a piece of her soul until there was almost nothing of Alice left.

Voices whispered from behind. "Look! It's the Deranged Duchess."

"Where?"

A couple to her left shared a laugh. The gentleman's boots clicked against the gravel of the path, to the rhythm of Roderick's footsteps, the footsteps she had dreaded each night as they grew louder, approaching her bedchamber...

She froze in fear, and her dog wriggled free, leapt to the ground, and ran ahead.

"Monty!" she set off after him, weaving between the other occupants of the park who moved aside to let her pass as if they could not bear to be touched by her.

She caught her foot against a stone, lost her balance, and crashed to the ground with a cry. The whispers increased.

Sad, mad, Alice...

Hold on to your children...

They should never have let her out...

Pain radiated through her knees, and she reached out to push herself up.

Two hands clasped her arms and pulled her upright. She struggled to free herself, but he tightened his grip, and she screamed as panic consumed her.

"Madam!"

The rich, deep voice brought her to her senses, and she looked up. It was not Roderick's ghost, but a living, breathing man. His expression bore the lines of experience, and gentle concern glowed in his mahogany eyes. An ancient, lined face surrounded by snow-white hair which thinned at the temples.

"Are you all right, Duchess?"

"My dog," she panted. "I've lost my dog."

"No matter," the man said. "Toddington, see to it, will you?"

"Yes, my lord," another voice spoke.

"I m-must..."

"Duchess, if I may be so bold, you're in no fit state to run about the park. You have an enormous tear in your dress. My man will find him."

"But..."

"My dear, I trust Toddington to find your dog, and you can trust me to care for you while he searches."

Trust. A state Alice would never see herself entering again. Yet, the deep familiarity of the man's voice softened the edges of fear.

A gentle hand took her elbow and guided her toward a bench where a couple were sitting. At a look from her savior, they rose and disappeared. He set her on the bench, then sat beside her. The smell of cigar smoke and woody spices drifted through the air. The comforting aroma of a benevolent uncle, which brought forth memories of happier times when Mama was alive.

"There!" he said. "Is that not better, Duchess? Or may I be permitted to call you Alice as I did when you were a child?"

She drew a breath to dissipate the panic, and a flicker of sadness clouded his expression.

"Perhaps you've forgotten me. My late wife and I used to visit your papa and mama when she was alive."

"Viscount Hartford?"

His eyes lit up into a smile. "There! You do remember."

Hartford had been a friend of Alice's parents, and Mama had always spoken of him with affection. He'd often visited when Alice was a child, a kindly old man who used to bounce her on his knee. His warm praise of her accomplishments when Mama had invited her to show him her drawings, poorly executed though they were, was that of an indulgent parent and in stark contrast to Papa's indifference.

After the viscountess died, his visits had thinned until Mama's own death, when they ceased altogether.

"Of course I remember you."

"Good." He took her hand. "You're freezing, my dear. Should you be venturing outside? Your papa will worry. As would your dear mama, were she alive."

A look of grief darkened his eyes.

"Forgive me if I'm taking liberties, but you're the very image of your mama. Save my beloved late wife, of course, your mama was the finest lady I had the honor of knowing. You're just like her."

Alice withdrew her hand, shame warming her cheeks.

"I'm nothing like her, Lord Hartford. I'm-I'm..." her voice broke, and she looked away. "You must know what I am. All of society speaks of it."

"I'm not so foolish as to take heed of every printed word issued by the popular press or every whispered word in the drawing room. I pay no attention to the cruelty of the gossip spread by an uncompassionate society."

He took her hand again. "I understand the limited choices women have in our world. You, my dear, are to be commended, for your endurance and ability to survive. You should be proud of what you have achieved."

She shook her head. "You have no idea what I've done, or you would not speak such nonsense. I'm nothing but a coward."

"That's enough of that," he said, his voice firm. "I'll not hear you say such things. If you cannot believe your own worth, what hope is there that others will see it?"

"I care not what others think," she said. "I seek only comfort and invisibility and to live out my remaining days in peace."

The beginnings of a laugh vibrated in his words. "My dear, to hear one so young speak so! You have your whole life ahead of you. If I had a fraction of your time left in the world, I'd seize it with both hands. As it is…"

He sighed, as if reliving a memory. "Your dear mama wouldn't want you wasting your life hiding away somewhere. Is there nothing you wish for yourself, nothing you wish to occupy yourself with? An occupation is the best cure for melancholy, my dear."

"An occupation? For a woman?"

"There are plenty of activities for a woman of your station which do not involve the production of useless objects to satisfy one's vanity. Is there nothing you'd want for others, if not yourself?"

His words brought forth the memory of the words of another, and she smiled.

"You remind me of Jane," she said.

"Jane?"

"I first met her when she visited me in Bedlam, after the first year when I was permitted to receive visitors. I'd asked her why she spent her time with the insane when she had all of society to amuse her. She told me she was thinking of others and not herself. She said society could go to the devil. I wish I could be like her."

"There's nothing to stop you."

"That's what she says," Alice said, smiling at the thought of her headstrong friend. "She has asked me to help. Not to visit Bedlam, I couldn't bear it, but at a shelter for women."

"Perhaps you should listen to her counsel," he said. "Do I know her?"

"Sir Robert Claybone's youngest daughter, Jane," Alice said. "I was acquainted with her sister, the Duchess of Westbury, when my husband…"

She shuddered at the memory of her marriage, and he squeezed her hand.

"I know of Miss Claybone," he said. "My son courted her briefly last season before he left to spend the winter in Paris. She's known to be something of a hellion, but I always thought her a delightful creature. Had she accepted his offer, she would have done him much good. If I were you, I'd seek her out. You will understand the plight of these women more than anyone."

Perhaps Hartford was right. Rather than spend her days regretting what might have been, she could use her past suffering to ease that of others. Jane had spoken of the hundreds of women abandoned to fend for themselves, women who endured the abuse of their drunken husbands, who strove to protect their children from brutish fathers. London's underbelly was full of them, but only in the past two years of her life had Alice become aware of the misery lurking beneath the glittering layers of high society. While others indulged in sweetmeats and drank tea in their drawing rooms, ordering their servants to close the curtains to shut out the world as if it did not exist, these nameless women suffered.

There was little Alice could do to change the world, but the prospect of changing it for a handful of souls was infinitely preferable to hunting for a second husband.

"My lord!" A man appeared, cradling a small brown bundle.

"Monty!"

She reached out, and the dog wriggled from the man's grasp and leapt into her arms, none the worse for his adventure.

"Oh, thank you!" she cried.

"You're welcome, ma'am."

"That was well done, Toddington," Hartford said.

"Thank you, sir. A sprightly little thing, for all his want of height. I found him sniffing at the edge of the water."

The manservant turned to his master. "My lord, permit me to escort you back to your carriage."

"It's early yet."

"But sir, the cold. Remember what Doctor Beckford said. You must take care, now that you…" his voice trailed off, and he cast a glance at Alice.

"I hardly think a morning in the park will see me off," Hartford replied. "The inevitable will strike me whether I shut myself inside or not. I might as well enjoy what little time I have left."

"Very good, sir."

"Come, Duchess, let me escort you home."

"I couldn't possibly…"

"Yes, you could. I insist," Hartford said. "Your gown is ruined. What manner of gentleman would I be if I let you roam the park in such a state? I'll wager your modiste, however talented she may be, would struggle to conquer such a tear. May I be so bold as to ask her identity?"

"Madame Chassigneux. On Bond Street."

"Of course! My Cassandra used to patronize her, as did your mama, I believe. But now's not the time for chatter. We must get you safely home."

He took her arm and steered her toward his waiting carriage, issuing orders to Toddington to help her in, then he placed a blanket over her knees. No wonder Mama had spoken so fondly of him! Rumor had it he'd courted Mama a year before she married Papa. How different Alice's life might have been had Mama married him instead. Kind, gentle, and with no concern for propriety, at least none which overshadowed the principles of human decency.

Viscount Hartford had achieved one thing, at least. He'd renewed her spirit and sense of purpose. And for that, he would ever have Alice's gratitude and affection.

CHAPTER FOUR

TWO WEEKS LATER, Alice walked along Vine Street, arm in arm with Jane Claybone, on her way to Mrs. Taylor's shelter for disadvantaged women, an establishment which, according to Jane, was sorely in need of resources.

A sense of trepidation rippled through Alice. Today she would meet women who'd suffered worse than her. She would see her own shame and pain mirrored in their eyes.

"You're doing a good thing, Alice," Jane said. "I trust you know that."

"Of course."

"You cannot expect their gratitude, many of them are too afflicted by circumstance to think rationally, but you have mine."

"A little money and a few hours to spare each week, it's not much."

"It's more than they get from anyone else, I assure you." Jane stopped outside a house near the end of the street. "Ah! Here we are."

The door opened as if someone had been watching them, and a woman's face appeared. She gestured to them.

"Get in, quick!"

They slipped inside, and it took a moment for Alice's eyesight to adjust to the dark. She blinked, and shapes came into view, a bare hallway leading to the back of the house and a staircase to the right. Their hostess, a thin woman wearing a plain, gray dress, led them into a small parlor which overlooked the street. She sat on a chair, bidding them to do likewise.

"Forgive me if I don't offer tea, *Your Grace*." She wrinkled her nose at Alice.

Jane clicked her tongue in annoyance but said nothing.

"Mrs. Taylor, I have no wish to be addressed as such," Alice said. "And I certainly have no expectations from you regarding social niceties or tea. I'm here to provide you with resources, not make use of them."

Mrs. Taylor's hostility thawed a little, and she relaxed into her chair. "I have no wish to sound ungrateful, Lady…"

"Alice, please."

"…Alice. The sum Miss Claybone spoke of will feed every mouth in the house with plenty to spare. But my shelter is not a whim for a lady to play at being the benefactress over. It's never empty. The rooms are often crammed with families seeking shelter and a little money to secure a permanent home elsewhere. I have no wish to become reliant on an income which may stop as quickly as it starts. I've pledged that every lost soul who passes through my door will not be ejected against their will. I cannot betray their trust."

Her harsh words belied the look of desperation in her eyes, the look of a woman who spent her life striving to better the lives of those less fortunate and relied on her own resources because she had nobody left to trust. To Alice, it was like looking in a mirror.

"Mrs. Taylor," Jane said. "I can vouch for my friend."

"How long have you known her, Miss Claybone?" Mrs. Taylor asked. "Long enough to deem her trustworthy?"

"Mrs. Taylor, "Jane said, "we both know the length of an acquaintance is not necessarily a suitable measure for the degree of trust we can place on them."

"Perhaps Mrs. Taylor needs to hear it from me," Alice said. "I, of all people, know it's better to form an independent opinion of another rather than submit to the persuasion of others."

She gestured toward Mrs. Taylor. "Nothing I say will persuade you to have faith in me, but I would not have it any other way. I would rather you trust me of your own volition and would hope that my actions over the coming months will earn that trust. I've learned that trust is a precious commodity which should never be squandered. You are right to guard it closely."

Mrs. Taylor's expression softened. "Your friend has told me much of you."

"Did she tell you I was confined to an asylum for two years?"

"Yes, but I thank you for admitting it yourself."

"Jane visited me there," Alice said. "I've always admired her determination to help others, which is why I wish to help you now. If I can make a difference to you and your guests, then perhaps I can atone for my past sins. I have pledged a regular contribution each month to an account established by Miss Claybone's lawyer. You may draw from it whatever you need. But I have no intention of simply furnishing you with money, then returning to my drawing room to forget you. I wish to help, to give your guests hope, to spend time with them so that they might learn to understand their lives are worth living and not to be defined by the men who have abused them."

"What hope can a duchess give to battered wives? What understanding could she ever possess?" the woman asked.

"A duchess, none. But through experience comes empathy. A man is a man, irrespective of the region of society he resides in."

Mrs. Taylor cast a glance at Jane who nodded. "Strip away the title, and Roderick Markham was nothing but a brute."

Alice bit her lip and curled her left hand in a fist, her usual ritual to drive out memories of *him*. Recognizing it for what it was, Jane placed a light hand over hers.

"Forgive me for mentioning him, Alice."

"And forgive me for doubting you," Mrs. Taylor said. "Would you be willing to help me today? Despite my earlier harsh words, my cook makes a tolerable biscuit, and it's nearly time to serve tea."

"Oh yes!" Alice cried. "I'm anxious to be of much use to you as I can while I'm here."

"Then let's get to work."

⟫⟫⟫✕⟪⟪⟪

JANE HADN'T BEEN wrong. As Alice slipped through the door to Papa's townhouse, her feet aching, she sighed at the memory of the faces of the women in the shelter. They barely spoke to her, let alone shared their experiences. It would take more than a few cups of tea to earn their trust.

It almost broke her heart to see the children, almost all of them thin with malnourishment. One young boy had subtly placed his body between his mother and Alice, as if he viewed her as a threat. His mother, a disheveled creature younger than Alice, sported a bruise on her cheek and an eye so puffy, it was almost closed. Her right hand was bandaged, and she struggled to drink her tea, her lip split and swollen.

Might Alice herself have ended up here? With a young child forced into adulthood too soon?

The tide of grief which her resolve held back, threatened to burst through. The children. All those children…

My children…

"Alice!" The harsh voice cut through her memories.

The butler took her pelisse. "His lordship wishes you to attend him in his study," he said.

"Thank you, Wilson."

Papa sat behind his desk, the same look of superiority and disappointment he bore when he'd interviewed her the day she returned from Bedlam. He'd lectured Alice on her willfulness and disobedience, his tone that of a disappointed parent forced to take a burdensome child back to maintain appearances.

Papa gestured to a box on the desk, a large, flat parcel bearing a familiar label.

"What is that, Papa?"

"I was going to ask you the same, child. I wasn't aware you'd visited Madame Chassigneux, but it pleases me to see you taking care over your appearance. It seems as if the account has already been settled."

He gestured toward the box. "Open it."

"Perhaps I may take it to my…"

"You shall open it here," Papa said. "Must I continue to instruct you in filial obedience?"

She lifted the lid. Beneath the layer of protective paper was a shot of pale, blue silk, not the vivid blue designed to attract attention, but a subtler shade of a mild spring sky. She pulled the garment from the box, and a handwritten note fell out and landed at her feet.

She picked it up.

"Read it to me," Papa said, his quiet tone signaling controlled anger. Defiance would only lead to punishment, so she opened the note.

"My dear Duchess.

Please forgive my forwardness in procuring a gown to replace the one which was ruined in the park when you sustained your accident. I took the liberty of selecting a shade I believe would be to your liking. I trust you are fully recovered.

Yours,
G.H."

"Who the devil is G.H?" Papa held an impatient hand out. "Give it here."

Silently, she handed the note across the desk. Papa's stern expression grew calculating as he read the gold-embossed letterhead.

George, Viscount Hartford.

"I see my daughter has secured herself an admirer. Perhaps the task of finding you another husband will not be completely insurmountable. I trust you've not been flaunting yourself improperly."

"No, Papa."

"Good," he said. "Given that I've managed to secure an invitation for you to attend Earl Stiles's house party, you can begin your efforts there. We must act swiftly."

A shiver of fear ran across her. "Papa, I have no wish to marry again. And I have already refused Countess Stiles's invitation."

"Don't be a simpleton, child!" he said. "You can't expect us to keep you forever. I must thank Hartford for renewing my hopes of success. Now go."

Dismissed as if she were a servant, Alice picked up the package and slipped out of the room. Only when she reached her bedchamber did she give free rein to her emotions. Monty whined in his basket, and she crossed the room and picked him up, seeking comfort in his warm little body as tears beaded in her eyes.

Hartford had acted out of kindness, but he'd only renewed Papa's determination to sell her to another man.

CHAPTER FIVE

THE CARRIAGE DREW to a halt outside Radley Hall, and Alice drew in a deep breath, praying the intake of cold October air would numb the rising panic. The dog in her lap stirred and yawned, stretching his paws before settling once more. She ran her hand along his back, her fingertips brushing the silky fur, and sighed.

A house party. A small group of people, but to Alice, it was a crowd of accusing stares, members of society gathered to indulge in frivolities while the less fortunate starved elsewhere. The women would gossip, and the men would trample the grounds, shooting every living thing in their path.

A footman opened the carriage door.

"Duchess."

She cringed at the title. Would she never be free of it? Ignoring his proffered hand, she tucked Monty under her arm and climbed out. She slipped on the bottom step, and he reached out to take her arm, but she shrank back.

"Leave me, please!"

At her cry, a group of guests who'd been chatting amongst themselves, turned to stare at her. One stood out from the rest. Tall and broad-shouldered, his dark blue coat and riding boots emphasized his athletic form. He frowned, then resumed speaking to his companions. Shortly after, male laughter echoed across the air.

Would she ever be free of Ross Trelawney?

"Duchess," the footman said, "I must insist…"

"That's enough, Mayhew," a female voice spoke. A voice from the past, which elicited more shame within Alice than any other. It was the voice of her former friend, the woman Alice's husband had almost destroyed. Since Alice had last heard the voice, it had grown in strength.

As had the owner.

Frederica stood before Alice in a green day gown. The dress emphasized the extraordinary color of her eyes and provided a sharp contrast to her red hair, which Alice had always thought contained a piece of the sun. Frederica had always been tall, but her inner strength rendered her statuesque.

"Countess." Alice dipped into a curtsey, but the woman tutted, pulled Alice into her arms, and kissed her on the cheek.

"I'll have none of that," she said. "We're friends, aren't we? So, I insist you call me Frederica, if you'll permit me to call you Alice?"

Alice nodded, and Frederica tightened her embrace. "You cannot imagine how glad I am to have you here, Alice. I was quite distraught when you refused my invitation at first." Moisture stung Alice's eyes, and she blinked, releasing the tears of shame. As if she understood, Frederica drew her closer.

"Today's not a day for sorrow, Alice," she said, "but a day for joy. For my friend has returned. Come, there's much we need to say to each other, and I'm anxious for you to meet my children. Let us take tea in the morning room."

"But, your other guests…"

The conversation among the others had resumed, but the man who'd laughed so animatedly, now appeared subdued as he stared in their direction. Frederica took Alice's hand. "Hawthorne can see to the other guests."

Alice flinched at the mention of the earl's name. Frederica led her inside and into the morning room where someone had already set out the tea. She gestured toward a two-seated chair beside the lit fireplace. Alice sat and settled Monty on her lap, stroking his fur to soothe her heartbeat. Frederica sat beside her and reached for the teapot.

Before the first cup had been poured, the door opened. A child burst through, dragging a toddler with her, followed by a young girl in a neat servant's uniform.

"Georgia!" the servant cried. "What have I told you about knocking when your mama has guests?"

Frederica set the teapot down. "It's all right, Sarah. You may leave us. But please notify the rest of the household we're not to be disturbed on any account."

The servant bobbed a curtsey and slipped out of the room.

At a nod from her mother, the child dipped into a curtsey. "I'm very pleased to meet you, Aunt Alice."

Frederica colored and held out her hand to Alice. "Forgive my forwardness, Alice, but I was concerned your title might be a little too *discomfiting* for you to hear. My daughter knows you as one of my dearest friends and asked how she may be permitted to address you."

Alice took her friend's hand and was rewarded with a squeeze as long, slim fingers entwined with hers.

"Aunt Alice will do very well," she said brightly, smiling at the eager-looking little girl. "May I know with whom I have the honor of acquainting myself?"

The child giggled. "Georgia Stiles. Very pleased to meet you."

There was no mistaking the child's identity. At seven years old, her height reached Alice's shoulders, and she would likely be taller than even her mother when she reached adulthood. As for her features, the resemblance to her father struck Alice like a blow. Deep-set, chocolate eyes regarded her thoughtfully.

The last time she'd seen those eyes was when Hawthorne Stiles had watched her while she was carried off to Bedlam, the day her actions had almost caused his death.

"I'm delighted to meet you," Alice said, "and who is your charge?"

Georgia tickled the toddler. "This is my sister, Eleanor. Would you like to see my drawings?"

"Of course." Alice smiled. "If you've inherited half your mother's talent, they'll be very fine, indeed."

"Perhaps you could show them to Alice tomorrow, my love," Frederica said. "It's time for Eleanor's nap. Run along and find Sarah."

"Yes, Mama. Come along, Ellie!" The child bobbed another curtsey and slipped out of the room, clutching her sister's hand.

"They're delightful," Alice sighed. "You're so blessed."

"I am, aren't I?"

"It's no more than you deserve after…"

"Let us not speak of it," Frederica said.

"But you must at least give me leave to apologize for what I did."

Frederica shook her head. "The fault lies with another. He's gone forever and does not deserve to exist in our memories. You were a victim as much as I, Alice. You suffered more than anyone."

"Everything I did was of my own volition."

"Was it?" Frederica asked. "Do you really believe that?"

"Yes," Alice whispered. "Why else was I punished?"

Frederica raised her eyebrows in question, but Alice shook her head to dispel the memory of the losses she had never been able to bring herself to speak of outright.

She sipped her tea, her hand shaking. Her friend remained silent, not the awkward gap in conversation which members of society feel the need to fill with inanities, but the companionable silence of true friends. A silence which told Alice that she was with someone she could reveal her innermost fears to.

"Frederica, m-may I ask you a question?"

"Of course, anything."

"I fear it may be impertinent. I have no wish to pry."

"Alice, I'm your friend."

"I understand your husband had a twin brother who died when he was just few hours old..." she broke off and caught her breath.

Frederica leaned closer. "Adam," she said. "What of him?"

"He died too early to be baptized..." Alice hesitated. "Forgive me, Frederica, but I heard a rumor about him, years ago."

"A rumor?"

Alice's cheeks warmed with shame, and she looked away. "I overheard Papa speaking of it. He told my stepmother the child was given a Christian burial, despite being undeserving."

"Undeserving?" Frederica stiffened. "I fail to see this is any of your..."

"Forgive me!" Alice cried. "I-I merely wanted to ask your opinion."

"My husband's brother was an innocent child who deserved his place in heaven as much as any other," Frederica said. "And he has it, whether or not a parson uttered a few incantations over him before he died. Hawthorne's father placed a stone in the family chapel to remember him by, and he will always be honored."

"Forgive me, Frederica," Alice said. "I meant no disrespect."

"Then why did you ask?"

"Because, I wondered if I might..." Alice hesitated, but shame stole her voice.

"Yes?"

"Might I...might I visit the chapel? And place a flower at Adam's memorial?"

"A flower?"

"A-a rose if you have any. A red rose." She swallowed her fear. "Four, if I may?"

Frederica frowned before understanding crossed her features, and she let out a low cry. Alice lowered her head, engulfed by shame.

"Oh, Alice!" A pair of arms drew her into a warm embrace as her friend pulled her close.

"Four! My poor, dear friend!" Frederica's voice grew hoarse. "Rest assured, I shall do everything in my power to make amends for what that man did to you. Now that we have resumed our friendship, I am determined that nothing and no one will come between us again.

Alice leaned into her friend's embrace. If Frederica could find forgiveness and love from the suffering Roderick had caused her family, perhaps Alice could begin to believe in human kindness once more.

⇛⇢✖⇠⇚

THE GRAVEL CRACKLED underfoot as Ross followed the path toward the chapel. The watery sun had failed to thaw the frost which had seized the landscape, and a faint set of footprints stretched in front of him.

But the cold would not deter him from his constitution before dinner. He drew comfort from the solitude. Almost six years after Caroline's death, the guilt still lingered. He often visited places of worship to speak to her of their daughter. Caroline had given him a child, his precious Amelia. For that, she would always own a piece of his heart.

But the passion had been absent, that bolt of flame from deep within, born of a visceral need for another. Kitty had met his physical needs for a time, but the need in his soul had only ever been satisfied by one woman, the very woman whose image he'd fisted his manhood to each night for the past month.

But *she* had deserted him, rejected him for a title. Yet now she sought to plague his peace once more.

What on earth possessed Countess Stiles to invite her here? Poor Frederica had suffered much at Markham's hands. She had almost lost her life, her husband, and her daughter. Alice was not directly responsible, but she must be held accountable for the part she had played, as the obedient, biddable wife of that monster.

As he neared the chapel, a rush of wings beat in the air above, and a cacophony of caws broke the silence as the crows launched themselves into the evening sky. He darted inside and shut them out.

A lone voice remained, and he moved deeper into the chapel. His heart jolted in recognition as the voice grew louder.

A solitary beam from the setting sun stretched into the vault, illuminating golden strands of hair.

Head bent in reverence, she knelt before a stone set into the wall, that ridiculous dog in her arms. Anger coursed through him as he noted the inscription carved into the stone. It was the memorial to Hawthorne's brother.

"What the devil do you think you're doing?"

She jumped at his voice and sat back. Pale, blue eyes stared back at him, red-rimmed and glistening with moisture.

"M-mister Trelawney." She swallowed, her throat bulging with the effort.

"Why do you invade your hosts' privacy?" he asked. "You have no right to be here! Have you no respect?"

"It is God's house," she said quietly. "He spurns no one."

"What about Frederica?"

"She gave me permission…"

"Of course she would!" he cried. "She wouldn't deny anyone, even one as undeserving as you."

"Undeserving?"

"You're nothing compared to her."

She dropped her gaze, her chest rising and falling, then looked directly at him, her eyes wide and clear.

"You love her."

"What man could not fail to love her?" he asked. "She's the best of women, who did not bring about her suffering at Markham's hands."

"But I brought about mine?"

"Yes," he said. "You did. You gave yourself to him willingly, and now you encroach on Frederica's hospitality. You'll always be a reminder of her ordeal at his hands." He gestured dismissively at her. "To think I once thought you were everything. You were an insipid little creature at best. Now you're nothing."

She leapt to her feet, a flare of anger in her eyes. He recoiled, expecting her to react, wanting to see the fire within her. But the brief flare of passion in her eyes died, replaced by indifference.

"You are, of course, correct in your conjecture," she said coldly. "Permit me to take my leave so you may enjoy your solitude. I fear you may need it more than I."

She dipped a curtsey, then swept past him, and left the chamber. Her footsteps were so quiet he could almost have believed she'd been a ghost.

He crossed the floor to the memorial stone. At the base was an offering. Four roses. Freshly cut, Alice must have left them.

He picked one up and held it to the light. Soft petals, the color of a rich burgundy, gathered together to form a teardrop. He lifted it to his lips and breathed in the sweet fragrance. A thorn caught his flesh, and a small red droplet swelled on the pad of his thumb, as if the rose were admonishing him.

He sighed, his anger bleeding away, as if the thorn had drawn it out.

She had not even defended herself against his vile words. Instead, she had donned the armor she used to wear to hide her true self from society and left the chapel. He could have withstood her screams, her cries, the false tears a lady sheds when she fishes for sympathy.

But he'd not expected her quiet dignity or her acceptance of his derision.

Sighing, he left the chapel and resumed his walk. An hour's exercise would soon rid his mind of any feelings of duty he had toward her.

DARKNESS HAD FALLEN by the time Ross returned to the hall. Candle-light flickered behind the windows, a row of reproachful, glittering eyes, watching him as he strolled back along the path. After changing for dinner, he waved away his valet, descended the stairs, still buttoning his jacket, and slipped into the parlor where the butler had just announced dinner. The guests were filing into the dining room.

He moved along the table until he noticed his place card adjacent to Frederica, who sat at the opposite end of the table to her husband. After the guests sat, silence fell, and she said the traditional grace with her soft voice. The murmur of voices resumed, together with the clink of cutlery as the footmen moved forward to serve the soup. Frederica fell silent, taking small sips of her soup, nodding occasionally to Dominic Hartford, who sat on her left.

"Westbury's not here tonight," Dominic said.

"No," Frederica replied. "His wife is unwell. Her pregnancy is proving rather a trial for her."

Dominic snorted. "Westbury's grown soft. He's already secured his heir. Most men wouldn't bother with a trifling matter as a wife's pregnancy."

"Westbury is not *most men*," she said. "I believe a man who tends to his pregnant wife possesses a rare degree of prowess."

Her eyes gleamed with love as she exchanged a glance with her husband across the table. Hawthorne's usually stoic face softened into the smile he only bestowed on his wife, then he glanced at Ross and his smile disappeared.

Ross sighed. A man might forgive many transgressions in a friend but falling in love with that friend's wife was a sin not easily forgotten. At one time, in an attempt to drive Alice from his mind, Ross had believed himself in love with Frederica. Hawthorne had overheard Ross's declaration and would have beaten him senseless had Frederica not intervened.

He cast his gaze around the table, from guest to guest. One face was noticeable by its absence.

"Do you search for anyone in particular, Mr. Trelawney?"

Frederica appeared engrossed in her soup, but she possessed the unnerving ability to observe, even when she wasn't looking.

"I don't understand you, Countess."

"I think you do."

"Very well," he said. "Where is she?"

"Returned to London. She sent for the carriage shortly after returning from her walk. I'd hoped she was recovering, but it appears she's far from it. She was determined to leave."

She lifted her wineglass to her lips, concern for her friend etched across her brow. "She seemed settled here this afternoon, before she left for a walk. At first, I struggled to understand what had given rise to such a change in her. Then I recalled *your* fondness for a walk before dinner."

She turned to face him. Frederica's gaze had always been unsettling, the color of her eyes capable of changing to match her mood. Now, the green was dark, forbidding, and searching.

"She was in the chapel," he said. "She had no right to be there."

"She had *every* right to be there."

"You don't understand, Frederica," he said. "She was kneeling at Adam's memorial!"

"Stop!"

Frederica set her glass down with a thud. The conversation halted, and the guests looked up.

"My love, are you well?" Hawthorne rose from his seat, concern in his expression. She motioned to him to sit.

"I'm quite well, Hawthorne. Please continue."

He resumed his seat, casting Ross a look of suspicion. At length, the conversation around them resumed, and the footmen cleared away the first course.

Ross sipped his own wine. "Forgive me, Countess, if I distressed you."

Frederica sighed. "It only distresses me that you think Alice unworthy to be my friend."

"She was Markham's wife!" Ross said. "You cannot forget what he did to you, and to Hawthorne."

"Do *not* mention that man's name! He does not merit one drop of our attention or our memory. Not after what he did to Alice."

Ross let out a snort. "He did nothing to her that she did not consented to."

Frederica lowered her voice to a hiss. "You fool! You believe every woman is consenting? He tried to violate me. I cannot begin to imagine what it must have been like to endure his violence on a daily basis."

"Alice married him, Frederica. It's not a violation if the woman is willing."

"Good lord." Frederica let out a sharp breath. "To think women are considered to be the weaker sex! I thought *you* had some intelligence, at least. We both understand what manner of creature Roderick Markham was. Do you imagine his nature changed when he entered the marriage state? A wife is obliged by law to service her husband's needs. That very same law permits her husband to undertake corrective action upon her. He may even use a stick, provided it's no thicker than his thumb. Even my beloved Hawthorne, for all the regard placed on him as a magistrate, can do little to pass judgement over the villains who beat or violate their wives when they're brought before him in court."

"Surely such behavior is confined to the lower classes?"

"You're a fool to say so!" Frederica said. "The possession of a title does not render a man incapable of the behavior of a beast. It merely means he is less likely to be brought to justice for it. And no wife, whatever class she belongs to, deserves to suffer at the hands of her husband."

"A woman reaps what she sows."

"Have you never made a decision which you came to regret? Imagine Alice's position, enduring a life with that man, suffering at his hands, knowing it was her choice."

Frederica leaned back as a footman placed a plate in front of her and waited until he moved on to serve Dominic.

"At least Alice is using her past suffering for good."

"What good can she ever hope to achieve?" Ross asked.

"She funds a shelter for battered wives."

"A whim, that's all. Many ladies throw their pin money at charitable causes in the belief it will buy them a place in heaven."

"You're wrong." Frederica sliced through her fish in a swift, deft motion, as if delivering a blow in a swordfight. "She visits there twice a week. She talks to the women, tends to their wounds, cares for their children, and speaks of it with such passion. I've never known such dedication in her, certainly not when we were friends. Now that she's shaken off the shackles of society's expectations, she can dedicate herself to what she truly believes in without fear of reproach."

"What does her father think of it?"

"I'll wager he doesn't know. She begged me to keep it a secret, so as not to draw attention to the women, the shelter, or to herself. I think she'd rather remain invisible for the rest of her life."

"Then why are you telling *me*?"

"Because you're determined to think the worst of her. At every turn, you seem to be looking for reasons to hate her."

Frederica's words, spoken with sadness and resignation rather than anger, did more to pierce his heart than any passionate admonishment she could have delivered.

His conscience resonated with her words, igniting the self-loathing which had festered deep within him. His determination to hate Alice arose from his broken heart and shattered pride, and the guilt which plagued him while he fought his need for her. That need had grown while he saw her married to Markham and continued to thrive, despite how much he'd tried to love Caroline.

Every time he looked at his daughter, he wondered what might have been had she been Alice's child instead.

He blinked, and a bead of moisture splashed onto his skin. Slim fingers touched his hand, wiping the tear away.

"Forgive me, Ross, I spoke out of turn. But I know that a man vehement in declaring one opinion, such as hatred for the woman he once courted, often does so to mask the fact that his feelings are quite the opposite."

She lowered her voice. "A man cannot help who he loves. Often, he strives to hurt the one he loves the most."

Frederica had endured so much, yet through it all, the love she bore her husband had remained unwavering, despite the actions of Roderick Markham, which had almost destroyed them both.

"That man has much to answer for while he rots in hell," Ross said.

"Aye, he does," she said quietly. "We must ensure his ghost remains defeated. Love, not a desire for retribution, is the only solution."

Ross resumed his meal with renewed purpose.

As soon as he returned to London, he'd pay Alice a call. Perhaps she might forgive his cruel words, as he would forgive her for breaking his heart.

CHAPTER SIX

"WE WEREN'T EXPECTING you today, but I'm grateful you're here, as always...Alice."

Mrs. Taylor colored as she always did when referring to Alice by name, her innate deference to a lady battling with her desire to comply with Alice's wishes.

Alice followed Mrs. Taylor into the parlor. Crates were scattered about the room, and a woman was packing items into them.

"Careful, Mrs. Brown," Mrs. Taylor said. "The china is fragile. It'll need two layers of paper to protect it."

"Yes, Mrs. Taylor." The woman nodded, then resumed her work.

Alice gestured to the activity. "What's happening?"

"We're leaving next week."

A ripple of dread coursed through Alice's body. "Are you in danger? Or have you been evicted?"

"No," Mrs. Taylor said, a smile stretching across her face. "It's such wonderful news! We have another benefactor. Miss Claybone came to tell us last week while you were in the country. He or she has pledged a regular payment into the fund held by Miss Claybone's lawyer, Mr. Stockton, and has secured us a larger residence on Boswell street, not far from here."

"Who is it?"

"They've asked to remain anonymous. But, think of it! I'll be able to house many more women. The house is twice the size of this one."

"And they want nothing in return?"

"I don't think so. Mr. Stockton has assured me the benefactor is not the type to make such a decision lightly, and they can be trusted."

Her eyes glistened with gratitude, and she took Alice's hand. "I must thank you, dearest Alice."

"What for? It wasn't me."

"Miss Claybone cannot think of anyone among her acquaintance who'd be so generous. It must be someone who thinks highly of *you*."

She wiped her hands on her apron. "And now I must be getting on. These crates are being collected tomorrow."

"What can I do?"

"Perhaps you could help Mrs. Brown with the china." She lowered her voice. "We've already lost two cups and a saucer. While I set little store on such things, I'd rather not have to spend the entire fund replenishing my entire tea set."

Alice removed her coat, tied an apron round her waist, then crossed the parlor to where Mrs. Brown was clumsily wrapping a plate in brown paper.

Mrs. Brown had been with Mrs. Taylor for almost a month. Alice had seen her arrive with her four-year-old daughter. The bruises which had adorned Mrs. Brown's face had faded to greenish-yellow. She looked up and gave Alice a warm smile.

"I'm pleased to see you, my lady."

"And I you, Mrs. Brown. How well you're looking!"

"Thank you. I'm delighted I'll be moving on soon."

Alice reached for a teacup and began wrapping it. "How so?"

"Mr. Stockton has found her a position," Mrs. Taylor said.

"I'll be laundering linen in a house in Hammersmith," Mrs. Brown added. "I'm to have a room of my own, and the housekeeper is letting me bring my Betty."

As if she'd heard, a little girl burst into the room, a familiar ragdoll tucked under her arm, with the enthusiasm only children possess, before their innocence is destroyed and their eyes opened to the dangers of the world.

"Lady Alice!" The child threw herself at Alice and wrapped her arms around her waist.

Swallowing the pang of loss which tugged at her heart, Alice embraced the exuberant little body.

"Dearest Betty!" she exclaimed. "How's my angel today?"

"Did you hear the news?" the child asked. "I'm to have a new home, in a big house outside London! I've never been out of London. What's it like?"

"It's green," Alice said. "So green. The air is clean and sweet. You'll love it."

Betty tipped her head up and turned her adoring gaze on Alice before wrinkling her nose. "Mama says I'll have to keep clean and take a bath every week!"

Alice suppressed a laugh at the horrified look on the child's face. "Won't you like that?"

"I'd hate it!" the child said. "But Mama says it'll make me respectable, and if I'm a good girl, I might be able to go into service there."

Betty held out the doll. "Must I give her back before I leave?"

"Of course not!" Alice said. "She's yours. I never looked after her well when she was mine, so it's high time she found a better mama to cure her loneliness."

"Won't you miss her?"

"I'll be happy knowing she's well looked after," Alice said. "And if you learn your letters, you might write and tell me how she's faring."

"Oh yes! Did you know I've called her Alice?"

"Dear, sweet, child!" Alice bent over and kissed the little girl on her forehead. Hot moisture pricked behind her eyelids.

As if she understood, Mrs. Brown placed a hand on Alice's shoulder before addressing her daughter.

"Run along now, Betty. Lady Alice and I have much to do."

The child skipped out of the room, hugging the doll.

"I'm so happy for you, Mrs. Brown," Alice said. "You and Betty deserve a new life, a safe and happy one."

"If only I could see you as happy, your ladyship. It comes so naturally to you."

"What does?"

"Motherhood," Mrs. Brown said. "It's in your nature. Betty adores you, and the other children here speak of you all the time. You were born to be a mother."

Alice turned her head away and bit her lip.

"You speak nonsense, Mrs. Brown," she snapped. "Come, there's no time for tattle. These tea things need packing, and we won't do that by gossiping."

An industrious silence fell while they continued packing the contents of the parlor into the crate.

When Mrs. Brown left to tend to Betty's supper, Mrs. Taylor ushered Alice to a chair.

"You've done enough for one day, Alice."

"Shall I come and help you unpack in your new lodgings?" Alice asked.

"You'd be very welcome, Alice, dear," Mrs. Taylor said. "But I've no wish to see you exhausted."

"I'm not tired, Mrs. Taylor."

"Perhaps not physically, but life takes its toll in other ways." She took Alice's hand. "Mrs. Brown meant no harm in what she said about motherhood."

"I know," Alice sighed. "I must apologize."

"There's no need, my dear. When a woman has experienced life such as Mrs. Brown, she recognizes when others have lived through the same. Did you never ask yourself why the women here warmed to you after only a few visits? They saw a kindred spirit, someone who endured the same horrors as they, and lived to tell the tale."

She led Alice to the front door. "My dear child, I am of the same opinion as Mrs. Brown. You were born to be a mother. And you understand a mother's grief. I saw it in your face the moment you laid eyes on the children here."

She drew Alice into an embrace. "There's none more than I who values your presence here, my dear. You've done so much. But you must not devote all of your efforts to others. You should reserve a little for yourself."

Alice took her leave and slipped out of the townhouse, wrapping her cloak around her to keep out the cold during her walk home. Only when she had turned the corner into Sussex Gardens did she realize her face was wet with tears.

⤛⤜

ROSS STOOD BEFORE the front façade of the de Grecy townhouse. The building looked the same as it had the day he'd left it seven years ago, a heartbroken man of twenty-five. Paint peeled around the window frames, the mark of the impoverished aristocrat. But de Grecy valued birth over fortune. No amount of wealth could render Ross worthy of that man's attention, for Ross's wealth had been acquired through trade. His great grandfather had struck tin near St Austell, and the profitable seam had amassed him a sizeable fortune. It had enabled his entrepreneurial fingers to dip into businesses all over England.

But none of that mattered to a man like de Grecy. Nor had it mattered to Alice in the end. Her cruel words resonated through his mind, how she apologized for her lapse in rationality in her fleeting attraction to a man so far beneath her in station. She had likened it to the fancy a lady of the house might have in a servant, a dark little fantasy to be ashamed of.

But had those words been her own? Frederica's admonishment at Radley Hall had sparked the seed of doubt in his mind. That seed had led him to this moment.

He knocked on the door which opened to reveal a familiar face of the butler who'd ejected him from the house seven years ago. Did he remember?

"Yes?" One simple word conveyed disdain and contempt.

"I wish to speak with Duchess Markham." Ross held out his card. The butler plucked the card and held it at arm's length with his fingertips, as if it might poison him.

"Wait outside." He sniffed and shut the door.

Yes, the butler remembered him.

Dear God, was it worth the humiliation to satisfy his curiosity over whether Alice deserved some credit, as Frederica believed?

He thrust his hands into his pockets and hunched his shoulders against the cold. A couple walked past. The man lifted his hat to acknowledge Ross, but the woman on his arm stared at him with curiosity, perhaps wondering what crimes he'd committed to suffer the incivility of being left on the doorstep. Or perhaps she wondered what crimes a man loitering in front of townhouses was capable of committing.

Eventually, the door creaked open. Ross took a step forward, but the butler blocked his entrance.

"His lordship is unavailable and will be for the foreseeable future."

"His lordship?" Ross asked. "But I came to see…"

"The duchess is out at present and has no wish to see you. His lordship asked me to give you this with his compliments."

The butler lifted his hand, holding something between thumb and forefinger, his expression laced with distaste, as if he held a soiled rag.

"Take it."

Ross held out his hand, and the butler opened his fingers. Four torn pieces of card fluttered into Ross's palm. As he inspected them, the door closed, and the butler's footsteps faded into the distance.

But Ross was not to be deterred, not until he'd heard Alice's dismissal from her own lips. He stepped onto the street and set off in the direction of Hyde Park.

⇒⇒⇒✕⇐⇐⇐

As Ross passed a cluster of silver birches, their bark illuminated by the sunshine, he caught sight of a familiar woman, arm in arm with an older man.

Jane Claybone bore little resemblance to her sister who was married to Ross's friend, Henry Drayton. Rather than possess her sister's lush figure, she had the wiry strength of a small terrier.

And the temperament. No wonder she'd broken off her attachment to Dominic Hartford. Woe betide any suitor of that hellion who sought to play away from home—she'd cut his vitals off with a butter knife and use them for earrings.

She ran wild all over London, thinking nothing of spending her days visiting the most undesirable places, hovels, brothels, makeshift hospitals... And Bedlam, the worst of them all, where the tortured souls beyond redemption were incarcerated.

The hellhole Alice spent two years of her life in.

He strolled toward Miss Claybone, forcing his lips into a false smile of greeting which would be wasted on such a creature. Her direct gaze and bad-tempered disposition toward his sex rendered her an unpalatable acquaintance at the best of times. But she had one redeeming feature.

Her friendship with Alice. Ross suspected Alice's involvement with the women's shelter resulted from that friendship.

As predicted, she scowled upon recognizing Ross. She turned to her companion, who had yet to spot him, and steered him away. Before they could disappear, he broke into a run.

"Miss Claybone!"

Her body stiffened, then she turned to face him.

"What do *you* want?"

"Jane…" her companion admonished her with the tone of an indulgent godparent who knew his charge would take no heed of his words but uttered them for the sake of propriety. He gave Ross an apologetic smile.

"Oh, hang it, Uncle George," she said, "you know I'm not one to indulge in social niceties with the undeserving."

"Miss Claybone," Ross bowed and turned to her companion. "Mister Stockton, what a pleasure."

The lawyer's eyes narrowed.

"While I may disapprove of the method of my goddaughter's inquiry, I find myself tempted to ask the same question. You look in a hurry."

"I wish to speak to Alice."

The lawyer's eyes widened at Ross's familiar address.

"I doubt she wishes to speak to you," Jane said. "Let's go, Uncle George. I've no time to waste on a rake."

"Miss Claybone, would you be so kind as to explain the reason for your pointed dislike of me? I know of no transgression I might have committed to merit such incivility."

She muttered an unladylike curse. Stockton made no further attempt to admonish her but regarded Ross with the knowing expression of a lawyer who was privy to the hopes and dreams of a multitude of souls.

Miss Claybone stepped toward Ross until they were almost touching. She had to tip her head up to meet his gaze, but for all the height differential between them, she was the more imposing of the two. Her eyes were an unremarkable shade, but a dark fire flashed in their depths, which threatened to ignite all challengers.

"Incivility!" she snorted. "What is a little plain talking compared to all that my friend has suffered!"

"So, you're content to believe everything told to you by the woman who humiliated me when she broke off our engagement," he said. "I thought you better than that."

"I don't care what you think!" Jane spat. "I visited Alice almost every week in Bedlam. I heard her screams in the corridors and can only imagine what horrors visited her mind at night. At first, she didn't recognize me—for a whole month they incarcerated her in a cell no bigger than a broom cupboard, manacled and strapped to her bed while they forced drugs down her throat."

She swept a hand across her face.

"And what did I endure between visits?" she scoffed. "I sat through dinner parties and balls where the gossips sought cheap gratification from relating stories of the Deranged Duchess and her latest exploits in the madhouse."

"There's nothing you can do when someone loses their mind," Ross said. "She was a danger to herself and to others."

"A danger of other's making!" Miss Claybone cried. "The brute who terrorized her and the whole of society, who looked the other way."

She jabbed a finger in his chest. "And what of you?"

He grasped her hand. "I fail to see what I've done to merit such censure."

She pulled free. "You bear the most responsibility of all," she said. "You understood her. And she understood you."

"She understands nothing!"

"You don't deserve her," she said. "You never did."

She sighed, and a tear splashed onto her cheek which, she brushed away with a gesture of resignation.

"Near the end of her time in Bedlam, she spoke of you, of how she regretted what she'd done."

"Regret born of guilt," Ross said.

"Is that your own guilt speaking?" she asked. "Like the man who beats his wife and convinces himself the fault lies with her because he's too cowardly to look at himself? My friend has every right to regret what happened, for her own sake. Her body and mind were destroyed while society looked on. But her biggest regret was you."

"Me?"

"Not her rejection of you," she said, "but what it did."

"Does she believe her rejection broke my heart?"

"No," Jane said. "But she viewed it as the first step to the life you lead now, to that of the rake. She told me that you were the sweetest, kindest man to walk this earth. She said that beneath the exterior of the man wanting to find his footing in society, lay the soul of a good man, the only good man of her acquaintance."

His heart sent a thread of guilt through his veins. Miss Claybone's words, spoken with such passion, brought forth his conscience, which always sat on his shoulder. When he'd married Caroline, when Caroline had died—even when he'd thrust into the welcoming body of a courtesan in the name of sexual gratification—his conscience had repeated the same word.

Alice.

"I'm sorry," he said.

"What for?" Jane exclaimed. "Standing by and watching while that man tortured her, or for ridiculing her destruction with your friends while she lay in a cell and prayed you found the happiness you deserved."

She paused and gritted her teeth, anger pulsing in her eyes. "Let me tell you, Mister Trelawney, like Alice, I hope you find exactly what you deserve! I pray that one day you endure the same horrors as she. Only then will I deem you worthy of my notice. May the devil take you!"

"Jane, that's enough!" Stockton said.

"You've said it yourself, Uncle George, Alice doesn't deserve such ridicule or such censure. You saw her for yourself in Boswell Street..."

Jane broke off, coloring.

"Boswell street?" Ross asked. "Is that where the shelter is? Is she there now?

"Leave her alone!"

"If you think I'd be intimidated by a petulant child whose behavior should merit a bloody good thrashing, you're mistaken," Ross said. "I must see her."

Stockton held up his hand. "I protest. If she wanted to see you, she'd seek you out."

"You've no right to tell me what to do," Ross said.

"No," the lawyer responded, "but I can point out the folly of your ways. What good do you think you would achieve?"

"I only wish to speak with her about what really happened," Ross said. "I need to know the truth, to reassure myself that she no longer suffers and is happy now."

"She still suffers," Jane said quietly. "And will for the rest of her life." She placed a hand on his arm and sighed. "I only want what's best for my friend. She has none to fight her battles for her. Her father only tolerates her presence, and the rest of society laughs at her. One day she'll be strong enough to weather the trials which life will forever place in front of her. But until that day comes, I am there to fight on her behalf."

"Then let me see her. Let me reassure myself she's happy."

"Only if you promise not to break her heart."

"I promise."

Jane sighed. "Very well. It's number twenty. I only tell you this so you can approach the house discreetly. Mrs. Taylor has no wish to draw attention to her establishment, the kind of attention you'd attract if you knocked on every door in the street demanding entrance like a typical boorish man. But if I hear you've upset her, I warn you, you'll find yourself waking in the middle of the night with a knife in your gut."

Hell's teeth! Was Alice worth all this trouble?

Yes.

The little voice broke through his thoughts. Miss Claybone had placed a mirror in front of him and revealed the ugly truth that lay beneath his righteous indignation.

The truth that he still loved her, had never stopped loving her.

And tomorrow, as soon as he saw Alice, he was going to tell her.

CHAPTER SEVEN

ALICE STRAIGHTENED AND rubbed her lower back. The kitchen cupboards were considerably cleaner than they had been before.

Her companion nodded with delight. "I can't believe how dirty they were before, your ladyship! You've worked ever so hard on them. They're almost sparkling!"

"Hardly that, Lottie," Alice said, affection warming her blood. "But you're most kind to say so."

Lottie smiled. She'd arrived at Mrs. Taylor's two days previously, a bruise on her cheek. Thin and malnourished, her pitiful gratitude for the bowl of stew Alice had ladled out on her arrival tore at Alice's heart.

Recognition punched her in the gut each time a new woman crossed the threshold—the same frightened look in their eyes, the look of guilt as if they believed they'd earned their suffering.

She bent down and continued scrubbing. The kitchen floor needed attention, and the best remedy for unwanted memories was hard work and idle chatter.

A young boy knocked on the door and opened it a fraction.

"Begging your pardon, your ladyship, there's a gentleman to see you. Shall I let him in?"

Lottie stiffened in fear.

"No, of course not!" Alice admonished. "You know men aren't admitted. What possessed you?"

"He insisted," the boy said, a thin veil of fear lining his tone.

A deeper voice vibrated outside.

"Is she here?"

The door opened more, and a broad male form stepped into the kitchen, his physical presence dominating the space. Lottie backed away.

Alice stood and looked up into eyes the color of steel, the same resolve in them which had once drawn her to him like a lost ship seeking out a beacon.

"Alice, I came to find you."

He'd always possessed the power to immobilize her with a single glance. Holding her in his gaze, he drew closer and reached for her hand. She jerked back.

"What are you doing here, Ross?"

"I rather think I should be asking that of you," he said.

Lottie whimpered, and Alice moved closer to her, shielding her with her body.

"What I do is none of your concern, Ross."

"It used to be," he said quietly. "There was a time when every waking moment, you were my primary concern."

"I ceased to be of concern to you a long time ago."

"At your own hand," he said.

"Is that why you're here, Ross? To admonish me? Harsh words might have ruled me in the past, but no more. When you've lost everything, including your mind, no man has power over you anymore."

He shook his head. "Now's not the time to discuss it, Alice," he said. "Do you have any idea the danger you place yourself in, being in a place such as this? Does your father approve?"

Anger flared at the mention of Papa. All men were the same. They all sought one thing. Mastery over the women in their lives, mastery over her. But no more.

She released Lottie's hand. "Lottie, please find Mrs. Taylor. Tell her to come immediately."

"Shall I give her a reason?"

"Say the kitchen is overrun with vermin."

Lottie slipped past Ross, giving him a fearful glance.

Her friend safe, Alice advanced on Ross.

"How dare you come here!"

"The last time I checked the law of the land, I understood a man had the freedom to go where he chose."

"What good has the law done for me or the women in this house? Do you have any idea the damage you're doing just by being here?"

"You must know, I wouldn't harm anyone here."

"I don't mean physical damage, Ross," she said. "Some of these women have endured years of abuse. Imagine what that does to their state of mind."

"You can trust me."

"What right do you have to demand my trust?" she asked. "The women here have entrusted us with their safety and anonymity. Your presence here has broken that trust." She picked up a knife from the table and waved it at him. "Like all men, you're convinced of your superiority, merely because of your greater physical strength."

"I only came here because I wanted to speak with you. Your father refused to admit me."

"What you want is of no consequence," she said coldly. "I care for nothing but the welfare of the women and children here, and I'll fight to my last breath to defend it."

She held the knife up, struggling to control the trembling in her arm. For a moment, he moved as if to take it from her, then he hesitated and backed away.

"Forgive me," he said. "I should not have come here."

He turned to go.

"Ross!"

His body stiffened as he stopped in the doorway.

"Can I trust you not to tell others about the shelter?"

"You can trust me completely." His eyes glistened, then he turned and left the kitchen.

But his feelings didn't matter. What mattered was that she would never place herself into a man's power again.

>>><<<

"I THOUGHT WOMEN weren't admitted into your card parties, Dom."

Ross raised a glass to his friend. The company of his libertine friends should have lifted his spirits. But with two of them married, the topics of conversation had degenerated from that of womanizing to parenthood.

He tipped his glass back and drained the contents. The liquid burned in his throat and he wrinkled his nose. Dom wore the veneer of the London gentleman but his funds, or perhaps his taste, didn't run to palatable liquor.

Dominic gave a wolfish grin and gestured toward the female silhouette by the window. "Come and meet our hostess."

The woman turned, and Ross halted, instantly recognizing her exquisite beauty, the tilt of her chin and loose-hipped gait calculated to titillate.

"Kitty?"

"Mrs. Bonneville, if you please," she said.

"Quite right, darling." Dom crossed the room and offered her his arm. "Such a familiar endearment has no place in a drawing room." He licked his lips. "We must save them for another chamber entirely."

"Dominic!"

"I trust I'll hear that name from your lips later tonight."

Kitty's mouth curled into a seductive smile which faltered as Ross met her gaze, before she resumed her attention on the two men who sat at one of the card tables, Viscount de Blanchard and Rupert Oakville.

Westbury appeared beside Ross, a full glass in hand.

"I see the delectable Catherine has found a new protector," he said. "Have you been supplanted, Ross?"

"No," Ross said.

"Any regrets?" Westbury asked.

Ross shook his head. "Don't tell me you had her also, Westbury."

Westbury let out a laugh. "My libertine days are long gone, and Kitty was always a little too grasping for my tastes. But she's making a mistake with Dom. He has no cash of his own, and I can't see his father loosening the purse strings. Old Viscount Hartford is no fool." He sipped his brandy and spluttered.

"Ye gods! I've tasted better in the gin parlors!" He set the glass aside. "Which proves my point. Dom's strapped for cash."

"Perhaps he hopes to relieve his guests of some tonight," Ross said.

"That explains why he invited de Blanchard, whom he loathes," Westbury said. "If I were a gambling man, I'd wager Dom intends to make a tidy profit."

"Out of de Blanchard?"

Westbury wrinkled his nose. "That fat lecher isn't known as the Mayfair Miser for nothing. He's careful with his funds. But a few glasses of this ditch water masquerading as brandy is enough to rot anyone's brain. By rights, I should warn de Blanchard, but I'd enjoy seeing him bested."

Ross couldn't hide his smile. "His nose still bears a kink from when your wife punched it, Westbury."

"And rightly so," Westbury's tone hardened. "Every chaperone in London would do well to steer their charges clear of him."

"He must be in his fifties, at least. His chances of securing a wife can't be high," Ross said.

"Most parents' ambitions outstrip any consideration for their daughters' scruples," Westbury said. "I pity any lady on the receiving end of his courtship. No title or fortune is enough to compensate a woman for having that bloated boar between her thighs."

A footman approached with a tray full of glasses, and Westbury waved him away.

"Come on, Ross. Let us witness de Blanchard's downfall."

As the evening drew to a close, Ross found himself standing alone by the window, watching de Blanchard as he swept a stack of coins and pledges across the card table and onto his lap, a smile of satisfaction adorning his fleshy features.

Dom sat opposite de Blanchard, his face having paled several shades throughout the evening.

The scent of orchids drifted into Ross's senses as a slender hand touched his arm and a female voice spoke.

"How much do you suppose Dominic has lost?"

"About eight hundred," Ross said. "Your plan failed, Kitty."

She shook her head. "Not my plan. Dominic…"

"I don't mean Dom's plan to best de Blanchard at piquet, and a foolish one at that, given Dom's lack of wits and weaker tolerance to liquor. I meant your plan to secure yourself a dividend. Unless, of course, you intend to transfer your affections to de Blanchard after tonight."

"Of course not!" she cried. "De Blanchard is nothing compared to Dominic." She gave a little gasp, as if she'd surprised herself with her outburst. Then she smoothed her face once more into the expression of the calculating Cyprian.

"Dominic's a wastrel," Ross said, "as proven by tonight's events."

"He cannot help what he is," Kitty replied. "None of us can. Not even you, Ross."

"He behaves like a boy, Kitty. You'll tire of him soon enough."

"He's misguided, that's all," she said. "High-spirited, an untamed stallion who lacked a firm hand when he was a colt."

"In other words, a spoiled child."

"His mother lavished him with love. After she died, all his father bestowed on him was disappointment."

Ross let out a snort. "I won't ask how you know that. Clearly a good hard ride loosens Dom's tongue."

She flinched and withdrew her hand. "I thought you, at least, might understand."

"Come, come, my dear," he said. "I'm sure every doxy in London has been fooled by the tale of an unloved son. Perhaps by eliciting your sympathy, he was able to negotiate a lower price."

She let out a sharp sigh. "When did you become so cruel, Ross?"

"Don't be naïve, Kitty. Dom's a rake. He knows what he's about."

"And why do you think he behaves the way he does?" she asked, her voice tightening. "Might it be because that's the only way to secure his father's notice? Perhaps he knew he'd never live up to his father's ideal of the perfect son, so he gave up trying."

"He'll secure his father's notice now that he's in debt to de Blanchard."

"Perhaps that's better than to always be ignored by him."

"How can you possibly know that?"

"Because I can read men," she said. "I understand their needs, motivations, and desires. It's how I've managed to survive so long in my profession."

Her usually hard, calculating expression softened. Then she blinked and turned her head away, focusing her gaze on the ashen-faced man at the card table who struggled to stand as de Blanchard held out a hand, thanking him for a most entertaining evening.

"You love him," Ross said quietly. "Don't you?"

Her chest rose and fell, then stilled as she closed her eyes. When she opened them again, the soulless courtesan had returned.

"Of course not, Ross," she said, "and I'd thank you not to spread such rumors among your acquaintances. They only serve to damage my livelihood."

She moved toward Dominic, and the vulnerable creature who had stood beside Ross moments before, morphed into the vibrant courtesan. Her bright laughter filled the air as she placed a hand on Dominic's shoulder. But this time, Ross saw beyond the façade, a slight shake of her hand as she reached for a glass of wine, little creases in the corners of her eyes, which narrowed as she whispered into her protector's ear.

Never had Caroline's dying words spoken the truth as loudly as they did tonight. Kitty played her part well, but Ross no longer saw the grasping doxy. Instead, he saw the living embodiment of Caroline's warning about loving without any hope of having that love returned.

A LIGHT BREEZE rippled across the Serpentine, broken only by the wake of a white figure gliding along with the current. The swan might exude the air of fragility and purity, but woe betide anyone she perceived as a threat.

Sitting on a bench near the water's edge, Alice clutched the roses in her hand and tipped her head up. The breeze drifted across her cheeks, which had been warmed by the winter sun. During her incarceration, she had lived for days such as this, cold winter days where the sun broke through the clouds to indulge in a final gasp before the frost set in. Lately, it had become her favorite time of year. Any force of nature which drove men and women indoors, thinning out the crowds, was to be applauded.

She drew her cloak around her to protect the bundle of fur on her lap.

"There you go, little one," she whispered, "safe and sound."

Monty stirred in his sleep, issuing tiny snores with each breath.

"May I see your dog?"

A child of six or seven stood before her. Golden hair in ringlets, she looked every part the angel. Her eyes were a clear gray, slanted in a distinctive almond shape which bore echoes of familiarity.

"Do you like dogs?"

"Oh yes!" The child's face lit up into a smile, her cheeks puckering into rosy pink apples. "I want a dog, but my papa won't let me."

"Why not?"

"He says I must learn to take care of an animal before he lets me have one. He said it's not like a doll which I can discard and place back into the toy box when I've outgrown it."

"He sounds very sensible."

"Oh, he is!" the child said. "But he still won't let me have a dog."

"Perhaps when you're older?"

"By then I'll be married," the child said, "and then I'll have to ask my husband. I don't think I'll like having a husband. He won't always give me what I want. Papa gives me what I want."

"Except a dog." Alice suppressed a laugh. "What's your name, child?"

"Amelia." The child stood upright and held out her hand. "Pleased to meet you." She nodded to the roses in Alice's hand. "I like your flowers. Would you like to meet Papa?"

Alice took the child's proffered hand and shook it. "I'm Alice."

"I like you, Alice," she said. "I wish I could stay here with you, but I must do as Papa says."

The child pulled her hand free and skipped toward the next bench where a man sat waiting. He stood, and Alice's stomach clenched in recognition.

No wonder the child's eyes were familiar.

He moved closer, the air shimmering with his presence.

"May I?"

She remained still, not wanting to disappoint the eager little girl who watched them intently. Taking her lack of refusal as assent, he sat beside her.

"Papa!" The child jumped onto his knee, and he wrapped his arms around her and kissed the top of her head. An instinctive gesture of love.

He looked up and their eyes met, and her chest tightened at the intensity of his gaze, that very quality which had drawn her to him in the first place, the expression which spoke of something deep within.

How could he still wield such power over her, render her weak and immobile? When surrounded by those who needed her, she could draw on her resolve. But here, in the quiet of the park, on her own, her resolve failed her.

"Did I do right, Papa?"

Ross Trelawney lowered his gaze, and a faint color bloomed in his cheeks.

"You did very well, angel," he said softly. "Why don't you look at the swans while I talk to your friend?"

"But Papa, I…"

"Now, Amelia."

The child jerked at his tone which, though quiet, vibrated with diamond-hard steel. A man not to be denied. As Amelia skipped away, Alice's resolve crumbled as she found herself alone, for the first time in seven years, with the man who'd possessed the power to master her mind and body.

>>><<<

AS HIS DAUGHTER danced across the path toward the water's edge, Ross reached out for Alice's hand.

She flinched, an insignificant gesture, but he recognized it for what it was and he withdrew. Compared to the avenging angel who'd expelled him from the shelter three days ago, she now seemed even more fragile than she had when he'd first seen her since her release from Bedlam.

Frederica's words echoed in his thoughts. Frederica had suffered at Markham's hands and though she had recovered, Hawthorne occasionally spoke of his concerns for her when her nightmares visited her. But Alice had endured five years in Markham's power. It made her display of strength at the refuge all the more remarkable, as if the woman before him was a phoenix rising from the ashes of her former self.

Yet here, in the peace and solitude, the victim resurfaced. Perhaps it was because she had time for her innermost thoughts to torment her.

"Your daughter is beautiful," she said quietly.

"That she is."

"You should cherish her, Ross. Children are a gift not to be taken lightly. It's a bitter lesson I've learned over the years."

"Why?" he asked. "You have no children."

Her body shuddered as if he'd dealt her a blow. The dog shifted in her lap as she curled her hands into fists, her knuckles whitening.

"Duchess?"

She flinched at his address, and he cursed himself. "Forgive me. Alice?"

She lowered her head.

"Alice, what's wrong?"

Distress vibrated through her body. She drew in another breath and sighed, caressing her dog as if he were the most cherished possession in the world.

Eventually she spoke, her voice so quiet, he thought he'd imagined it.

"Sarah."

She paused and drew another breath.

"Anna."

The world around grew silent, as if even the trees waited to hear what she had to say.

"Thomas, and Ross."

She caught her breath as if she'd been stabbed, then looked away. She seemed absorbed in a distant feature of the park, as if in doing so she could divert his attention elsewhere. It must have been a trick she'd learned while married to Markham. Her way of surviving.

Four names.

One for each rose in her hand.

"The memorial," he said. "In the chapel at Radley Hall. You placed four roses there."

Her head moved in a slight nod. "They died," she whispered. "They all died. For my sins."

"Your sins?"

She nodded. "I was a poor wife. I disobeyed him. But when he punished me, it wasn't just I who suffered."

She bit her lip and turned her clear gaze on him, the blue of her eyes pale in their honesty, her pupils dark pits of loss and despair. "Any creature can render themselves hardy against pain, until eventually one feels nothing."

She shook her head and tears fell from her eyes. She lifted her hand and wiped the tears away.

"But the pain of four souls on my conscience is more than I could bear. I welcomed Roderick's punishments because I deserved them. When the first child, my Sarah, left my body, I knew then that I deserved each and every punishment administered afterward. It was the only way I could atone for killing her. But when the rest followed..."

She caught her breath. He touched her hand and she recoiled.

"I was a poor wife. I didn't love him. I didn't even try. Perhaps if I'd made more of an effort, he wouldn't have needed to punish me. They'd be alive were it not for me."

She lowered her voice, as if making a confession. "I killed them."

His skin tightened in horror. Not only had she suffered Markham's beatings, but it had cost her four children.

But the most pitiful thing of all was her belief that she deserved it.

"You cannot blame yourself, Alice."

"If not I, then who?"

"Papa!" Laughter echoed across the park as Amelia chased the swan along the water's edge.

"Not too close to the water, angel!" he cried out.

The woman beside him fell silent and drew the dog into her arms, cradling it lovingly. A ridiculous creature, yet he now saw it for what it was.

But there was one thing he had yet to understand.

"Why did you visit Adam's memorial at Radley Hall?" he asked. "What possible good could come from it? I don't understand."

"No, you don't, do you?" she asked, her voice cold and hard. "I went there because Adam was another who never had a chance at life. But he was loved, given a memorial and honored."

"I still don't think…"

"I care not what you think!" she cried. "My lost babies were never honored. But perhaps if I honor Adam's memorial, he might find a place in heaven for mine. It's my only comfort. I'll never have a child of my own. All I can hope for is that the ones I lost have not been sent to purgatory for my sins."

Instinctively, he reached for her, the urge to ease her suffering too strong. She pushed him away and stood, cradling the pug in her arms.

"Don't touch me," she snarled.

"What would you have me do, Alice? I can't bear to see you suffer."

"Leave me alone!" she said. "Instead of indulging in torturing me, you should take better care of Amelia. Count the blessings you have, Ross. Your daughter is to be treasured and does not deserve to be used for your own purposes."

He recoiled at the force of contempt in her gaze. She called out to Amelia and waved, and his daughter waved back, then she set off along the path and disappeared.

CHAPTER EIGHT

THE SUN HAD long since set when Alice returned home from Mrs. Taylor's. Her feet ached, and she longed for a bath. She smiled to herself. The child, Betty, hated baths. Alice had said goodbye to Betty and her mother only that afternoon as they left for Hammersmith. Alice knew the owners of the house, an American who'd amassed a fortune privateering, and his wife. They were kind souls who would treat Mrs. Brown well, and they had promised to seek out Mrs. Taylor when they were next in need of a servant. Alice had even managed to procure a pledge from Mrs. O'Reilly to contribute a regular stipend to her fund.

She removed her pelisse and handed it to Wilson, then crossed the floor. With luck, there'd be enough hot water for Lizzie to fill her a bath.

"Alice!"

Her body flinched at the voice which came from the morning room, and she changed course and pushed open the door.

Papa stood beside the fireplace, the glow of the flames rendering his skin a pale orange. Beside him sat her stepmother, the usual look of distaste on her face.

Lady de Grecy gestured toward the rug in front of them as if Alice were an errant servant brought to stand before her mistress.

"Am I not permitted to sit, Kathleen?" Alice asked.

Her stepmother's lips thinned at the address.

"Alice..." Papa growled. Ignoring him, Alice crossed the floor to a chair and sat.

"Show some respect to your mama."

"Mama is dead," Alice said. "I will give your wife the same degree of respect she gives me, but she is not my mother."

"Ungrateful child!" Papa hissed.

Beside him, Kathleen's lips curved into a slight smile. In some households, it was the woman who ruled. Alice saw it in her friend Frederica, who ruled her husband with compassion and gentle kindness, though she always deferred to him outwardly. But in households like Papa's, where the poison bled through the atmosphere, only a woman of a very particular disposition could weave her own web of influence.

Kathleen inclined her head toward Papa, who touched her shoulder and continued.

"I trust you'll show more respect to your husband."

Fingers of dread ran across the back of Alice's neck. "Husband?"

"Yes," Kathleen said. "Your Papa has been working hard to secure a home for you."

"A home?"

"You cannot expect to remain here forever," Papa said. "You're fortunate I agreed to take you back after your..." He paused and looked at his wife.

"Your *rest cure*," Kathleen said, a smile on her face though her eyes remained cold and hard.

"Your rest cure," Papa echoed. "Your mother and I have secured two interviews with you tomorrow, each with a prospective husband."

"But I don't want..."

"Be quiet!" Papa roared, his face darkening. Kathleen placed a hand on his arm in an outwardly act of gentle benevolence, but malice glittered in her eyes.

"Charles, don't distress yourself," she said. "I'm sure your daughter will do her duty. How many times have I told you she needs understanding and a guiding hand?"

"Of course, my love," Papa smiled at her before resuming his attention on Alice.

"Consider yourself fortunate I'm giving you a choice, daughter."

"A choice?" Alice asked. "I can refuse them, if I so wish?"

Papa shook his head. "Of course not. I shall permit you to choose which of the two suitors I have obtained, but this time tomorrow, you *will* be engaged."

Alice rose to her feet. "Did you place an advertisement at Whites for the first man to relieve you of the burden of the Deranged Duchess? How much did you offer as a dowry to rid yourself of me?"

"Spoiled child!" Papa hissed. "To think I took you in, on your stepmother's persuasion, I might add, when I could have left you in that madhouse where you deserved to be after your behavior!"

"My behavior?"

"You failed in your duties as a wife, a duchess, and a daughter. I trust you'll not fail again, but this time tomorrow, you'll no longer be my burden."

"May I ask who you plan to sell me to?"

"You'll find out tomorrow," Papa said. "Now go to your chamber and think on your good fortune. If you do not marry one of these men, I'll have you sent back to the asylum. A word from me will have you readmitted, and this time, I'll ensure you're kept there indefinitely. Now get out. Wilson will see you to your chamber."

The resolve which had been thriving in her veins since she'd found a new purpose in her life drained from her body. The butler stood in the doorway, a slight smile on his face. For as long as she could remember, Wilson thrived on moments such as this.

As she approached the doorway, Wilson placed a hand on her forearm, fingers of steel curling round her wrist as he guided her to the foot of the stairs. There was nothing she could do. In a world ruled by men, she was the property of Papa. As a wife, she'd be the property of her husband. But as a madwoman recently released from Bedlam, she was also, in the eyes of the authorities, a danger to society. Papa was right, one word from him she'd be incarcerated forever. She'd be hunted down like an animal, netted and shackled, hauled back to her cell…

"Duchess?" Wilson tightened his grip.

"Unhand me," she said as coldly as she could.

Pulling her arm free, she climbed the staircase toward her chamber. There was nowhere else to go. The prospect of matrimony, terrifying though it may be, paled in significance compared to a lifetime in a madhouse.

⫸⫷

"HOW MANY TIMES have I told you! Do as I bid!"

Crimson lips parted to reveal large, white teeth, sharp edges glinting with readiness to sink into her flesh.

"Roderick, no!"

"Be silent!"

She tried to move, but a weight pressed her to the bed. Fighting for breath, she lashed out. She opened her mouth to scream but no sound came.

"You pathetic creature!" the voice snarled. "Barren little bitch! How many murders are on your hands! How many children have you killed?"

"Roderick, stop!" she cried. "I'm innocent!"

"Innocent!" the voice snarled, crashing into her mind, tearing through her senses, each word punctuated by a blow. "You've destroyed good men, murdered innocent children. Useless, fucking whore!"

"No!" Acid pain tore through her. She reached out and clawed at the monster on top of her. Her hands met skin, and she dug her fingernails in, tearing through the layers of flesh. The monster disappeared and was replaced by dark shapes surrounding her.

"Madwoman. Deranged. She needs restraining."

The voices were muffled, as if she were drowning underwater. Cold metal scraped at her skin as the shackles confined her.

A harsh light glinted and stretched to an elongated shape. It moved closer and snapped into focus, a large needle, dripping, moving closer.

"Hold her down."

With a scream, she punched a fist forward, smashed through the wall and sat up, gasping for breath. Her chest almost burst as her heart strained, thudding as if it, too, were desperate to escape.

She blinked and focused on her surroundings.

She was in her chamber. Alone. A solitary candle flickered in the air. It was almost burnt out. Through the window, a thin sliver of light stretched across the sky, the first sign of the dawn.

Her nightmare had visited her again.

She drew the bedcovers aside and swung her legs over the side of the bed until her feet met the solid floor, something to anchor her to reality. She reached for the decanter on the side table and poured a glass of water. The cool liquid soothed the ache in her throat.

Dear God, it had been so real!

Would she spend the rest of her life doomed to purgatory, to be haunted by the memory of him, and of what he did, of what she had allowed him to do?

Would she ever escape the cries of the children whose lives were on her conscience?

She padded across her chamber, the fibers of the rug soft against the soles of her feet, so unlike the stone floors of her cell, until she reached the bureau beside the window, its handles shining in the candlelight.

She opened a drawer, grasped the neck of the bottle inside and held it up. Still more than half full. She turned it to one side and ran her thumb across the printed letters on the label.

Laudanum.

She pulled out the cork and sniffed the contents. The familiar sweet smell stung her senses, and she placed the bottle to her lips. One spoonful had always been enough to pacify her. But if she were to finish the bottle, she would find eternal peace from the laughter and derision of society, freedom from the slavery of marriage.

You were an insipid little creature at best. Now you're nothing. Less than nothing!

Roderick had been right. If she disappeared from the world, it would make no difference at all.

One swallow and she could end it all. It was the only power she had in a world where the women were owned, abused, incarcerated, then tossed aside. Roderick's voice cut through the dark, the harsh words of hatred which were always the precursor to pain.

Go on, you pathetic little creature. Do it.

With a cry, she flung the bottle across the chamber where it landed with a smash of splintering glass. An owl screeched outside, and she crossed the chamber and leapt onto her bed, covering herself with the bedsheet as if to shut out the ghosts who'd witnessed her sin.

She did not even possess the courage to end her own life—not if it meant she would join Roderick Markham in hell.

"YOUR LADYSHIP?"

A timid voice drew Alice back into consciousness. Sunlight stretched across her chamber and illuminated the figure of her maid.

"Forgive me for waking you, your ladyship. The master awaits you in the morning room."

"Have I slept late, Lizzie?"

The maid nodded. "Begging your pardon, I didn't want to wake you. You need rest."

The memory of last night returned, and Alice sat upright and looked about the chamber, but there was no evidence of what she'd almost done.

Had she imagined it?

"Your table must have toppled over in the night," Lizzie said, not meeting Alice's gaze. "Splintered glass everywhere! I took the liberty of clearing it up before you woke. I trust I did not do ill?"

"Thank you, Lizzie," Alice said. "Forgive me for making such a mess."

"There's naught to forgive, my lady. Let me help you dress before his lordship grows impatient."

Lizzie could not be more than fifteen years of age, yet she took Alice's hand and led her across the chamber as if Alice were the child, smiling at her in sympathy as she selected a morning gown and helped Alice dress.

She steered Alice toward the dressing table and sat her in the direct path of the sunlight. Alice closed her eyes while the maid's gentle fingers tended to her hair.

"There!" Lizzie said brightly. "Your papa cannot help but be proud of you."

Alice slipped out of her chamber and descended the stairs to her fate.

As she knocked on the morning room door, Papa's voice called out, laced with impatience.

He stood in his usual position in the morning room. Her step-mother was absent, most likely taking tea at Almack's. The maintenance of Kathleen's position in society was worth more than the welfare or happiness of her husband or stepdaughter. But Alice was grateful for her absence. She preferred facing one enemy rather than two.

"Ah, here she is. I must apologize for my daughter's lack of punctuality."

Another man was in the room, standing by the window. He turned and smiled, the sun forming a halo in his soft gray hair.

"What a pleasure to see you again, my dear."

It was Viscount Hartford.

Alice glanced at Papa. Was he going to admonish her for the gown Hartford had bought her?

"Alice…" The warning tone in Papa's voice sent an involuntary shiver through her. It was the same tone Roderick had used to indicate his displeasure, the precursor to punishment.

"V-viscount Hartford?" She stepped back.

"I have not given you leave to go!" Papa said before turning to his guest. "Please forgive my daughter's incivility, Lord Hartford."

Hartford merely smiled. "No matter, De Grecy. Perhaps she did not expect a visitor today?"

"She's expecting two," Papa said.

Her skin tightened in understanding. Hartford was one of the suitors Papa had chosen. In his desperation to rid himself of her and secure her a title, he was willing to give her to a man old enough to be her father.

"I take it I have a rival," Hartford said. "May I inquire as to his identity?"

"Viscount de Blanchard will be visiting later," Papa said smoothly.

Alice's stomach churned. De Blanchard had a reputation for preying on unsuspecting young women such that most debutantes' fathers steered clear of him. Nausea threaded through her, and she stumbled forward. Hartford crossed the room, issued a swift bow, and took her arm.

"What a pleasure to see you again," he said. "Let me escort you to a seat."

His grip was solid and reassuring, and he led her to the chair by the fireplace. It was the chair Kathleen usually occupied. Kathleen was very particular about her ownership of it, but Papa said nothing. Perhaps the prospect of ridding himself of his daughter for good was worth risking the wrath of his wife.

The world slipped sideways, and Alice took a deep breath.

"Alice!" Papa admonished. "Aren't you going to thank…"

"That's quite enough, de Grecy," Hartford said, an undertone of steel in his voice. "Give me leave to attend your daughter in peace. I understand in circumstances such as this, a man must be granted a private audience with the young woman concerned."

Papa opened his mouth as if to reply, and Hartford stood, his body stiff and erect. Papa lowered his gaze and backed out of the room. As soon as the door closed behind him, Hartford sat beside Alice and sighed, once more betraying his age, as if the effort of defending her against Papa had drained him.

For a moment, he sat beside her in silence, the only sound the ticking of the clock over the fireplace and the faint beating of her heart in her ears. Finally, he spoke.

"Forgive me for such an unexpected visit. I won't insult your intelligence by asking whether you know why I'm here. You must think me an awful cad."

He reached for her hand, and she flinched. Understanding crossed his expression, and he sat back.

"I'm sorry," he said quietly. "It was a mistake on my part to come. But I've always felt a sense of obligation to you, for your mother's sake. If you would rather marry de Blanchard, say the word, and I'll leave this house forever."

She closed her eyes as if to shut out the world. But the world existed whether she could see it or not. The limitations of her choices closed around her. Refusal to obey Papa, which would result in incarceration, or marriage to a lecher with a reputation for debauchery…

Hartford sighed. "I *do* have a rival."

"No!" she cried. She looked up into his kind eyes. "I-I'm sorry, Lord Hartford. I have no choice in the matter. But you do. You cannot want to marry me."

He reached for her hand and hesitated. "May I?"

She nodded, and he covered her hand, his skin smooth and papery to the touch.

"I'm not long for this world, but before I leave it, I want to do as much good as is within my power."

She understood.

He sighed and squeezed her hand. "I'm no fool," he said. "Just because I'm old doesn't mean I lack wits. In fact, I possess the experience through years of observation of human behavior."

"What do you mean?" she asked.

"I can only imagine what you endured during your first marriage, and I'll not speculate on it now, lest it distress you further. I understand a man's actions are more to be believed than his words, but I give you my word that I'd never treat any living creature in such a manner. I know the choices which have been placed before you. Your Papa is not the epitome of discretion. I offer myself to you as one of those choices if all others are too abhorrent to bear."

"And w-what would you expect..." Alice stuttered over the question, at the shame of having to ask it.

"I expect nothing in return, my dear," he said, "except a little companionship. When I said I was not long for this world, I spoke the truth. My heart is failing. My surgeon is a very frank young man, and he has given me no more than six months."

He gave her an indulgent smile. "I must confess, it was initially from pure selfishness that I offered to court you when your papa was brokering you around Whites. I long for the companionship of a good woman. A woman who'll care for me because she wants to, not because she's paid. I've heard much of your exploits at Mrs. Taylor's, my dear. The tender care you've given those poor women is to be admired. If you might indulge me with a small portion of that care during the few weeks I have left, you would make me the happiest of men."

"You're suggesting a marriage of convenience?"

"A marriage of indulgence and affection," he said. "In exchange for companionship, I offer you friendship and freedom. You'd be free to indulge as much of your time and money on your refuge, particularly now the women have settled into their new lodgings."

"How do you know about that?"

He colored and looked away.

"It was you?" Alice asked. "The anonymous benefactor?"

"I'm afraid so, my dear," he replied. "Rest assured that whatever answer you give me, the stipend shall remain. I've drawn up a letter of intent with the trustees of my estate. The refuge will want for nothing whether you marry me or not."

He lifted her hand and kissed it. "Before I speak further, I must ask you a question," he said. "Is there anyone else who you wish to marry? For if there is, I'll withdraw my offer and leave you in peace. I don't believe in forcing a woman against her will."

The memory of Ross still ached—his words of contempt, how he'd used his daughter for his own ends thinking nothing of the child herself and, finally, his accusation, the disdain he'd shown for her lost children.

Moisture stung her eyes, and she blinked and shook her head.

"No," she said. "There's no one else."

Hartford lowered himself to the floor on one knee.

"Forgive me for being so indulgent, my dear, but I find myself wanting to indulge in a little gallantry. Marry me, Alice, and you'll want for nothing. Safety, peace, and security—a life where you can heal in mind and body, where you can begin to live again. I will pledge an annuity to you after I am gone so that you're never beholden to a man again."

"Lord Hartford, please don't kneel, think of your heart."

He struggled to his feet and let out a low chuckle. "Not the most passionate response I've had to a proposal."

The door burst open, and Papa strode in.

"Well?" he said. "Has she accepted?"

"Not yet," Hartford said.

"Foolish child!" Papa muttered under his breath. Hartford strode toward Papa.

"I'll thank you to show more respect to your daughter," he said, then he turned and bowed to Alice.

"I shall return tomorrow for your answer." He began to retreat, as a ship in the night, the ship which the marooned man on a desert island clings his hopes and dreams of escape to.

"No!" Alice blurted. "There's no need. I'll give you my answer now."

She rose to her feet, ignited at last by a sense of hope, that now her body was free from incarceration, her mind and soul might follow.

"I would be honored to accept your proposal," she said, then turned to Papa. "Please inform Viscount de Blanchard that I am no longer available to receive him."

CHAPTER NINE

THE DOOR OF de Grecy's townhouse seemed to absorb the sunlight, as if the very house were devoid of a soul. De Grecy might have warned Ross never to return, but Ross was determined to see her.

After watching the house for almost half an hour, he spotted her through a first-floor window, her face clear in the rays of the setting sun which cast a warm glow on her features. He stepped forward and knocked on the door.

It was for her he risked returning. Her revelation had cut through to his soul. What agonies she must have suffered! Four children—four! If Amelia came to harm, it would destroy him, and he was intelligent enough to understand that a mother's bond with her child would always be stronger than a father's.

That sacred bond existed between Alice and the children she'd lost, manifested in the trembling of her body and the hoarseness of her voice.

And in the way she treasured that silly dog.

What did her father know, or understand, of her pain? In all likelihood, he was the reason for her belief that she had sinned and deserved her losses.

A father should never use a daughter to further his own ends. His duty was to prepare his daughter to enter the world and thrive in it, with independent thoughts and beliefs.

Perhaps that was why Alice had been so angry with him when he'd used Amelia to engage her. She, of all women, would know what it was like to suffer at the hands of an ambitious parent who thought only of his own objectives.

But no more. Ross didn't need de Grecy's approval to marry Alice. She was hardly a debutante. And society, in its cruelty, would now consider their marriage an elevation of *her* status, not his. How many times, after she'd rejected him, had he wished their roles were reversed such that he was the more respected of the two?

Now, fate had presented him with his wish. But when a man makes a pact with the devil, he must be prepared for the price. Wishes were granted in many forms. A man craving wealth might achieve it through the loss of a parent. He might wish his mistress ceased plaguing him, then discover she'd been murdered. Or he might wish the woman who spurned him to suffer as much as he did, only to discover that she had been brutalized into insanity and grief.

The door opened to reveal the butler.

"His lordship is unavailable."

"I'm here to see his daughter," Ross retorted.

"She is out at present."

"You lie." Ross wedged his foot in the door. "I saw her upstairs. I wish to speak with her."

"Wait here." The butler ushered him into the hall, then disappeared into the house. A door opened and closed in the distance, and a shape emerged from the darkness.

"I thought I'd made myself clear. You're not welcome."

De Grecy had aged since Ross had seen him last. His hair had thinned, the glossy black now peppered with gray and thinning at the temples to produce a deep widow's peak. It gave him a sinister air as if he were permanently frowning.

"My daughter does not wish to see you, *Mister* Trelawney."

"I'll not leave until I've heard it from her lips."

"She'll afford you no such courtesy," de Grecy sneered. "Neither will her fiancé."

"She's engaged?"

"Hartford won't want to see her spurned suitors littering the place. I had a devil of a job finding a good match for her, and you'll not ruin it."

Ross snorted. "A good match? Dominic Hartford is a rake. He'd never offer for her."

"My daughter is engaged to the viscount."

"Dominic's *father*?"

"Yes," de Grecy said, a smile of triumph on his lips. "What his son does is of no concern of mine. He can have her, too, if he wishes."

Dear God! Had de Grecy sold Alice to a man old enough to be her father?"

A clatter of hoofbeats approached outside, then stopped. The butler opened the door, and an old man walked in. The faint smell of spices and old cigars lingered in the air for a moment until another, sweeter smell, overpowered it—the unmistakable scent of flowers.

"Ah!" de Grecy said, his tone growing obsequious as he gave the viscount a stiff bow. "Take no need of that *gentleman*. He's leaving."

Hartford turned his gaze on Ross. Soft brown eyes regarded him thoughtfully before he lifted his head and a broad smile crossed his lips.

"My dear, Alice!"

"George!"

Ross froze. A single word, spoken with such love.

She stood at the top of the stairs, a smile of affection and relief on her face. With the smooth movement from years of breeding, she glided down the stairs and held out her hand to the bent old man she'd sold herself to. As she reached the bottom step, she glanced at Ross. A flash of pain crossed her eyes before they hardened.

"Daughter," de Grecy said. "Take your guest to the morning room while I see our visitor out."

Without casting another glance at Ross, she took Hartford's proffered arm and let him lead her through a door halfway down the hall.

"It's time you left," de Grecy hissed. "Find someone of your own class to dally with. My daughter's not for sale."

"No," Ross said. "She's already bought and paid for."

After the front door had closed behind him, he turned his back on the house and descended the steps to a coach-and-four bearing the Hartford crest. The horses shook their heads with restlessness, and one scraped its hoof on the street. The clink of the metal in the harnesses echoed off the stone wall of the house.

"Careful there, sir!" the driver cried. "That gelding spooks easily."

"How so?" Ross asked.

"It was mistreated, before the stable master took him in on his lordship's insistence."

The animal eyed Ross warily, and he held both palms up to show he meant no harm.

"Is he dangerous?"

"Not really, sir," the driver said. "He'll not take a rider again, but he's happy enough in a four." He tipped his hat. "Mind how you go, sir."

Ross nodded and hunched his shoulders against the cold which had descended with the disappearance of the sun, and he set off along Sussex gardens. Only when he'd reached the end of the road did he realize where the scent of flowers had come from.

Hartford had been carrying four roses when he called on her.

"I NOW PRONOUNCE you man and wife."

The church was barely full. Though Papa had wanted a fanfare to proclaim his success in ridding himself of Alice, Hartford had insisted on a quiet, evening wedding to ensure privacy from overly curious journalists.

As each day had passed during their brief engagement, the old man's insight and kindness became ever more apparent. Alice's faith in mankind would never be completely restored, but at least some kind souls existed among the men of the world.

The vicar closed his bible and nodded, waiting for the bridal kiss. Hartford drew her close, and her body froze as she fought the instinctive urge to flee. But rather than show irritation at his wife's apparent rejection in front of witnesses, he smiled and brushed his lips against her forehead in a gesture of fatherly affection, then patted her hand and led her down the aisle.

Papa and Kathleen sat on one side of the church, together with Alice's oldest brother, John. Her middle brothers, Roger and Andrew, were unable to secure leave from the army. The groom's side of the church was notable in its emptiness.

Dominic Hartford had refused to attend.

But why would he attend? A second wife, to a much older man, was generally understood to have married to further her own ends. Alice had only to consider her stepmother to understand that. Kathleen, having seen two husbands into their graves, had secured her third purely to regain her footing in society, to enable her to attend balls and parties on the arm of a viscount.

Now, Kathleen stood next to Papa as Alice passed down the aisle on her new husband's arm with a smile of satisfaction on her lips at having rid herself of her stepdaughter.

As her new husband led her toward the carriage, she spotted a lone figure across the street. Though he stood as still as the statues which graced Hyde Park, pain radiated from his expression—pain she had caught a fleeting glance of the day she'd rejected him.

He took a step toward her, then hesitated. He thrust his hands into his coat pockets, turned away and disappeared down the street.

Hartford helped her into the waiting carriage, and they set off for her new home. Each turn of the wheel took her away from her old life and toward the new.

She was a wife once more, the property of another, having sworn an oath to fulfil the duties which came with marriage. The maintenance of the household would occupy her during the day. But as for the night…

"Are you well, my dear?" The soft, rich voice beside her pulled her from her thoughts, and she jumped as his hand covered her own.

"You're quite safe with me," he said.

She merely nodded and fixed her gaze out of the window and focused on the buildings they passed as the carriage rolled toward Mayfair. If only they moved slowly enough to enable her to count the bricks of each townhouse they passed. An object of interest to occupy the mind was the best cure for the fear swelling inside her—the fear of the night to come.

Hartford sat back and closed his eyes. At close range, he looked older. His skin had a gray pallor, the creases around the mouth and eyes evidence of his age. But there was something else. He looked strained, even in repose. Perhaps Dominic's absence had affected him more than he'd admitted. Her first task as Viscountess Hartford would be to reconcile with her stepson. Not to take the place of a mother, at nearly thirty years of age, he was older than her, but to show him she wished for peace in the Hartford household.

When the carriage drew to a halt, her insides continued to churn as if they rotated as violently as the wheels jolting over the cobbles. Hartford eased himself out of his seat. A waiting footman helped him out of the carriage, then he stood, holding his arm out, and she took it.

A row of servants had gathered to greet their new mistress, and each one bowed or curtseyed silently as she passed, showing no emotion. Their blank faces had been schooled not to betray their own emotions but, rather, to reflect those of their master. One or two of the younger servants cast her a curious glance, no doubt wondering why a woman married a man nearly forty years her senior.

At the end of the line the butler waited. Unlike Papa's butler, his smile bore a look of benign obedience.

"Welcome, your ladyship."

"Fossett, some tea in the drawing room, if you please," Hartford said, before he turned to Alice. "Or perhaps my wife would prefer a brandy?"

"N-no thank you, Lord Hartford," Alice stammered. Her stomach lurched at the mention of their relationship.

He took her hand, the gesture most likely intended to comfort, but it only served to increase the maelstrom within her.

"George," he said. "Remember, there should be no formalities between us."

"G-george."

"That's better. Are you tired, my dear?"

"Yes."

"Then we should retire. Come." He looked over his shoulder. "Fossett, see to it that her ladyship's maid prepares her belongings."

"Yes, my lord."

Alice let her husband lead her up the stairs. Perhaps it was for the best that there had been no wedding breakfast, for she would have expelled it. The knots in her stomach tightened, and her chest constricted. The walls seemed to be closing around her, and the stairs shifted under her feet. Hartford tightened his grip.

"Steady, my dear," he whispered. "Not far to go now. The bed-chamber is only a few steps away."

Bedchamber...

They arrived at a large oak door which was half open. Dark panel-ing lined the walls of the chamber inside, deep red curtains stretching from floor to ceiling. But what drew her gaze was the large, four-poster bed at the far end of the room. The breath caught in her throat.

She bit her lip to suppress a whimper, and tears stung at her eyes. She lifted a hand to wipe them away and cried out as he caught it and squeezed her fingers.

"Alice," he whispered. "My sweet Alice, you have nothing to fear from me. Have I not promised to take care of you? Do you fear that because of my sex I am incapable of gentle behavior?"

He kissed her fingers, and she flinched instinctively. Disappointment flashed across his eyes and he sighed. "I see I must be patient."

He patted her hand. "Goodnight, my dear. I'll see you in the morning when you have rested. Fossett will send your maid to tend to you."

He released her hand, then retreated along the hallway. Before he disappeared, she called out. "George?"

"Yes, my dear?"

"Are you not going to lie with me?"

He shook his head and smiled, as if indulging in a private joke. "Whatever for?"

"It—it's a husband's right." She cast her gaze down, shame warming her cheeks. "A wife has her duty."

He shook his head. "My dear Alice, my days of making love to a pretty woman are long gone. I didn't offer marriage to you for physical gratification or, for that matter, for the pleasure of having a woman at my beck and call."

"Please," she whispered, "if you're going to do the deed, I'd prefer if it were tonight. I will oblige you, if it's what you want."

He cursed under his breath, and she closed her eyes to shut out his contempt. Soft footsteps drew near, and a hand took hers.

"Look at me, Alice."

She blinked away the tears and looked up. Kind, brown eyes regarded her thoughtfully, pity and concern in their expression.

"Alice, I do not refuse to lie with you out of any lack of regard for your beauty, but out of my respect and affection for you. I'm no fool, despite what my son and the rest of society thinks. I am able to see beyond the surface. I often watched you with your late husband. I knew his father well, we were at Eton together."

A ripple of fear threaded through her at the mere thought of Roderick, even though Hartford hadn't mentioned his name.

"Let us not pursue it further," Hartford continued. "It only remains for me to say that I believe after what you endured, you've earned yourself a little peace. And I intend to ensure you have it."

He held out his hand. "May I?"

Slowly, she extended her hand to his and closed her fingers around it. With a smile of gratitude, he lifted her hand to his lips.

"I shall see you in the morning, my dear. Tomorrow marks the first day of our life together when we travel to my estate in the country. I'm sure the fresh, Dorset air will restore your health and spirits. I intend to devote my time, however much of it I have left, to restoring the balance of peace in your world."

He bowed once more, then disappeared. Shortly afterward, her maid ushered her into the chamber, then helped her to undress and led her to the bed. She pulled back the covers to reveal a warming pan.

"Goodnight, your ladyship." The maid bobbed a curtsey and left Alice alone, feeling, for the first time, cared for and protected.

CHAPTER TEN

THE JOURNEY TO Dorset took three days and two nights. Alice's new husband had already made the arrangements, and at each inn they stopped at, supper awaited them in a private room. Each night he kissed her chastely on her forehead, in the manner of a doting uncle, then left her in peace until the morning.

By the time they reached Belfield Park, her fears had almost completely dissipated. Away from the public atmosphere of London, Hartford still maintained his gentleness toward her. Surrounded by the peace and quiet of the countryside, his kindness seemed only to increase.

As the carriage passed farmhouses and barns, the tenants ran outside, hailing their lord and welcoming him back. So unlike the ride to Markham Hall after her marriage to Roderick. Here, the tenants clearly loved their lord. Children raced out of the houses and ran alongside the carriage, calling out in greeting. Hartford lowered the window and called back, smiling and waving at the people.

The hall, a building of soft, gray stone, stood bathed in the winter sunlight. Highlights of pink and orange glowed in the windows, warm lights to welcome her home. As the carriage drew to a halt beside the steps leading to the main doors, a footman opened the door and Hartford stepped out, turning to hold his hand out to her. She took it, and he squeezed it affectionately.

"Welcome home, my dear."

She climbed out of the carriage, Monty in her arms, and shivered as the chill of the winter air brushed across her face.

"Are you quite well, Alice?"

She nodded and let him lead her to the steps. A row of servants stood to greet her, one on each step, ascending to the main doors where the butler and housekeeper stood, the butler dressed in black and the housekeeper in a trim, dark blue gown, a set of keys hanging from a belt around her waist.

Each servant acknowledged Alice as she walked up the steps past them, the footmen clicking their heels and issuing a bow, the maidservants bobbing curtseys, all welcoming her home in soft, reverent voices. The butler, a man older even than Hartford himself, bowed and gave her a warm smile, his gray eyes twinkling in the evening light. For a moment, they reminded her of another pair of eyes exactly the same color.

"Welcome, my lady," he said, giving her a bow. "I hope you'll be happy here. I must say what a pleasure it is that Belfield Hall has a new mistress." He turned to Hartford. "And you, my lord, welcome home."

"Thank you, Hastings," Hartford said. "Is her ladyship's gift ready?"

"Aye, my lord."

"A gift?" Alice asked.

"Of course." Hartford smiled. "But you must wait for it, my dear. I will show you once we've taken tea."

"It's ready in the morning room," the housekeeper said.

"Thank you, Mrs. Sumner." He took Alice's other hand. "Come, my dear. Let us take tea then, if you're not too tired, I'll show you what I have planned for you."

WHAT I HAVE planned for you.

Roderick had used almost the same words as a precursor to one of his punishments—when she had committed an infraction of his many rules concerning her behavior.

While Alice had taken tea with her husband, she remained subdued, containing her fears within herself. Hartford was nothing but kind.

Now, as the gravel crunched underfoot as they strode together outside, the fear magnified into terror, and her body shook.

"My dear, are you well?"

She took a sharp breath and shook her head. "Forgive me, George, I'm a little out of spirits."

"I understand."

"I'm not sure you do."

He sighed. "You think me devoid of observation, Alice? I'm well aware that the ailment you suffer, though not of a physical nature, is just as crippling as my own. I see how you strive to hide it."

He patted her hand. "You need time to heal, and I must learn to recognize the signs. Ah! Here we are."

They reached a courtyard with a row of stables along the far end.

"Hello there!"

A groom appeared from behind the stables. He removed his cap and approached them with swift footsteps, giving them a bow when he stopped.

"Begging your pardon your lordship, I did not realize you'd be here so soon."

"My wife, sadly, has the appetite of a bird," Hartford said, "and we finished our tea sooner than planned. Forgive me, I was eager for her to see her gift."

"As you wish."

The young man bowed again, then disappeared through one of the stable doors. Moments later, he emerged with a gray mare.

"What do you think, my dear?"

"She's beautiful," Alice breathed.

"Go and see her."

She removed her gloves, and the animal watched her warily as she moved closer and held her hand out. A faint puff of breath blew from the animal's nostrils, which quivered as she placed her hand on its forehead. The fur was smooth and silky, and she ran her hand down the animal's nose, tracing the markings on the fur with light fingertips. The animal's ears, which had lain back, twitched and lifted, a sign of trust.

"There, there," she breathed, and she moved close enough to lay her head against the mare's flank. The animal gave a snort and shifted toward her.

"I've heard you're a formidable horsewoman," Hartford said, his voice deep with indulgence. "I see I've made an excellent choice, not only in my wife, but in her gift."

"My gift?"

"Yes, my dear," he said, smiling. "Did you think just because I'm an old man, that I'm not so gallant as to want to present my bride with a gift? I'm sure Artemis will provide you with many opportunities to enjoy the fresh air."

"Artemis?"

"A fitting name, don't you think? The goddess of the hunt and of good health. You might wish to bring her when we attend Westbury's house party at Ravenwell Hall next week."

"House party?" A ripple of dread ran through her, and she shrank back. The last house party she attended, she'd fled before dinner had been served. As if it sensed her fear, the horse stamped its foot and shook its head.

"A wider acquaintance would be good for you," Hartford said. "Westbury is an excellent young man, and I believe his wife is sister to your friend, Jane Claybone. If you are to recover your spirits and regain your independence, you must make the first steps. And I believe these will be the easiest steps you can take. It's only for a few days, my dear, then we can enjoy Christmas in peace."

He smiled, his eyes twinkling. "I'm also anxious for them to see how fortunate I am in my choice of wife."

Alice stroked the horse's flank, the action intended to give her as much comfort as the animal. "Who else will be there?"

"Just a small party. Earl Stiles and his wife—I understand you're friends with the countess? One or two of Westbury's other friends will attend, but I can assure you, his wife is very particular when it comes to selecting guest lists. As such, you're unlikely to find any of them less than welcoming toward you."

"Are you certain?"

A flicker of doubt crossed his face. "My son will be there. Westbury and he are old schoolfriends. But don't let that worry you, my dear. My son may be a fool, but he's intelligent enough not to insult my wife."

"But a whole company of people," she shook her head. "I don't know if I could bear it."

"Westbury's house parties are informal affairs, and he prefers his guests to come and go as they please. I suspect the only occasion everyone will be together is at dinner and the hunt. You may join in as many or as little of the activities as you wish. You can remain by my side the whole time if you prefer, but I would have you spend time in the company of others your own age. You have your whole life ahead of you, whereas I..."

He broke off, a smile of resignation on his lips.

"Come, my dear. Let us return inside."

The groom, understanding the cue, took the reins from Alice's hand and led the mare back into the stables.

She linked her arm with her husband's, and together they returned to the house.

CHAPTER ELEVEN

ALICE LOOKED UP from her plate of scrambled eggs as a clatter of hooves echoed outside.

Hartford glanced at his pocket watch.

"Who on earth can that be at this hour?" he asked. "My steward is not due until nine."

"Perhaps your doctor?"

Hartford smiled. "I've not sent for him, my dear. I've had no need to send for him. I'm in the peak of health thanks to you."

Blushing, Alice resumed her attention on her breakfast. Voices echoed outside, and the door opened to reveal a familiar figure dressed in a dark blue jacket and riding boots. He took off his hat and gloves and handed them, along with his riding crop, to the nearby footman.

"Dominic!" Hartford rose from his seat to greet his son. "To what do we owe the pleasure?"

"This is my home," Dominic said, an edge to his voice.

"And you're very welcome in it," Hartford replied.

"May I join you for breakfast?"

"What say you, my dear?"

"Please do," Alice said. "Shall I retire? I have no wish to intrude on your conversation with your son."

Dominic moved toward a chair, and a footman hurried to pull it out to let him sit, while another rushed forward and set a place before him.

"I'd rather you stayed," Dominic said. "What I have to say concerns you both."

Alice set her fork down, unable to control the trembling in her limbs. Dominic glanced at her, then sighed.

"I'm come to pay my respects," he said, a subdued expression on his face, "which are long overdue. And to apologize to you, madam, for not paying them sooner."

Though he smiled, his eyes lacked the warmth of his father's. Nevertheless, he was making an effort, and any gesture of cordiality, in a world which held her in contempt, was to be treasured.

She returned the smile. "There's nothing to forgive, Dominic," she said. "I fully understand your feelings. Don't forget I lost my mother, too. Nobody can replace your mother, and I have no intention of doing so. I hope we may be better acquainted in time and that you'll come to see me as a friend."

"Then with your permission, I'd like to stay for a few days, perhaps travel with you to Ravenwell Hall for Westbury's house party."

"I'll defer to your papa, Dominic," she said. "But I would very much like it if you did."

"Please do, Dominic." Hartford lifted his teacup as if in salute. "And I must say how proud I am of you."

"Splendid!" Dominic rose to help himself to breakfast from the side table, a spring in his step.

Alice exchanged smiles with her husband. But as Dominic sat down, he cast a swift glance at her, his eyes narrowing momentarily. It was as if the ghost of Roderick Markham looked out at her. But when he blinked, the moment was gone.

She drained her teacup and summoned her resolve. She would not let Roderick's memory taint her new life. Dominic might be hotheaded, but he was prepared to welcome her into the family. If she were able to show she did not intend to supplant him as the primary focus of his father's love, they would soon become firm friends. Then she would have two allies in the world of men.

Her hopes for a happy, settled family life only increased as Dominic's visit wore on. He was a source of entertaining after-dinner conversation, regaling her with his sharp observations on the less desirable members of society. When he likened de Blanchard to a bloated boar whose face had been boiled in grease, she burst out laughing, something she never believed she'd do again. But what warmed her to him the most was the attention he gave his father.

Alice and Dominic found a common ground in tending to the old man when the rigors of the day overwhelmed him. Dominic insisted that he, rather than the servants, help him upstairs after he suffered a sudden loss of breath, and he proved a useful helpmate when Alice administered Hartford's medicine.

Even the weather shone on their new-found cordiality. The morning of the third day of his visit dawned bright and sunny, and the mist gave way to a clear sky, a marked contrast to the rain which had plagued them the day before.

Alice itched to bathe in the sunlight and breathe the fresh air, which always cleared away her memories. Dearest George possessed such insight, that she had no need to make any request of him. As the three of them were eating breakfast, he gestured toward the window.

"My dear, why don't you take a turn about the park today?"

"I–I don't know, George," she said. "Should I not remain by your side?"

"Nonsense!" he laughed. "As capable as you are at tending to me, I can bear my own company for a few hours. With the nights drawing in, you must seize every opportunity to enjoy the sun. Perhaps my son would accompany you."

"It would be my pleasure," Dominic said. "I will see you by the main doors, Alice."

For a moment, a predatory look glittered in his expression, then he bowed and took his leave.

Hartford leaned back in his chair, contentment in his expression.

"At every turn, my son surprises me. Just when I think he's settled into the life of a rake, he shows some mettle. Perhaps when I depart this world, the estate will be in good hands after all. The trustees will be relieved."

Alice rose from her seat and crossed the breakfast room to her husband, taking one of his hands in her own.

"George, please don't say such things. Let us enjoy life here and now."

He patted her hand affectionately. "You're right, my dear," he said. "But I must accept my own mortality and ensure my loved ones will be well looked after. My son, my estate, and now you, my dear Alice. The trustees control my affairs, but I want you cared for after I'm gone. But I realize I have no worries on that score. My son is as devoted to you as I, and he's promised that you shall be taken care of."

For a moment, his eyes took on a vacant look, then his smile resumed.

"But as you say, now is not the time to speak of such things. Go and enjoy your walk, my dear."

THE FOREST, WHICH lined the path, thinned out to reveal a small summer house tucked away in a forgotten-looking corner. The surrounding trees were almost completely bare, their branches poking toward the sky as if pleading for the onset of spring.

"This is my favorite part of the park," Dominic said. "I used to play here as a child, when..." His voice faltered as he gestured toward the building.

A solitary statue of a woman stood like a sentinel at the entrance, the once-white marble now tainted with a greenish hue. Her face bore a look of determination as if she might come to life and defend her charges against marauders.

"She's beautiful," Alice said.

"I had her commissioned from a stonemason in Weymouth." Dominic approached the statue, placed a hand on the carved face, and brushed the lips with his thumb. "I've not seen her for some time. She's as beautiful as I remember. Worth every penny, despite what *he* said."

"Is she Venus?"

"No," he said. "She's from Greek mythology, a seer whom nobody believed. She warned of the folly of trusting those pretended to be allies, but was ignored, and it led to a massacre."

"You speak of Cassandra and the downfall of Troy?"

"Cassandra…"

She would have missed his quiet whisper were it not for the ache in his voice which resonated with her own grief for a lost parent.

"She's a memorial to your mother."

His body stiffened.

"Do you miss her?" she asked.

He turned and looked back toward the main hall. Bathed in the morning light, it dominated the horizon with benevolent care. Silent, solid, and caring. Like the man who ruled over it.

Dominic sighed. "My home. And it will be all mine one day. Very soon."

She turned to face him and he smiled, but his eyes remained hard.

"You shouldn't speak of such things, Dominic. Not while your father…"

"My father." he said, his voice rising. "The man who never forgave me for being my mother's son."

"He loves you, Dominic," she said. "He was most upset when you didn't come to our wedding."

He gave a snort. "Doubtless he cared more for his bride's sensibilities. I've always been a disappointment to him. I remind him too much of my mother."

"He loved her," Alice said. "He speaks of her often."

"No," Dominic said, his voice hardening. "He didn't love *my* mother. He loved yours."

"How can you say such things?"

"Because they're true. He spoke of Lady de Grecy too often. Mother bore it because she loved him. Why do you think he married you, Alice? He couldn't have your mother, so he waited until he could bed the daughter he wished he'd had. It's disgusting."

She recoiled at his obscenity. "No!" she cried. "You cannot think..."

"I'll think what I like in my own home," he snarled. "You expect me to stand by and watch while you drain his funds with your cow-like eyes and pleading demeanor?"

"How dare you insult me so!" she cried. "I have no such intentions on your father."

"You may have fooled him, but you'll find me a better protector of my inheritance," he said. "Only last night he told me how he wanted to make sure you were *taken care of*. Perhaps that's his notion of generosity toward his son, by sharing out his wife."

His shadow lengthened and stretched into another shape. The familiar hateful silhouette seemed to expand, the bright sunlight rendering the shadows black as a familiar voice echoed in her mind. The echo increased, whirling into a vortex, filling her mind with darkness.

Hateful, barren little bitch! Why must you always be such a disappointment? You'd be nothing were it not for me. Come here. Here, I say!

He lunged for her, and she let out a scream and lashed out at the nightmare. Her fingernails met flesh, and she curled her hand, tearing at her assailant. Blood pounded in her ears as iron-hard arms wrapped around her, morphing into the chains they'd secured her with in her cell when the nightmares had conquered her wits. He held her close, and she leaned forward and sank her teeth into warm flesh.

"Christ!"

With a roar, he released her, but she was not done yet. Never again would a man take her unwilling. She fisted her hand, drew her arm back, then rammed her fist into his stomach.

He toppled onto the ground with a cry, and she backed away. Her vision cleared and she blinked. Roderick's ghost had disappeared, replaced by the man who lay before her.

He pushed himself upright. Blood dripped from a wound on his hand and three parallel lines crossed the left side of his face, reddening where she'd broken the skin.

"At last, she reveals herself," he said. "The Deranged Duchess has come to haunt the shades of Belfield." He touched his cheek and winced. "I now bear the mark of a madwoman. But I'll not permit you to infect my father with your insanity. When everyone sees what you've done to me, you'll be sent back to Bedlam. And I, for one, intend to ensure your incarceration is permanent."

He rose to his feet and moved toward her, and she picked up her skirts and fled into the forest, as if the demons of Bedlam were snapping at her heels.

"Come back here!" he cried.

Her foot caught on a stone, and she pitched forward and fell, the hem of her dress tearing. Like Roderick had always been, Dominic was too strong and too fast for her. Her best chance was to remain hidden. Like a deer, she remained still, waiting for his footsteps to crash through the undergrowth.

But instead, she heard his voice.

"You can't run forever, Alice. Belfield Park is mine. That decaying old bastard won't live forever, then I'll have you hauled back to your cell before he's cold in his grave!"

She struggled to her feet and continued into the forest. It thinned out into a field dotted with sheep. The rain from the past two days had soaked the ground, and mud seeped into her shoes.

The sheep lifted their heads as she passed, their jaws moving side to side as they continued to chew, then lowered their heads on realizing she posed no threat. For a moment, she envied them. They had such simple needs, food, water, and shelter. But the simple life was not one she craved any more. She had a purpose, not only the lost souls at Mrs. Taylor's who depended on her, but the kind, loving man whose son was biding his time, waiting for his death.

Despite his superior strength, Dominic Hartford would never conquer her. Nor would any man again.

She followed the perimeter of the field until the hall became visible again. The huge building promised to be a haven among the perilous waters. But within resided someone who needed her as much as she needed him.

⟫⟩⟨⟪

BY THE TIME she reached the house, her feet were soaked, the soles covered in blisters. Her gown was six inches deep in mud and her hair in disarray. The footman at the door recoiled in horror, presumably thinking a farm urchin had come to visit, then regained his composure on recognizing his mistress.

The butler appeared beside him.

"Good lord, your ladyship, what on earth happened to you?"

"I'm sorry, Hastings. I had an accident."

"Quite so," he said. "His lordship asked that you attend him immediately."

"Might I be given leave to freshen up first?"

The butler glanced at her gown, his lips forming a straight line. "He was very particular in his instructions. You're to go to the morning room directly."

The footman coughed nervously, and Alice's stomach churned in apprehension.

"I will, of course, do as my husband wishes."

As if escorting a mud-stained disheveled woman were an everyday occurrence, the butler led her to the morning room with the bland formality of the upper servants. He knocked smartly on the door and pushed it open.

"Her ladyship has just returned."

The knot in her stomach tightened. Her husband sat beside the fireplace as usual, but he seemed to have aged since breakfast. His skin had a gray pallor, the wrinkles more prominent. His hands were clasped on his lap, the fingers thin and bony, blue veins visible beneath the translucent skin which stretched across the backs of his hands.

"George…"

"Not so fast!" Dominic stood beside the fireplace, leaning on the mantelshelf, a lazy smile on his lips. He stood upright and folded his arms. "I wondered when you might return. I expected it to be earlier, but I presume you needed sufficient time in order to straighten out your story."

"That's enough, Dominic," Hartford said. "Let her speak for herself. I'm anxious to know how my son sustained his injuries, after which my wife returned home in such an unseemly state."

"It's as I said, Father." Dominic gestured toward her. "You only have to look at her to see what she is! She's been deceiving you. I mean no disrespect, but a woman such as her would not marry a man of your age for love. She set her cap at you to secure another title, and as soon as she secured your affections and promises of money, she offered herself to me. How many other men has she promised her body to?"

"As you have said, Dominic, but…"

"When I refused, she became violent. I've never seen such fury! Just like the rumors I warned you about, Father. Rumors of madness. She was so strong it was a struggle to fend her off." He gestured toward his scratched face. "See what she's done to me!"

"I do," Hartford said. "But she, too, does not appear to be un-scathed."

"She threatened to turn you against me, Father. Like I said earlier, I had to get here first before she cast another spell on you."

Dominic knelt beside his father and took his hands. "Can't you see what she's doing? You're the laughing stock of society, the man ensnared by the madwoman."

Hartford bent his head over his son's hands, and Dominic lifted his hand and caressed his father's cheek.

"You know it to be true," he said, "don't you, Father? Please, for your own sake, take action before it's too late."

Alice stepped back, powerless against a son's tender words, no matter how false they might be. Hartford looked directly at her. The despair and utter sadness in his expression tore at her heart.

"Alice," he said, his voice grave. "Have you nothing to say?"

Father and son watched her, their features so alike. When all else failed, blood ties would always be the strongest.

What had Dominic said about Cassandra? She was forever cursed by mistrust, never to be believed.

"No, George," she said. "I have nothing to say. Nothing I have ever said changed a man's opinion of me when he'd already formed it."

Hartford nodded, resignation in his eyes. Slowly, he withdrew his hands from Dominic's grasp and clasped them together as if in contemplation.

At length he spoke, his voice so quiet, she almost thought she'd imagined it.

"I want you to leave," he said.

"Bravo, Father." Dominic stood, a smile of triumph on his lips.

She took another step back.

"Stop!" Hartford's voice rooted her to the spot. He jabbed a finger at his son.

"I meant *you*," he said. "You think me a fool? That two days of simpering and smiling would convince me you're no longer the reprobate I've always known you to be? I wondered to what lengths you would go to discredit my wife in my eyes."

"She lies!" Dominic said.

"My wife has said nothing," Hartford snapped, "but you have spoken several times. You must think me a simpleton if you believe mere words would convince me. I only have to look at my wife to see the state you've left her in, to understand what you've done."

He rose to his feet, the color returning to his cheeks. "Alice, come here."

She moved to his side, and he drew her into his arms, seemingly not caring for the mud on her gown which smeared against his jacket. "My dearest Alice, you never have to explain yourself to me, for I understand you better than most. I'm only sorry you thought so little of me as to believe I'd think the worst of you. I must strive to prove myself a better man."

He caressed her hair, then hardened his voice. "As for you, Dominic, I want you gone from this house. You are no longer my son!"

"No!" Alice cried. "Please, George, do not cast him out."

"Why, Alice? Why would you speak for him?"

"He's your son!" she cried, and her voice broke. "A child is a gift to be cherished. Please don't do anything you'll regret. You have no idea how fortunate you are to be blessed with a child."

He sighed and held her against his chest, his heartbeat faint against her ear. "I understand, my dear, and I know why you believe it to be so. To think you'd plead my son's case only serves to show me that I am doubly fortunate in my choice of wife. But I must insist. For your peace of mind and mine."

"You old fool!" Dominic made an explosive sound of rage. "But I'll have my day, Father. Mark my words, you'll both be sorry when that day comes."

He strode out of the room, slamming the door behind him, and he shouted at the footman before he disappeared. Soon after, the crunching of hooves against gravel signaled his departure.

Hartford let out a sigh.

"I'm glad that's over." He released Alice and held her at arm's length, his gaze falling on her torn gown.

"I see I must write to Madame Chassigneux once more." He took her hand. "Forgive me, Alice, it was most remiss of me to leave you standing there in such a state. But I wanted to see for myself what my son had done before making my decision."

"What made you doubt him?"

He drew her hand to his chest and held it over his heart.

"My dear Alice, I knew from the moment you uttered your vows that you were the purest soul on this earth, to whom no one can compare. Like my impending mortality, the one unwavering factor in my life is my faith in you."

He leaned forward and kissed her forehead. "Now, run along before you catch a chill. Hastings will see to it that you're looked after and, if you would oblige me, I wish to enjoy a quiet supper tonight with my lovely wife."

He rang the bell, and Hastings arrived. In a quiet voice, he issued orders that Lady Hartford be tended to with the greatest care.

As she sank back into a warm bath, Lizzie's gentle hands washing the mud out of her hair, Alice allowed herself to relax. At every turn, Hartford showed unwavering devotion and compassion toward her. Perhaps, at last, she had found peace.

CHAPTER TWELVE

ROSS CLUTCHED AT the reins of his mount as the delicate ripple of female laughter burst through the cold, damp air. At least someone was enjoying this godforsaken weather, probably some of Westbury's guests wanting to exercise their horses before the hunt. But if this rain persisted, Westbury would be a fool if he didn't call off the hunt altogether.

Though he wasn't in the mood for socializing, the familiarity of the laugh stirred a memory of happier times and compelled him to steer his mount toward the voices.

A woman dressed in a dark blue riding habit had her back to him, but her horsemanship was evident in the ease with which she sat in the saddle. Her companion displayed less skill as his mount fidgeted while the two continued to talk. He threw back his head and laughed at something the woman said, and Ross recognized him. Barely out of boyhood, Edward Drayton.

Edward was Westbury's bastard son, though woe betide any man who mentioned his lineage in front of his father. Or the duchess, for that matter. Westbury's wife was all fire and spirit, and she loved her stepson as if he were her own. She ruled over her husband as effectively as Westbury ruled over his estate. But her steel core was enveloped in a lush, womanly body and the kindest, most loyal of hearts.

The perfect woman. Or she would have been, were it not for another…

The woman laughed again. Recognition punched him in the gut, and he almost lost his grip on the reins.

Alice.

It wasn't the victim he'd come to know in the past weeks. This was a different Alice, the animated, laughing creature he had first come to love.

He spurred his horse into a trot and approached them. The young man failed to notice him, his adoring gaze locked onto his companion. But she turned her head. The laughter in her eyes faded as Ross drew his horse to a halt. Her dignified expression seemed to resonate with the dark blue of her apparel.

He curled his hand around the reins. "I suppose I must congratulate you on your marriage, Lady Hartford. It seems only last week I heard of your engagement."

Edward cast Ross a nervous glance. Alice said nothing but set her mouth into a firm line.

"I trust the viscount is well," Ross said.

She curled her lip and looked straight at him, tipping her chin up.

"Have you nothing to say to me, your ladyship?"

She glanced sideways at the young man. "Edward, would you be so good as to see to Monty? I fear he's very particular about the company he keeps, and he seems to have taken a liking to you."

"But, Lady Hartford," the boy stuttered. "Lord Hartford entrusted me with your care and made me promise to remain by your side. Your dog can wait a little longer, surely?"

"I shan't be long, Edward," she said, her voice steady despite the turmoil in her eyes. "My husband need never know. I don't want him worried."

"Very well." The boy nodded to Ross, then spurred his horse and disappeared into the mist, his mount throwing clods of earth into the air behind him.

"Why deceive your husband, Alice?" Ross asked. "Are you afraid of him?"

She narrowed looked away, her gaze following the route Edward had taken.

"He worries if I venture out unescorted," she said. "I am thinking of him."

"Are you?"

She sighed. "I care not what you think, Ross."

"Then why send the boy away?"

"Because if you have some new admonishment or insult to say, I'd rather Edward were not included in it."

"I merely came to congratulate you on your marriage," he said.

"Your congratulations are welcome," she replied, "though I wonder at the mode of delivery."

"Can you blame me?" His voice lifted a pitch as the muscles of his throat tightened. "Society will say that you married, with a noteworthy degree of haste, a rich old man in possession of a title."

"And you think I care what society says?"

"I care, Alice," he said. "It pains me to hear them gossip. If I could spare you from it, I would."

"You must believe me a simpleton if you think I don't know what they're saying about me," she said. "But I owe them nothing. My reasons for marrying Hartford I shall keep to myself. You—and the rest of the world—are at liberty to think of me what you will."

She moved her hands to steer her mount, and he reached out and took her wrist. Eyes wide with fear, her body stiffened, and her mount shuddered as if it felt the tension in her.

"Unhand me, sir."

"Not until I have satisfaction."

She wrenched her hand free. Her mount reared up, and she steered it round, controlling it with expert hands.

"Shall I give you the satisfaction you crave?" she cried. "Very well. I married Hartford because he's the only man in London who does not look upon me as a creature to be ridiculed or pitied. I know what they all call me, Mad Alice, they say, the Deranged Duchess! Beware or she'll eat your children and scratch your eyes out!"

She lifted a hand and wiped her eyes in an angry gesture.

"Hartford is the only man who sees beyond the caricature. He's never judged me. He doesn't treat me as an inferior or as an object to own and conquer. He gives me freedom and choices. He stood up to Papa and defended me when he had no need to. I have nothing to give him, Ross, nothing! Yet still he wants to take care of me and treat me with kindness and affection. What is wealth, or a title, compared to that?"

Guilt stung him, and he reached out to her.

"Oh, Alice," he said, his voice hoarse, "he's not the only..."

She lifted her hand, brandishing her riding crop.

"Don't come any closer!" she cried. "You dare criticize me for following the footsteps of every other woman in society. Why single me out, Ross? Society holds me in contempt for what I am. But you..." She bowed her head. "Did I hurt you so badly that you harbor such hatred for me?"

"No," he whispered. "Dear God, no, Alice, I could never..."

But before he could finish, she spurred her horse into a gallop and was gone.

⟫⟫⟩⟨⟨⟨

ALICE SIPPED HER sherry and relaxed into the armchair. She had not wanted to leave George, but he'd insisted on her joining the party while he rested, assuring her he would join them before dinner was announced.

The parlor door opened. Clearly another guest was also in need of an early drink before the rest of the party congregated.

Her heart skipped as Ross entered the room.

"Oh," he said. "Pardon me, I didn't expect anyone else to be here this early. Would you like me to go, if you prefer solitude?"

She shook her head, "No, please join me, if you don't mind my company."

"I would never mind your company," he said. His brow furrowed and an expression of discomfort flashed in his eyes.

"Lady Hartford..." he hesitated. "...Alice. Permit me to apologize."

"What for?"

He gave her a pained smile. "Everything. The things I said, the pain I caused."

"You never caused me pain, Ross," she said. "Any pain I endured was of my own doing."

He crossed the floor and took her hand. A thrill coursed through her as his fingers curled round hers. "You did nothing wrong, Alice."

She withdrew her hand. He moved away, toward the decanter and poured himself a drink, then sat, watching her.

"Are you happy?" he asked.

"Yes, Ross," she said. "I'm happier than I've been for many years."

He smiled, his eyes gleaming a soft silver. "Then I must be content with that. Forgive my rudeness this afternoon when I said society was gossiping about you. If Hartford makes you happy then nobody has the right to judge—least of all myself."

He leaned forward, his expression growing in intensity. "Does he treat you well? Are you granted freedom?"

She smiled. "I am more free than I have ever been. I have my friends, my horse. He even permits me to visit Mrs. Taylor."

"Unaccompanied?"

"Yes," she said. "He was reluctant at first, but he understands the difference between protection and incarceration."

"It was good to see you riding today," he said. "I never knew a more accomplished horsewoman." His mouth curved into a gentle smile. "Do you recall the day you challenged me to a race in the country?"

"Yes," she replied. "I remember telling you how much easier it was for a man because he rode astride, and you offered to lend me a pair of your breeches."

"If I recall," he said, "I did so because you told me I would be unable to make an acceptable fashion statement if I were to wear your riding habit. Apparently green velvet with red trim didn't suit me, though I still maintain to this day that I would have found the cut of the skirt flattering to my figure."

The light dancing in his eyes transported her to another time. She let out a laugh as she recalled the day he'd attempted to put on her riding jacket and split the seams across his broad chest.

"It's good to hear you laugh," he said, "and I'm glad you're visiting Mrs. Taylor."

"I thought you disapproved."

"I did at first, but I have grown to understand the fulfilment achieved through helping others, through giving those women a safe place to stay, finding them employment. Mrs. Taylor is to be admired for her ability to make such a small income stretch so far."

"She has learned to use her funds wisely," Alice said.

Ross smiled. "That she has. Why, only the other day she told me that a mere five shillings can…" He broke off and sipped his drink.

"You seem to know a lot about Mrs. Taylor," she said.

He nodded toward the glass in her hand. "Shall I pour you another?"

"Please do."

After refilling her glass, he took the chair next to hers.

"I found myself admiring your mount this afternoon," he said.

"George was most obliging to gift Artemis to me," she replied. "By all accounts her previous owner mistreated her, but she thrived under George's care."

"And will you also thrive?" he asked.

"He gives me peace," she said. "One might say he's like a father—or how I imagine a father ought to be."

His body relaxed and he nodded and smiled, as if in relief.

"Then permit me to offer my best wishes for your happiness. I had procured a gift for you, but I feared you'd deem it impertinent."

"A gift?"

"It's a little worse for wear, I'm afraid. I intended to give it to you several days ago, but I have not had the opportunity, and I couldn't bring myself to discard it."

He reached into his pocket and withdrew a small, round object. Though shriveled, she recognized it, nonetheless.

A single orange.

Her chest constricted at the memories brought forth by his offering, and she closed her eyes. But the memories only strengthened. She opened them again and avoided his gaze.

"Ross... Mr. Trelawney... I-I'm sorry, I cannot accept it."

He reached for her hand then drew back. He smiled but the expression in his eyes spoke of regret and sadness.

"Alice," he whispered. "I..."

The door burst open and a number of guests entered the room, laughing, accompanied by Westbury and his wife.

"Alice!" the duchess cried. "There you are! Edward's been looking all over for you. He's anxious to know whether he can set aside some of tonight's ragout for Montague. I must say, I've been concerned about the prospect of him entering adulthood and exposing his heart to the wiles of some fortune-hunting debutante. But it seems that any young woman wishing to entrap him must compete with a pug."

Ross rose to greet Westbury. Jeanette watched him, her eyes narrowing, before she resumed her attention on Alice.

THE DISCOMFORT, WHICH had plagued Ross from the moment he'd seen Alice that afternoon, intensified while he watched her at dinner. She was all smiles and affection toward her husband, showing such tender devotion while she helped him with his meal and leaning toward him while he whispered in her ear. Her father had sold her to a man old enough to be her grandfather, but did she have to play at being his lover in public?

Lover...

The soup solidified in his stomach, and he pushed his bowl away.

"Are you unwell, Mister Trelawney?" He looked up to see their hostess had leaned forward, her face illuminated in the candlelight.

"I'm quite well, thank you, Duchess," he said, reaching for a glass of water.

Dominic sat across the table. He looked as out of sorts as Ross felt. His dark gaze was fixed on his father and stepmother, the muscles in his jaw pulsing as if he gritted his teeth to control his fury.

The rage in Dominic's eyes only seemed to increase as the meal wore on, at every smile his father bestowed on Alice, every tender word of thanks as she helped him. By the time dinner was over, Ross's own view of the world had been dulled by the wine.

As the gentlemen retired for brandy and cigars, leaving the ladies to adjourn to the drawing room for tea, Ross leaned on the man-telshelf, nodding to the passing butler who filled his glass almost to the brim. He tipped it up and swallowed it in a single gulp. The taste exploded on his tongue, sending heat through his veins.

"A man after my own heart."

Dominic stood before him, flanked on either side by their host and Rupert Oakville. Once the three most celebrated libertines of society, their little band of debauchery had disintegrated on Westbury's marriage, though Oakville and Dominic still enjoyed the delights of seduction.

"You seem out of sorts, Trelawney," Westbury said. "I trust it's nothing to do with our hospitality."

"No, of course not, Westbury," Ross said. "Your wife is, as usual, an exemplary hostess."

"With one flaw," Dominic slurred, a dribble of brandy on his lips. "Her choice of guests." He lifted his glass to Westbury. "My friend, I warned you not to let that madwoman into your home."

"I can't think who you mean, Dom," Westbury said. "Perhaps it's time to join the ladies in the drawing room."

"And engage in small talk with *her*?" Dominic spat. "She's even emasculated Father to the point where he's not man enough to join us for brandy. Instead, he simpers off with the ladies to gossip about embroidery or some such nonsense! She's condemned him to a life of insipidity, and for what? To rob me of my inheritance." He waved his glass around the room. "Everyone here will agree with me. She's turned him into the laughing stock of society, and her insanity will drive him into an early grave."

Ross tightened the grip on his glass as a knot of anger uncoiled in his stomach, like a snake preparing to strike.

Westbury cast a swift glance at him before turning his attention to Dominic. "Dom, I think you've indulged in a little too much of my brandy. Perhaps you should drink tea instead."

"Tea!" Dominic snorted. "Is that what your wife has reduced you to, Westbury? A witless sop whose manly parts sit in her palm? There was a time when you were a real man."

"What, like you?" Westbury gestured toward the scratch marks on Dominic's face and his bandaged thumb. "If you take a lady unwilling, she's bound to fight back."

"That wasn't a lady." He glanced at Alice. "I was bitten by one of father's bitches."

"That's enough, Dom," Westbury said sharply. "I suggest you retire for the evening."

"And make myself scarce while she seduces my father in public?

Did she ask you to rid yourself of me so she could continue to whore herself out to the father while the son is conveniently out of the way?"

The tide of anger spilled over. Ross curled his fingers around the glass, and with a sharp crack, the glass disintegrated, scattering shards onto the floor.

"You take that back, Dominic! You've no right to speak of a lady thus," Ross demanded.

"Lady, indeed!" Dom said. "I hear you courted her at one point before she discarded you for Markham. She must have been a bloody good fuck for you to defend her still. Perhaps I'll have a go if it's being shared around. Why pay for a doxy to service me when there's one residing in my father's bed!"

"How dare you!" Ross cried. He swung his hand back and smashed into Dominic's smiling face. He went for another hit, but Westbury pulled him back.

"You dog! I should knock you senseless!" Dominic cried. He rushed toward Ross, but Oakville blocked him. In his state of inebriation, he presented little challenge.

"Come on then!" Ross cried, struggling in Westbury's grip. "Nothing would give me more pleasure!"

"That's enough!" Westbury roared. The room fell silent.

"May I remind both of you, you're guests in my home. If you wish to remain so, I suggest you refrain from such unseemly behavior."

"I don't care!" Ross cried. "He's insulted a lady's virtue. Dominic, I'm calling you out."

Oakville rolled his eyes. "Don't be a fool."

"On the contrary, nothing would give me greater pleasure than to finish off any man who defends that slattern," Dominic said. "What say we meet at dawn?"

"Don't you bloody dare!" Westbury hissed. "If you have a score to settle, you settle it like gentlemen."

"A duel is the only resolution for a gentleman," Dominic said.

"Not on my land," Westbury replied. "I won't allow it, and if my wife catches you engaging in a duel, she's likely to shoot you both herself."

Ross's anger, fueled by his instinct to protect Alice, began to lessen, and he held out his hand. "Dom, shall we shake on it?"

Dominic spat at his feet. "Not until you bleed, Trelawney."

"So be it."

"Then I've no alternative but to throw you both out," Westbury said.

"Perhaps the deed may be done with as little hurt as possible," Oakville said. "How about you spar with swords, and the first one to draw blood is declared the winner?"

"Suits me," Dominic said, his words slurring.

"Ross?" Westbury lifted his eyebrows.

"Very well," Ross sighed. He turned his gaze on Dominic who, though fueled by anger, looked ready to pass out at any moment. "If I win, Dominic, then you never insult your stepmother again."

"As you wish," Dominic said. "But if I win, Trelawney, then I can do as I like, and you are to desist from sniffing round her."

"That's settled then," Westbury sighed. "Dom, Oakville will act as your second and I'll second Ross. For now, I suggest you both retire. Neither of you is in a fit state to join the ladies tonight."

"Ladies!" Dominic snorted.

"That's enough!" Westbury said. "Get out of my sight, both of you. We meet at dawn tomorrow."

"As you wish." Ross gave their host a stiff bow and left the room. Not long after, Dominic joined him in the corridor and held out his hand.

"Till tomorrow, Trelawney."

Ross took it. "May the best man win."

Dominic tightened his grip and pulled Ross closer.

"Take care," he said. "A commoner should always look over his shoulder when he challenges his betters."

"First blood," Ross said. "You heard Westbury."

"The first blow is usually the deadliest," Dominic replied, a cold smile on his lips.

A shiver of fear rippled through Ross at the expression in the other man's eyes.

"This time tomorrow, Trelawney, I'll have silenced you for good." He bowed with mock courtesy, then turned his back and disappeared, leaving Ross alone in the corridor, his only companion his conscience and the faint sounds of the guests chattering in the drawing room.

CHAPTER THIRTEEN

A LICE SLIPPED OUT of a side door and headed toward the stables. George encouraged her to ride Artemis daily, and her preferred time was dawn, when the rest of the world slept. Dawn was like a rebirth. Light conquered the darkness as the sun rose from the horizon, heralded by the birds bursting into song.

Her hostess, in her kindness, was happy to oblige Alice in her wishes, and had promised the services of the head groom.

Raised voices came from a field beside the stables, and Alice followed the path toward the field. Two men stood, facing each other.

Another two stood a few paces away, and the tallest lifted his hand and held up an object which looked like a piece of cloth. He called out, and Alice recognized Westbury's voice. The object fluttered to the ground, and she caught a flash of sunlight glinting as the two men in the center raised their arms. They were brandishing swords.

She had stumbled across a duel.

The two swordsmen circled each other, swords aloft. Then, they charged and the clash of steel echoed through the air. One of the combatants sprang forward, slicing through the air, but his opponent dodged the blow and darted back. They circled again, the movement bringing them closer to Alice's vantage point.

They were well matched, each man able to read the other's attack and block the blow. They danced around each other, alternating between attack and defense, as if adhering to a gentlemanly code of conduct, giving each other a fair turn at drawing blood.

She held her breath. When duels were fought, the combatants rarely walked away uninjured. Would a man die today?

One of the duelers lifted his head, and her heart jolted in recognition. She let out a cry.

"Ross!"

He stopped in his tracks, and his opponent seized his chance. He charged toward Ross and thrust his sword forward. Ross fell to the ground, and his opponent held his sword aloft as if preparing to deliver the fatal blow.

Alice screamed and ran toward them.

"Stop right there!" Westbury's stentorian voice roared through the air.

Alice obeyed, immobilized by the strength of his voice. Ross's opponent held his sword in the air, not moving.

"Dominic, put that damned sword down," Westbury snapped. "You've had your blood."

"But..."

"I said to put the sword down!"

Dominic let the weapon fall, and the fourth man, who she recognized as Viscount Oakville, rushed toward it. Westbury bent over Ross and helped him up. Ross tried to move but yelped as he took the first step. A small stain appeared halfway down his thigh, a diagonal slash darkening and growing wider.

"My God!" Alice cried. "You're hurt!"

"Get away from here, Lady Hartford," Westbury said. "This is no place for a woman."

"It bloody is," Dominic growled. "It's her fault we're here."

"Be quiet, Dom," Westbury said. "Get back to the hall, have a brandy and be thankful the better swordsman didn't win. Were he not distracted, Trelawney would have sliced you in two." He cast a glance at Alice, a glimmer of accusation in his eyes, and she lowered her gaze.

"I'll not stay under your roof while *she* remains there," Dom snarled.

"Very well," Westbury said. "Oakville, help Dom to pack. My carriage is at his disposal should he wish to return to London."

Grumbling, Dominic let Oakville lead him across the field.

"Come on, Ross," Westbury said, circling his arm round the other man's waist. "Let's get you seen to."

Ross straightened and shook his head.

"It's just a scratch. No need to make a fuss."

"If you say so." Westbury turned to Alice. "Your ladyship, I suggest you continue with your morning ride. Can I trust you to be discreet?"

"Of course," she said, "and in turn, may I trust you to send for a doctor?"

"There's no need," Ross growled. But his expression belied his words. The skin around his eyes bore slight creases, and the strain in his voice resonated in her bones, until she could almost feel his pain.

"Mister Trelawney, please," she said. "For your own sake, have your wound tended to."

"Leave me be." He wrenched his arm free of his friend's and sauntered across the field in Dominic's wake.

"Your Grace…"

"I think you should respect my friend's wishes," Westbury interrupted her. He couldn't completely disguise the dislike in his voice. And why should he? He, too, had witnessed her disintegration into madness, after she'd jeopardized the life of his friend Stiles.

She turned her back and resumed her path to the stables. The warm greeting Artemis gave her when she recognized her mistress tore at her heart. If only men were like animals in that they didn't judge her for past sins.

BY THE TIME Alice returned to the hall, the fresh air had blown away her nightmares. Lizzie helped her into her day dress in silence. The maid understood when Alice's need for quiet was at its most intense. With nimble fingers, she set Alice's hair, then placed a light hand on her shoulder.

"There you are, your ladyship," she said, her face coming into view in the dressing table mirror. "I swear you're the prettiest of all the ladies here."

"Don't speak nonsense, Lizzie," Alice admonished her, but she gave her a quick smile and placed her hand over Lizzie's thin little fingers. "I trust you're being looked after well here?"

"Oh yes!" Lizzie said. "Mrs. Barnes, the housekeeper, has been taking such great care of me! Why, only last night she admonished one of the kitchen maids for saying that you were..." She blushed and looked away.

"Saying I was what, Lizzie?"

"I'm sorry, ma'am."

Alice nodded. "There's no need to speak of it again, Lizzie. But if you have any more trouble, let me know. Is that clear?"

Alice studied the mirror. The face staring back at her looked healthier and happier than it had for a long time. Lizzie might be forgiven for flattering her, but beauty would never atone for insanity. Not only was she gossiped about among the highest echelons of society, but also by the lowest.

By the time she approached the dining room, breakfast was almost over. Two men sat at the breakfast table.

"Good morning," she said.

They looked up, and she froze. Viscount Oakville nodded a greeting, but his companion, Dominic, sneered at her. She crossed the room to help herself to breakfast, her stomach growling. Westbury's cook was, by all accounts, the best in the kingdom.

"May I inquire after the health of your friend?" she asked, keeping her tone light.

"Our friend?" Oakville raised his eyebrows.

"I've no time for games," she said. "Has a doctor seen to Mister Trelawney?"

"Whatever for?" Dominic snorted. "He's unharmed."

Oakville took a mouthful of food and chewed it, a thoughtful expression on his face. "You're concerned for his welfare?"

"As I would be for anyone who sustained an injury."

"I'd leave the matter be," Oakville said. "It's not for a woman to meddle in the affairs of men."

"As you wish," she said. "I trust you're both well and sustained no injuries from your—excursion?"

"Perfectly so, I thank you, Lady Hartford," Oakville said. He looked pointedly at Dominic who sighed.

"I'm quite well also…" Dominic hesitated and rolled his eyes. "How must I address you?"

"You may address me as you see fit," Alice retorted.

He might be the epitome of incivility, but at least she could refrain from taking the bait.

"Well, thank the Almighty you're not wanting me to call you *Mother*," he said.

She closed her eyes and swallowed. Dominic wouldn't understand the pain his childish insult caused her, that while she longed for a child of her own, she would never have one.

"Lady Hartford, are you all right?" Oakville leaned forward, concern in his expression.

"Of course." She pushed her plate aside and rose from the table. "I find I'm not hungry. Please excuse me."

She dared not approach their host for help. Westbury was an imposing man at the best of times, and he had made his dislike of her plain. There was only one man she could appeal to.

Smoothing down the front of her skirt, she made her toward the orangery where George would be spending his morning.

Her husband reclined in a wicker chair, a blanket over his legs, and Monty in his arms. His eyes were closed, but his hands caressed the little dog in a smooth, gentle motion.

He was not alone. A small group of guests were at the far end admiring the exotic plants while their hostess pointed out their features. One of them turned toward her and his gray gaze followed her as she crossed the floor to her husband.

The pug's tail quivered with delight, and he gave a little yap in greeting.

"Hush, Monty!" she whispered. George opened his eyes and smiled.

"My dear wife, Montague is merely expressing his, and my, pleasure on seeing you."

George glanced at the group as they moved about the room. Though he might try to disguise it, Ross bore a slight limp. To the casual observer there was nothing amiss, but Alice could feel his pain in her heart.

She took her husband's hand and sat beside him.

"I trust you enjoyed your ride this morning, my dear?" he asked.

"Perfectly so, thank you, George."

"Then why does my wife look so distressed?"

"I—I hate to ask a favor of you, when you've given me so much. But would you mind if I sent for our doctor?"

"Are you unwell?" Concern lined his face, and a shiver of guilt ran through her.

"I'm quite well," she said, "don't distress yourself. It's merely a whim. A trifle, really. I can bear the cost from my pin money, so you're not inconvenienced."

"But why ask for the doctor if you're well, my dear? Can it not wait until we're home?"

"I know where he lives, George, I can ride there myself to save taking the carriage. I want to ride."

He shook his head. "Doctor Beckford is over an hour's ride from here, Alice. And you've already been out today. Are you not tired?"

"I'm sorry," she said, casting her gaze down. "Forgive me, it was a foolish request."

He patted her hand. "Nothing you request from me will ever be foolish, my dear." He glanced at the group of guests again, then nodded, a knowing expression in his eyes.

"Ah, I might have known," he said. Then he raised his voice.

"Alice, my dear, I'm feeling rather unwell. You must send for Doctor Beckford!"

Jeanette crossed the floor, concern in her expression.

"Lord Hartford, are you ill?"

"It's no cause for alarm, Your Grace," George said, "but I must have my doctor."

"There's no need for that," Jeanette said. "Henry can send his man for Doctor Lucas."

"You're most kind," George said, "but I insist on my own doctor. My wife knows where to find him."

"Lady Hartford?" Jeanette asked. "You're sure?"

"Of course," Alice replied.

"I insist," Hartford said, his voice taking on the undertone of steel he'd used against Papa. "And I will not be gainsaid. Perhaps your groom can saddle my wife's horse forthwith."

"What's all this?" Westbury's tall form approached, towering over Alice, and she cringed under his scrutiny. But Hartford, despite the differential in age and state of health, was not to be cowed.

"I beg you to oblige me, Westbury."

"If your wife must go, she can have our carriage."

"No," Hartford said, his voice firm. "I insist she go on horseback, a carriage would take too long."

"Very well," Westbury said, and he waved a footman over. "See to it that Lady Hartford's horse is saddled this instant. And send for her maid immediately to tend to her."

⋙✦⋘

BY THE TIME Alice returned to Westbury's estate with the doctor, her riding habit was filthy. Heaven knew what Lizzie would think of her. Such unladylike behavior would only perpetuate her reputation as Mad Alice.

The ride to the doctor's house had taken less than an hour, but the return journey took longer. Artemis had begun to tire, and Doctor Beckford, though an accomplished rider, was unable to match Alice's pace.

As they approached the main hall and dismounted, two grooms ran toward them to take the reins.

"This had better be worth it, your ladyship," the doctor grumbled as he reached for his medical bag. "I'm soaked to the skin. As are you. You could catch a chill."

"Alice, at last!" Jeanette ran toward her, holding an umbrella.

"We were so worried when the weather took a turn for the worse! Let's get you inside."

"I must see to my husband," Alice said.

"Not in that state," Jeanette replied. "You must change into something dry, and I'd suggest a hot drink." She held her hand up to stay Alice's protests. "I'll never forgive myself if you took a chill. You should have taken the carriage. I don't know what Henry was about permitting you to go on horseback."

"I insisted."

Jeanette sighed and linked her arm through Alice's. "Come along. The sooner we can present you to Lord Hartford safe and well, the quicker he'll recover."

A wave of panic rippled through Alice. "Recover? Has he taken ill?"

Jeanette gave her a puzzled expression. "Isn't that why you sent for the doctor?"

Heat warmed Alice's cheeks despite the cold, and she looked away, but not before she saw the indulgent smile on Jeanette's lips.

"Let us say no more about it." The duchess led Alice inside, issuing instructions to the footman to take the doctor directly to Lord Hartford.

⇶⇷

WHEN ALICE RETURNED from her chamber, dried and changed, a footman escorted her to a small, south-facing parlor set apart from the main reception rooms. The view from the windows, which must be breathtaking in finer weather, was still to be admired, even though the colors had been dulled by the rain which battered against the glass. The room overlooked a lake, lined each side by trees. At the far end, a bridge arched across the water at such an angle that were the water still, the reflection, together with the original, would form a perfect circle.

George sat beside the hearth where a fire crackled with the comforting aroma of wood and smoke. In the chair beside him, a bundle of fur lay on a cushion, each rise and fall of its body accompanied by little snores. As if he sensed his mistress's presence, the little dog's ears twitched, and he stretched out a paw settling once more into the rhythm of contented sleep.

The doctor stood beside Alice's husband, arms folded, his medical bag unopened on the floor.

George's face lit up into a smile as she entered the room.

"Alice!" he said, holding out his hands. She rushed forward and took them. His fingers were warm against hers and he frowned.

"Your hands are cold, my dear. I was so worried when I saw the rain. I should never have permitted you to ride." He patted the chair beside him, and she took it, lifting Monty off his cushion and placing him on her lap.

"A fool's errand," the doctor said. "Your health has not deteriorated since I last saw you, Lord Hartford. In fact, I think it's improved a little. I fail to understand the need for such urgency."

"Doctor Beckford, I pay you for your services, do I not?" George asked.

"Yes, my lord, but given your state of health, you must understand what I feared when your wife arrived at my door, begging me to attend to you. You know, as well as I, that your time…"

He glanced at Alice, and George nodded for him to continue.

"Your time must come soon. But here, I find you healthier than you've ever been! While I marvel at your renewed vitality, I must ask myself why you sent for me under such urgency? After more than an hour on horseback in damned awful conditions, I might add, I find there was no need for me at all! I do have other patients who would not appreciate their doctor catching a chill."

He sneezed as if to prove his point.

"There's one small service you can perform, Beckford." George took Alice's hand. "Would you be so good as to find Mister Trelawney and escort him back here?"

"Can you not send another?" Beckford asked.

"No, Doctor Beckford, it must be you." George nodded to the footman at the door. "The man here will help you find him."

The doctor picked up his bag and huffed. "Lord Hartford. I am a doctor, not a footman."

"And I pay you very handsomely for your services," George said, an edge of steel to his voice. "If you are concerned about the use of your time today, you're at liberty to double your fee."

He gestured toward the window. "The weather is closing in, and I'm sure you've no wish to ride out in it again. Westbury has assured me you're welcome to dine here and remain until the rain eases."

"Very well." The doctor bowed and left the room.

George squeezed Alice's hand. "I'm glad you're safely back, my dear." Though he smiled, an undercurrent of sadness lined the tone of his voice and for a moment, the weight of his illness seemed to bear down on him. Despite the doctor's declaration on how he looked, he understood his own mortality.

"Perhaps you might indulge me, Alice, in waiting for me in your chamber." Hartford nodded toward Monty. "I'm sure your little friend would relish your company for a while."

"As you wish, George."

She stood, cradling Monty under her right arm. Hartford lifted her hand to his lips and kissed it before patting the back of her hand and linking his fingers with hers.

"Don't worry, my dear," he said. "I'm sure he'll be all right."

CHAPTER FOURTEEN

THE MURMUR OF his friends' voices had faded, replaced by the throb of pain in his leg. Ross took another sip of brandy. The liquid burning against his throat shifted his focus momentarily from the pain.

Damned fool he was, he should have taken up Westbury's offer of a doctor, but he couldn't bear to see the look of triumph on Dominic Hartford's face. As the superior swordsman, having achieved a fencing blue at Oxford, Ross should have bested him easily.

And he would have, had he not heard her cry, a plaintive sound which had tugged at his heart.

"Mister Trelawney? Sir?"

He jumped at the voice which cut through his thoughts, and the glass slipped out of his hand and landed on the rug with a thud.

"I say, old chap, are you all right?"

Westbury and Oakville had looked up from their conversation, Westbury watching him intently with his dark eyes.

"Of course." Hiding his discomfort, Ross bent down to retrieve the glass. Fortunately, the rug had a deep pile. Westbury was no miser, but he wouldn't relish the destruction of his finest crystal for the sake of a lovesick friend.

Lovesick…

Ross uttered a snort to dispel the very notion and shook his head.

"Sir?"

The footman who had so rudely interrupted his thoughts stood before him, together with a stranger, dressed in a plain, gray jacket and cream breeches. The newcomer's hair was wet, as was the edge of his jacket, and his breeches, streaked with mud near the top of his boots. He gave Ross a stiff bow.

"Sir," he said, "I have been asked to escort you to another part of the house."

"And you are?"

"Andrew Beckford, at your service."

"I don't know you, Mr. Beckford."

"No, but a fellow acquaintance has made a particular request to see you. I'm to take you to him this instant."

"And he is?"

"Viscount Hartford."

Ross sighed. No doubt Hartford had learned of his son dueling with Ross and wished to admonish him. At least the old man had the decency to do it in private. But how had he found out? Had *she* betrayed them? Her behavior at dinner suggested a level of intimacy with Hartford like that of a husband and wife. Perhaps they indulged in post-coital gossip.

His stomach knotted at the image of the two of them, that lush body of hers he'd once believed would be his, in possession of a wrinkled old goat who likely puffed and sweated his way to completion while she cast aside her self-respect…

"Very well." Grimacing as he placed his weight on his injured leg, he followed Beckford to the door.

Beckford nodded to the footman. "Thank you, you may leave us now. We'll call you if we need you."

"Very good, sir." The footman disappeared, leaving Ross alone with the newcomer.

The further along they walked, Ross's resolve to stem the pain began to waver, and he bit his lip to shift his focus away from it. When they reached a staircase, he drew a sharp breath as his leg jarred against the first step.

"Are you all right, Mr. Trelawney?"

"Of course!" he snapped, gritting his teeth, but at the next step, he let out a grunt of pain.

"Forgive me," his companion said. "I can see you're in pain and favoring your left leg."

"I fail to see that's any of your business, Mr. Beckford."

"It's *Doctor* Beckford," his companion said crisply. "Now I see why Hartford asked me to find you."

"It's just a scratch," Ross said. "No need for…"

"If I may contradict, I've not been a doctor for over twenty years not to be able to recognize pain in another, however valiantly they try to conceal it." He nodded toward Ross's right thigh. "The evidence speaks for itself."

Before Ross could protest, a lean, muscular arm circled around his waist.

"Let me help you. We're nearly there."

Ross nodded, unable to deny the pain any longer. As if his admission gave his body free rein to recognize the injury, his legs buckled beneath him, and he let the doctor support his weight as they climbed the remaining stairs.

"How long have you known Lord Hartford?" Ross asked.

"I've tended to his family for decades."

"Does he enjoy good health?"

The doctor smiled. "His lordship is in unusually good health considering. In general, he's not a well man, but the transformation in him this last month has been extraordinary."

"Transformation?"

"He's not long for this world, Mister Trelawney. But the viscountess has achieved in a short space of time what I've been unable to in six months."

"The viscountess?"

"That pretty wife of his. She's most attentive. Few women in society would marry a man over twice their age then strive to extend their lifespan. Hartford is to be envied."

Envied indeed. And now Ross was about to come face to face with the happy couple. Beckford pushed open the parlor door and helped Ross inside where Hartford sat waiting for them beside a glowing fireplace.

But *she* was nowhere to be seen.

"Ah!" the old man said. "As I thought." He waved to a couch beside the window. "Beckford, I believe your visit will be justified after all. See to it that this young man has all the care he needs."

"With respect, Lord Hartford," Ross said, "I don't see it's any of your..."

"I insist," Hartford said, his voice firm. "If you're irresponsible enough to sustain an injury and not seek proper treatment for it, then you've relinquished your rights as a rational creature to decide your own fate in this room. Once you've been tended to and your rationality restored, you are at liberty to do as you please."

He lifted his lips in a smile. "Permit me the liberties of an old man if you may, Mister Trelawney."

The liberties of a dying old man.

Ross sighed. "As you wish." The doctor led him to a couch beside the window, and Ross limped after him.

Hartford rose from his seat. "I'll give you some privacy now, Trelawney. It's time I joined my wife. Beckford, please add any costs incurred to my account."

"No, Lord Hartford, I can pay for my own..." Ross protested, but a sharp word from the viscount cut him off.

"I will brook no argument. Consider the matter settled."

Without another word, he left the room, closing the door sharply behind him. Ross sank onto the couch, surrendering to his wound, and let the doctor tend to him.

"THAT BLOODY HURT!"

"I expected no less. And be thankful. It means the nerves are un-damaged."

Ross's head swam with pain. Not only content with opening the wound again with a knife, the doctor had rubbed in some concoction which caused it to sting, then sliced through it with a needle again and again, all the while muttering about the folly of male pride.

Rather than being deficient, the doctor's bedside manner was non-existent.

"Consider yourself lucky, Mister Trelawney. An inch or two to the left, and that blade would have severed an artery. You would have lost your leg, and very likely your life."

The doctor's tone reminded him of his schoolmaster at Harrow, a man he'd loathed who had looked down on him for his lack of aristocratic origins.

"It's my life to lose, damn you!" he hissed through gritted teeth.

"You may care little for your life, but you should consider the feelings of others who do."

The doctor was right. What would Amelia think if he were to die? He might be a poor father to her, had been a poor husband to her mother, but he was all she had.

The doctor cleared away his instruments, then reached into his medical bag and drew out a small bottle.

"Here, take it."

"What is it?"

"Laudanum. The infection shouldn't spread, but you'll need to bathe the wound at least once a day. Take one spoonful of this for the pain if it becomes too much."

Ross closed his fingers round the phial, but the doctor held it firm, a frown on his face.

"Make sure you take it, Mister Trelawney. I've no time for heroics."

"I will."

"I'm serious. I don't care what caused your injury, though I'm not so naïve as to be incapable of recognizing the spoils of a swordfight. But you're still in danger if the wound becomes putrid."

He released the phial, and Ross pocketed it in his jacket.

"Are you able to stand?"

"I'll try."

Holding the couch for support, Ross lifted himself up, bearing his weight on his good leg before slowly transferring the weight to the other. Save for a small twinge, the pain had lessened to a dull throb.

"Better?"

"Yes, very much."

Despite his stern demeanor, the doctor had acted with crisp efficiency. Swallowing shame at his own behavior, Ross held out his hand.

"May I thank you, my good man."

"No need to thank me, I'll be handsomely paid for my services."

"Are you sure I cannot settle the account?"

The doctor shook his head. "There's little point in you inconveniencing yourself unless you wish me to be paid twice?"

"Then," Ross said, "I must ask you to thank Lord Benevolence."

"I think," the doctor replied with a smile, "you'll find that in this case, benevolence is to be found in the female form."

I'M SURE HE'LL be all right.

Alice concentrated on the embroidery in her hands in an attempt to ease the churning in her stomach. She had conquered her fear for

Ross, the fear which had driven her on as she urged her horse through the rain. But George's words had replaced the fear with guilt.

Old he may be, but her husband was no fool. By the very nature of her fears for another man, she betrayed him.

And he knew.

You make a poor wife, Alice…

She closed her eyes to shut out Roderick's words from beyond the grave, but it only served to intensify the image of him, of the fists he'd used to subdue her with.

She heard a soft knock on the door.

"C-come in."

The door opened to reveal her husband.

"May I join you?"

"Of course," she said. "You have no need to ask."

"I do, my dear," he said. "No man has a right to expect anything from a woman, not even his wife."

"Please, sit."

He settled into a chair beside her and smiled. She turned her attention once more to her sewing and waited for his admonishment, but he remained silent.

She'd survived everything Roderick inflicted on her, endured incarceration, weathered the condemnation of the world, yet it had not broken her.

But it paled in significance compared to what she was about to endure. The disappointment of this kind, gentle man. Guilt overcame her and she spoke, her voice wavering.

"I-I'm sorry, George. Forgive me."

He tutted and placed a fingertip under her chin, tilting her head until their eyes met. His expression showed understanding and a deep-set sadness.

"My dear Alice, you've nothing to be sorry for. If anything, I should apologize to you." He smiled and the creases in the corners of his eyes deepened.

"I should have realized," he said. "You were engaged to Mister Trelawney at one point, were you not?"

She nodded, and the motion released a tear which slid down her face.

"So, my son spoke the truth, in that, at least."

She cast her gaze down.

"No, my Alice," he said quietly. "Look at me."

She blinked, her vision blurred by tears of shame and guilt, and looked at him.

"Why did you break off your engagement to him?"

At the very least, she owed him the truth.

"I didn't want to," she said. "Papa and my stepmother…insisted. They knew Markham wanted to court me, and they persuaded me to act in the family's best interests."

"What about *your* interests?"

She shook her head. "They're of no consequence."

He released her chin and sat back, his chest heaving in a sigh of resignation.

"I'm sorry, my dear," he said, "so sorry I married you."

She let out a cry, and he caught her hand. "No, my dear, you misunderstand me. I'm not sorry for myself. My dear, sweet, Alice, I count myself fortunate to have such a gentle wife. But I am sorry you tied yourself to a sick old man like me, when your heart belongs to another. I had no right to offer for you. Forgive me, my dear."

Another tear rolled down her cheek, and a gentle finger brushed it aside.

"I don't love him," she said in a small voice.

"My dear," he said, "take it from one who's seen more of the world than he cares to. You probably don't even realize it. I didn't spot it myself until today."

"I don't understand."

"I saw your fear, Alice, when you asked me to send for the doctor. It was the deadliest form of fear there is. Fear for a loved one."

"Forgive me, George."

"There's nothing to forgive," he said. "Our marriage is one of friendship and mutual affection. You've made me the happiest of men, my sweet Alice."

He drew his arms around her, and she brushed her lips against his.

"George…"

On impulse, driven by the need to prove her fidelity, she clasped her hands round his neck and deepened the kiss, and his eyes widened in surprise.

The door burst open, and Westbury tumbled into the room, flanked on either side by Ross and Oakville.

"There they are!" Oakville cried. "We wondered where you'd got to!"

"You missed an excellent morning's shooting, Lord Hartford," Westbury said.

Oakville laughed. "With such a pretty wife in his possession, I'll wager Hartford would rather bag a different bird than the rest of us. But have a care, Hartford, you should leave that sort of thing for the bedchamber!"

Ross stood in silence, his dark eyes taking in the scene before him: Alice in the arms of her husband, her lips parting as they broke free from the kiss. He curled his lip in distaste, then turned and disappeared.

Chapter Fifteen

ARTEMIS SHOOK HER head and snorted as Alice grasped the reins. Pent-up energy vibrated through the mare's body as if eager for the hunt. The baying of the hounds only served to increase the excitement.

The master of the hounds stood among his charges, talking with Westbury who stood beside an enormous black gelding. At a nod from the master, Westbury lifted his foot into a stirrup and with a smooth, powerful movement, mounted his horse.

Though still a little afraid of him, Alice had to admire Westbury's skills at horsemanship. Beside him, his wife looked less comfortable in the saddle. Having been raised on a farm, doubtless she would have preferred to ride her horse like a man. In times past, Alice would have sneered at such an unladylike habit, but she found herself admiring the duchess.

Their eyes met, and Jeanette steered her mount toward Alice.

"I'm so pleased you were able to join the hunt, Lady Hartford."

"You're too kind."

"Your husband was, I know, most anxious that you enjoy yourself today. I've heard much of your horsemanship. My son has spoken of little else."

Behind her, Edward struggled to mount his horse, almost losing his balance on the mounting block. His father barked an order at him, and he redoubled his efforts and launched himself onto the saddle on his stomach, almost toppling over the other side.

Alice couldn't hide her smile.

"Ah!" Jeanette exclaimed. "I see your husband was right, even if your entertainment is at my son's expense." She gave Alice a conspiratorial wink. "Both Edward and I have had—how shall I put it—less than aristocratic upbringings. I fear we'll never be perfectly at home in a hunt. Edward takes no pleasure in the need to chase a defenseless animal only to tear it to pieces when it can run no further. I, however, have a more pragmatic view having seen the evidence of a fox's work myself. A farmyard littered with carcasses is not a sight for the fainthearted."

She smiled. "But today's not the day for philosophizing. We must indulge in the pursuits of the idle rich."

The sound of a horn echoed across the courtyard, and the party set off. Alice glanced around her. The men, each astride powerful hunters, took the lead, the women following. Though Westbury was by far the tallest of the party, Alice's gaze was drawn to another. A familiar figure steered a dark brown animal with a black mane, almost as large as Westbury's horse. He rode alongside their host, his back ramrod straight. While Alice had been talking to Jeanette, the uncomfortable feeling she was being watched had pricked at her, but each time she glanced at him, he was looking in the opposite direction.

But now was not the time to be concerned about him. All she wanted was to be at one with her horse and let the fresh air banish her troubles.

DESPITE HER HORSEMANSHIP, Alice remained at the rear of the party. Though she took pleasure in the ride, the prospect of witnessing the kill held no pleasure for her. The main party plunged into the forest and out of sight.

Once again, an uneasy feeling of being watched needled at her senses. Did Roderick's ghost seek to torment her?

"Come on, Artemis!" The bright tone of her voice belied the fear circling inside her, and she urged her mount toward a patch of light between the trees.

When she emerged from the other side, the rest of the party had disappeared, though the trail of hoofmarks had torn up the landscape to mark their route. She steered Artemis to the right and urged her into a gallop, following the line of a beech hedge. A horse was gaining on her, powerful by the sound of it. Fear spiked within her, and she glanced behind.

It was no ghost, but a mortal man. Another rider. Alice wanted to be left alone. But before she could ride away, the other rider hailed her. Unwilling to show incivility, she slowed Artemis to a canter.

Her pursuer drew alongside her mount, and she realized her mistake as cold eyes, glittering with disapproval, met her gaze. Had he been watching her for the entire ride?

"What are you doing riding off like that?" Ross asked. "The duchess will only worry."

"I felt unwell," she said. "I decided to return to the house."

"You're going the wrong way."

She resumed her attention on the path ahead and maintained her course. Perhaps he'd tire of taunting her. She was in no mood for a confrontation.

"At least look at me when I'm speaking to you!"

She jerked at the reins and drew Artemis to a halt, circling about to face him.

"I'm answerable to no man, Ross."

"Except the old man you sold yourself to."

"Leave me alone," she said. "You don't understand."

"Oh, I understand," he said. "I saw you, fawning over him. Women all over England sell themselves. The price may differ, but the commodity is always the same."

He drew his horse alongside hers, forcing her into the hedge. Artemis reared up, and a pheasant burst out from the hedge with a screech. Alice lost her footing and slipped sideways, clawing at the reins for purchase.

"Whoa!" she cried. The horse ignored her command and gained speed. She clung to her mount, but her hands slipped against the leather reins. Another hedge loomed up ahead, blocking her path.

"Dear God! Alice!" A shout echoed behind her, but she was unable to turn.

Artemis surged ahead, then launched into the air. Alice felt a brief sensation of weightlessness followed by a shudder as the animal's hind legs clipped the hedge. The horse landed and fell sideways, Alice landing hard on the ground.

By the time Alice pushed herself up to a sitting position, Artemis had disappeared.

Her beautiful horse!

A thunder of hooves approached, and before she could stand, another horse launched itself over the hedge. Its rider turned the animal in a tight circle, then dismounted and rushed toward her.

"Alice! Are you hurt?"

Strong arms pulled her into a tight embrace. He bent his head until his chin touched the top of her head.

Ross sighed as his heart hammered against her ear.

"Oh, my love, what have I done? You could have been killed! Dear God, I would never have forgiven myself!"

He pulled away and held her at arm's length, looking her up and down.

"Are you hurt?"

She shook her head. "I don't think so. But my horse, I've lost my horse."

"What is a horse compared to you?" His voice broke, and his

whole body shuddered. Moisture glistened in his eyes.

"Nothing matters except you," he whispered. "Nothing."

He cupped her chin and drew her close, his breath warm against her mouth.

"Oh Alice, my love!"

Soft lips caressed her mouth.

"Ross…"

She melted into his embrace, drawing comfort from his solidity and strength, and he gave a low groan of anguish.

"What a fool I've been," he said, his voice hoarse. "A damned fool to let you go again!"

With a cry of need, he claimed her mouth. His tongue begged entrance, and she granted it, her body craving to surrender. Murmuring her name, he deepened the kiss. Desire ignited her body as if a flame had burst from within, and she melted against him.

"You feel it, too, don't you, my love," he whispered and peppered little kisses along her neck.

"Ross…"

"That's it," he whispered, "say my name as I claim you."

His words broke the spell, and she pushed him away.

"Alice, what's wrong?" he asked. "You want me, don't you?"

She shook her head. "We can't do this!"

"Why not?" he asked, an edge to his voice. "It's what you want, isn't it?"

"I'm sorry," she said. "I don't know what came over me. I'm married. You shouldn't have kissed me."

"You were willing," he said. "No, not willing. You begged for it!"

"I was in shock, after the fall. I thought you were my husband. I trust you'll forgive my lapse of judgement."

"Your *lapse of judgement*?" he snarled. "Or were you seeking a lover? Tell me, how do I compare to your husband?"

"Please, stop!" she cried. "I made a mistake. Forgive me, Ross. I have no wish to seduce you. I want to find my horse and return to my husband."

Pain etched across his forehead, an echo of the pain she had inflicted when she broke their engagement a lifetime ago. But it could not match the pain which clawed at her insides. She had loved him then, even when he'd cursed her for rejecting him for Markham. And she still loved him.

But for his sake—and for the sake of the dear, kind man she'd married—she must reject him once more.

The pain in his eyes diminished, leaving the numb, cold expression of the rake she had turned him into.

"Very good, madam," he said, his voice stiff. Permit me to escort you back to your husband after which I'll promise never to inconvenience you with my presence again.

Ross led her to his horse, which had waited patiently beside the hedge. He lifted her onto the saddle, then swung himself up behind her. She closed her eyes and tensed while they rode back to the hall, not once speaking a word.

❧⟫⟪❧

THE BAYING OF the dogs echoed around the stables. Each stall was occupied, and grooms were running to and fro with brushes and bales of hay. The hunt had returned.

"I wondered where you'd got to, my dear." George stood in the center of the stable yard.

"Madam, your husband awaits." Ross dismounted, then held out his hand to her.

She took it, and strong, lean fingers laced through hers as he helped her off his horse.

George gave Ross a look of suspicion, then resumed his attention on her. "Alice, my dear, you look rather the worse for wear."

Shame warmed her cheeks. She'd lost her hat and her riding habit was streaked with mud. "Forgive me," she said.

Her husband glanced at Ross, who shrugged his shoulders and set off toward the house.

"Not so fast, young man," George said. "I'd like a word with you."

Ross stopped and turned to face him. "What about?"

"Alice," George said, "perhaps you'd care to return to the house while I speak to Mr. Trelawney."

She shook her head. "Husband, the fault lies with me. I've lost Artemis…"

He sighed and drew her hand to his lips. "What matters most to me is that you are safe. Westbury's men will find your horse."

"George, I'm sorry."

"My dear, you've done nothing wrong. Now, would you be kind enough to indulge an old man who desires nothing but your good health?"

"Of course."

He smiled and kissed her forehead, and she returned to the house. She turned back before leaving the stable yard, but both men remained where they stood, waiting for her to leave, as if neither wanted her to know what they had to say to each other.

CHAPTER SIXTEEN

ROSS WATCHED ALICE leave. She turned to face him before she left, sorrow reflected in her eyes.

Why was it that a man had no choice over where his heart lay? With countless women in society willing to accept his hand if he offered it, and twice as many in the brothels of London eager to entertain him for a coin why, then, did he love the one woman he couldn't have?

Try as he might, he could not hate her, nor did he harbor the indifference he'd once professed.

He loved her.

His actions had been driven by jealousy, which had almost consumed him when he'd seen her locked in an embrace with Hartford. But a woman had the right to kiss her husband. The devil perched on Ross's shoulder might try to convince him of her being a seductress, but Ross knew her too well. She was not the pampered lady who hunted titles, but a tender-hearted woman with a genuine affection for her husband, even if that affection was not the burning passion she'd once felt for Ross.

But what of the old man himself? Had Hartford married her for love? Would he suffer the pain of not having that love returned, as Caroline had with Ross himself?

"Lord Hartford, do you wish to discuss my horse?" Ross asked.

"You must think me an old fool, Mister Trelawney," Hartford

replied. "But you'll find me quite the opposite."

"I hardly think of you at all," Ross said. "It's cold, and I wish to return to the house. What do you want?"

The viscount tapped his cane on the ground. "I want you to stay away from my wife."

So, Hartford saw him as a rival. Ross almost laughed at the cliché. An old man, married to a woman half his age, warning off every young buck in the vicinity through fear of being cuckolded.

Hartford's mouth curled in a wry smile. "I see what you're thinking. Don't you think I know what the gossips say about me—and my wife?"

Ross looked away to hide the shame in his eyes.

"Yes," the viscount said, "you may well avert your gaze. I've lived in this world longer than most, which gives me greater insight into the hearts and minds of others. But I'm the first to admit I can be wrong. For example, in your case, I'd have thought you better than to succumb to prejudice."

"Forgive me sir, I…"

"I've not finished." Hartford moved closer. Though Ross stood nearly a head taller, the viscount's inner strength gave him the greater stature.

"My reasons for marrying Alice, I'll keep to myself," Hartford said. "Think of me what you wish. But if you consider, for one moment, that she accepted my hand for material gratification, then I've been gravely mistaken in my belief as to your character."

He nodded toward the house where Alice had long since disappeared. "Roderick Markham's father and I went to school together. A wicked boy he was then, taking pleasure in tormenting defenseless creatures and bullying the weak. I watched his son grow up. I'd not believed it possible, but Roderick surpassed his father in cruelty. I once saw him beat a horse so savagely, the animal had to be shot. And he thought nothing of doing it in front of his guests."

Fire blazed in Hartford's eyes.

"Imagine what such a man would do to a living creature in his power behind closed doors. Such as a wife. Imagine it, Mister Trelawney. Think what she might have endured. Day and night. For *five years.*" The old man shook his head. "Not even in my blackest nightmares can I entertain the notion of what my Alice has endured."

The mention of her name sent a ripple of shame through Ross. But a hand clasped his arm and thin fingers curled around his elbow, their frail appearance belying their strength.

"You don't deserve the love of a woman like her, Mr. Trelawney. Neither do I. But I've pledged to take care of her. She has earned a little peace, and until I draw my last breath, I will fight to ensure she has it." Hartford released his grip. "Now, if you'll excuse me, I must tend to my wife."

He gave Ross a stiff bow then took his leave. Ross remained in the yard with his guilt and watched the viscount tap-tap his way across the stable yard.

Shortly afterward, he heard a clatter of hooves. A groom led a gray mare toward the stable door. The animal had lost its saddle and bore a slight limp. Its ears were flat against the back of its head. Eyes wide, it shied as Ross moved toward it.

"Easy, girl! Best keep back, sir!" The groom patted the mare's flank and led her straight into a stall.

The expression in the horse's eyes mirrored what he had seen so often in Alice's gaze. Like an abused animal, beaten and cowed, she needed to be coaxed back into life again. Ross had failed—completely and utterly—so self-absorbed was he in his own wounded pride and consumed by guilt over Caroline's death.

But his guilt was selfish. He hadn't considered Caroline's feelings— nor Amelia's, the child who had lost her mother. He'd thought only of himself. He had watched, bitter with resentment while the woman he loved had married a monster. He'd laughed with his friends while she rotted in an asylum—then taunted her for marrying the only man to treat her with kindness.

Yes—Hartford had every reason to think ill of him. But he couldn't hate Ross as much as Ross hated himself. The viscount was right in saying what mattered most was Alice's happiness. The best Ross could hope for was to be permitted to admire her from afar.

CHAPTER SEVENTEEN

ALICE PICKED UP a carrot and rinsed it. The steady action and contentment from helping Mrs. Taylor in her kitchen served to calm her nerves.

A fortnight ago, she had returned to London with George, who promised her a peaceful Christmas in town. Dominic was nowhere to be seen, and save a remark about gaming hells, George said little in response to her inquiry as to his whereabouts.

Without asking, George understood her need to be occupied, rather than languishing as the lady of the manor, and almost as soon as the carriage had drawn to a halt outside his townhouse, he encouraged Alice to resume her visits to Mrs. Taylor.

A child slipped though the kitchen door and wrapped his arms round Alice's companion—a thin, young woman with a bruise on her cheek. The woman smiled and ruffled his hair.

"Is that your son, Mary?" Alice asked.

"Yes, that's my Adam." Mary smiled. "My pride and joy."

"And how old are you, Adam?"

"I'm nearly five," the boy replied. "Old enough to take care of Ma."

"I don't doubt it," Alice said. "Would you like to help us? We're making stew for everyone."

"Yes, please!" the boy said. "Edward sent me here to help. He might be a nob, but I like him, don't you?"

"Yes, I do," Alice replied. "Though he's the son of a duke, he spent his early years living around here. He knows Mrs. Taylor well, and she trusts him to be discreet."

Edward Drayton had returned to London after the house party and was proving a useful helpmate at the shelter. Despite Westbury's lack of enthusiasm toward his son's friendship with Alice, his wife encouraged it. Alice found herself making another friend in Jeanette who, like Frederica, had forgiven Alice for her involvement in the incident with Roderick. Westbury, however, remained aloof toward her. But Edward, though he possessed his father's dark, searching expression, viewed Alice with compassion and understanding. Alice didn't know whether that was due to Jeanette's influence as his stepmother or his early life on the street, but she valued it all the same.

She gestured toward the sink.

"Would you like to wash the vegetables, Adam?"

"Can I chop them?"

"Oh no," Alice said. "Knives are dangerous, and you mustn't hurt yourself."

Adam's lip curled into a frown, and Mary placed a hand on his shoulder. "Adam, my love, Lady Alice is right. Be a good boy and do as she says."

"Very well," the boy said. "May we go to the park later, like we did this morning?"

Alice set her knife down. "You went outside, Mary? In the daytime?"

Mary looked away, her cheeks reddening. "Forgive me, I know we're not supposed to, but Adam loves looking at the swans."

Distress lined the young woman's features, and Alice didn't have the heart to chastise her. She took her hand, her heart aching as Mary flinched.

"I understand," she said. "But you must be careful. Mrs. Taylor values discretion, as do all the people here. Next time, take Edward with you. He…" She stopped at a knock on the outside door.

"Ah! That must be him now, with the rib of beef the butcher promised us."

Alice crossed the floor to the door beside the sink and lifted the latch. The door flew open, and a man burst into the kitchen. Hair unkempt, a sour smell of ale on him, he rushed toward Alice and knocked her to the floor.

"Jake!" Mary screamed.

"Da!"

At the boy's voice, the man turned and snatched him into his arms. The boy cried out and tried to struggle free.

"Adam!" Mary wailed in fear.

"You think you can leave me?" the man cried. "You think you can take my son away from me?"

"Jake, put him down, please!" Mary cried.

"No!" the man said. "He's *my* son." He tightened his grip, and the boy whimpered in fear.

"You're hurting him!"

"I'd never hurt him, Mary. You're turning him against me—his own father."

Mary backed away, her body shaking with fear.

Alice struggled to her feet and forced the tremor out of her voice. "And who, might I ask, do you think you are, coming here uninvited and in such an unseemly manner?"

He hesitated, a shimmer of uncertainty in his expression, then he backed away, still holding the boy, until he reached the fireplace.

"My name's Jacob Whitworth. This boy is my son and that woman is my wife."

"What makes you think you can come in here uninvited?"

"Didn't you hear me, woman? I'm her husband!"

"You think that gives you the right to treat her as you see fit?" Alice asked, coldly. She gestured toward Mary who was trembling uncontrollably. "Is that what a husband is expected to reduce his wife to?"

"She vowed to obey me!"

"And you vowed to beat her if she didn't?"

The man's eyes narrowed, a flicker of guilt in his expression before he clasped the boy to him once more.

"I don't care what you think—bleeding nob, telling the likes of us what to do. You know nothing of hardship."

"Oh, you think?" Alice asked, moving closer. "Just because I'm clothed in silk rather than cotton and attend balls rather than dog-fights, that means I'm happy and fulfilled? You don't think someone in my position can understand helplessness, or fear, or pain?"

"Understand this," the man said. "Mary's place is with me, not in some fancy home with the likes of you poisoning her against me."

"None of us have said anything about you," Alice said. "But we are not blind." She gestured to Mary. "Are you trying to tell me your wife sustained that bruise walking into a door?"

His eyes narrowed and a flicker of pain crossed his expression as he loosened his grip on the boy. Adam tried to wriggle free.

"Let me go, Da!"

Alice moved closer until she was within arm's reach. "Do as he says, Jacob."

"No!" he cried. "I won't lose my son!"

"Look at him!" Alice cried. "He's frightened out of his wits! You think by terrorizing him you'll get him back? Is that what you did to your wife?"

"My Da said…he told me…" Jacob's voice caught, and he shook his head. "I'm not weak," he said. "Whatever he tells me, I'm not weak! I just want my wife and son to come home."

He blinked, and for a moment, Alice saw the look of a frightened child. She held out her hand. "Give the boy to me."

"I can't," he said, his voice wavering. "She'll only leave again—take him from me." He shook his head and let out a quiet whisper. "Please…"

Pain shone in his eyes, and Alice recognized it for what it was. She had seen it in the mirror almost every day. It was the pain of one who lived according to the rules of others—rules enforced by fear and brutality.

"I understand, Jacob," she said.

"You know nothing," he said. "Someone like you will never worry where the next mouthful is coming from." He shook his head. "I lost my job, but you probably think I deserve it, don't you? Seven pounds a year. Seven bleeding pounds! But that's nothing to you."

"I can help you," Alice said, "but first, you must give me the boy."

"No!" Jacob cried. "If I give him to you now, you'll set the runners on me." Jacob nodded toward his wife. "She'll relish the chance to see me hang. When I lost my job, she told me I was worthless."

Adam wailed in fear, his cheeks streaming with tears, while his mother sobbed.

"Mary!" Alice said, forcing her voice to become sharp. "Your son needs you—you must be strong for him."

The woman grew quiet, but her husband still clutched at the boy.

"Jacob, you've done nothing to merit the gallows," Alice said. "I can see you're hurting. I want to believe you're not a bad man. Prove it now by releasing the boy."

"Then I'll have nothing to persuade her to listen to me!"

Alice moved closer, wrinkling her nose at the sharp odor of sweat. "Take me instead."

"For what purpose?"

"As surety. Let me help."

"Why would you help me?"

"I wouldn't be doing it for you. I'd be doing it for Mary and Adam."

For a moment he hesitated, then he released the boy and lunged toward Alice and grasped her arm.

"Adam!" At his mother's scream, the boy ran across the kitchen.

Jacob wrapped an arm around Alice's waist and pulled her close against him until the stench of unwashed man and musty clothes threatened to fill her with nausea. Before she could react, she caught a flash of light against metal and something cold and sharp pressed against her neck.

Mary screamed.

"Don't move," he snarled, his breath hot and sticky in Alice's ear, "or I'll slit her throat."

Alice had not known he had a knife.

CHAPTER EIGHTEEN

ROSS SWIRLED THE brandy in his glass, watching the amber liquid form a vortex. His nostrils quivered at the tangy scent of the liquor. He smiled to himself. Frederica had once told him the best way to discern a good quality wine was by the aroma. She possessed an extraordinary degree of perception, which most ladies lacked. Together with her intelligence, she made a formidable woman. Hawthorne, the man who had secured her hand and heart, swallowed his brandy in a single gulp, then leaned back in the wingback chair, smiling in satisfaction.

And well he might. That very morning he'd announced Frederica was to furnish him with another child.

Lucky bastard.

Ross loved Amelia as any father might, but she needed siblings. Would he ever have what Hawthorne enjoyed? A loving wife to tend to his home, warm his bed, and fill his heart and home with children?

As if to taunt him, Hartford's laugh filtered across the clubroom. That old devil was the luckiest of them all. For he had secured Alice's hand.

Hawthorne caught his eye and raised an eyebrow. *Damn the man!* He seemed to read Ross's innermost thoughts. No wonder he was such a successful magistrate. Sometimes Ross wished his friend would not look at him so closely. He'd long since been cured of his infatuation toward Hawthorne's wife, having recognized it for what it was. A pathetic attempt to purge all thoughts of Alice from his mind.

With a sigh, he drained his glass. He should be getting home to his daughter. Amelia would be waiting. With the unconditional trust and admiration only a child possessed, she was blind to his manifold faults—his lack of care, his ill temper, and most of all, his longstanding obsession with the one woman he could never have.

"Hey!"

A cry from outside the clubroom cut through his contemplation as sharply as the brandy had severed his self-pity. The door burst open, and a slim youth rushed into the room.

"Where do you think you're going, you reprobate! Stop him!"

A footman unceremoniously dropped a tray and lunged at the uninvited guest. Surprisingly spry on his feet, for he must have surpassed Ross in age by at least thirty years, he caught the boy as deftly as an angler bagging a salmon with his net.

"Let me go, damn you!"

The boy's accent, which stemmed from the gutter, belied the cut of his jacket which, unless Ross was mistaken, originated from one of Savile Row's finest establishments.

Ross called out. "Edward!"

The boy stopped struggling, and the footman addressed Ross. "Do you know this young *gentleman?*" His lip curled in a sneer.

"He's the Duke of Westbury's firstborn son," Ross said, rising from his chair as if to challenge the footman to refer to Edward's illegitimacy. However, the man had the sense to release the boy.

"Perhaps, Mr. Trelawney, sir, you might remind the young master of the rules of decorum."

Edward snorted. "Oh, shut up you…"

"That's enough, young man!" Ross said sharply. "What on earth possessed you to force your way into here? For one thing, you're too young and for another, your father's not in town. If he were, he'd give you a thrashing."

"I'm not here to see Papa," Edward panted and he pointed across the clubroom. "I'm here to see him!"

"Lord Hartford?"

The old man lifted his head. "You wish to see me?"

"It's your wife!" Edward cried. "She's in danger. A man's got her."

A cold hand gripped at Ross from the inside, turning his blood to ice.

"Where is she?" Hartford asked, his voice tight.

"Mrs. Taylor's," Edward panted. "I ran all the way here."

"Have you informed the runners?"

"No."

"Foolish child!" Ross cried. "You left her alone with a houseful of women?"

"I don't trust the authorities," Edward panted. "They don't care."

There spoke the voice of experience—the boy who had been brought up on the wrong side of the law. Though clothed in the garb of a duke's son, Edward would never forget his origins.

Hartford struggled to his feet. He curled his fingers round the handle of his cane, but his body swayed with the effort and his breath wheezed as he tried to speak.

"I must go to her…"

"No." Ross rushed toward him and held him steady. The old man looked up at him, knowledge and understanding in his clear brown eyes. Shame warmed Ross's cheeks at the memory of their last encounter. But fear for her overshadowed propriety, and the promise he'd made to himself to leave her alone.

"Forgive me, Hartford, you're in no state to help her," Ross said. "She wouldn't want you risking yourself. Let *me* go."

"Nonsense," Hartford said, "I must protect my wife."

"He has a knife," Edward said. "His wife and child are there. I know the type. He looked desperate. I saw him through the kitchen window."

Ross tried to swallow the tight ball of terror in his gut.

Dear God. Alice...

The murmur of voices around him seemed to fade while deep within his mind he heard her screams, the screams which had haunted him at night while he lay alone, trying to imagine the horrors she'd lived through.

Had she endured marriage at that bastard Markham's hands, followed by two years in Bedlam, only to be cut to death when she had found peace?

A hand touched his elbow and gentle fingers curled around his sleeve, anchoring him once more to the firm ground. He blinked, and the image swam into view. A kind, benevolent face, brown eyes glistening with understanding.

"She'll be well, Mr. Trelawney," Hartford said. "She's suffered much, but it's made her strong."

Fear lurked behind Hartford's expression, glimmering in the dark depths of his eyes. *Dear God*—though Hartford feared for her himself, he was, even now, trying to reassure Ross.

Hartford coughed and leaned forward, clutching his left arm.

"Alice..." he croaked.

"I'll find her," Ross said. "Edward, tend to Lord Hartford. Take him home."

"Thank you, young man," Hartford said. "Bring her back to me safe and well."

"I will, sir," Ross said. "You have my word."

As he sprinted toward the door, he took one moment to look back at the husband of the woman he loved.

He uttered a silent prayer that he would be able to fulfil his promise. But a small voice in the back of his mind whispered that, even now, Hartford might be a widower.

CHAPTER NINETEEN

LUNGS BURSTING WITH pain, Ross paused outside Mrs. Taylor's house to draw a breath. Though it was a little over a mile from Whites, he felt each and every step. He hollered at the crowds to stand aside, sprinting past without even a thank you. Some, he shouldered out of his way. Doubtless, the newspapers would remark on the spectacle in the morning. But what did appearances matter compared to the woman he loved?

Lights flickered in the upper stories, but the ground floor seemed to be in darkness. As he slipped round the back toward the kitchen, he saw a single candle through the window, casting shadows which danced across the kitchen table. He moved closer, and voices could be heard from inside, together with the sound of a woman crying.

He pushed the door, and it creaked on its hinges.

"Stay back!" a voice cried. A woman sat at the table, sniffing and crying, a child in her arms. At the far end, by the fireplace, he saw the shape of a man holding a woman captive. Pale blue eyes widened as she recognized him, and she drew in a sharp breath.

"Don't come any closer!" the man barked, and she let out a hiss as his left hand moved against her throat. The edge of a blade glinted in the candlelight.

Ross raised his hands in a gesture of appeasement. "I'm unarmed."

The man nodded toward the table. "Sit over there, where I can see you."

After Ross complied, the man loosened his grip on his captive.

Alice let out a small sigh. "What are you doing here, Ross?"

"Edward said you were in danger."

Her captor tightened his grip, and she gasped in pain. "I knew it! You've sent for the runners!"

"No," Ross said. "I've come alone."

"I'm in no danger, Ross," Alice said, her voice betraying only the slightest of tremors. "Ross, this is Jacob Whitworth. He's only twenty-two. Jacob has been telling me a little of himself, that's all. I'm quite safe."

Ross studied the young man. Not long out of boyhood, his thin face bore a hint of a beard. As the man's gaze kept flicking about, guilt and inadequacy glimmered in his eyes, and a shock of recognition rippled through Ross. It was the guilt of a man who understood his own failings toward his family. Ross saw the very same expression each time he looked in the mirror.

"Ross," Alice said. "If you've come alone, I would have you swear it. I made a promise to Jacob that I would not deceive him."

"I swear," Ross replied, and he looked into her eyes, voicing his love for her in the only way he could.

"I would never lie to you," he said. "You know that, Alice. You know *me*."

She closed her eyes for a moment. When she opened them again, they glistened. Jacob gestured toward Ross. "Is he your husband?"

"No, I'm not," Ross said, fighting to keep the regret from his voice. "Her husband tasked me with finding her, and I promised to return her to him, safe and well. You'd want that, wouldn't you, Jacob? A man should take care of his wife, shouldn't he? He's pledged to honor and protect her—not just from others, but from himself."

The man's hand shook, and Alice winced.

"You can lower the knife," Ross said.

"No," Jacob said. "You'll only have me arrested."

"We won't," Alice said. "I promised you, Jacob, and I won't break my promise. I can see you're a good man, and you love your wife."

Jacob shook his head, unshed tears in his eyes. "I'm a failure," he said. "I've lost my job and now my wife. I was born to fail. That's what my da told me."

"A parent should never say that to their child," Alice said. "A father should encourage his son, help him, rather than bring him down."

"What would you know?" Jacob's voice shook. "You're a bleeding do-gooder, who's never experienced hardship or disappointment."

"You're wrong," Alice said. "I know what it means to fail. A parent's disappointment in a child is not dependent on class. Every father possesses fists, and all bodies will bruise if beaten."

"You were never beaten," Jacob said, "not like me and my sister."

"Yes, I was," Alice said, her voice quiet. "By my father, my husband..."

"But you sent for your husband," Jacob said.

"He died," Alice said. "I have a different husband now."

"And does he beat you?"

"No." Alice gave a gentle smile. "He's the kindest, gentlest man that walked this earth. He takes care of me, though I'm surrounded by scandal. Despite his own frailty, he weathers the scorn of society and the ridicule of his peers." She blinked, and a bead of moisture rolled onto her cheek.

"He does it for me, Jacob." she said. "He does it because he cares for me. There's no greater gift a man can give to his wife."

"A man must control his wife," Jacob said, "to show his strength. That's what my da told me."

"Where's the strength in terrorizing those you swore to protect?" Alice shifted in Jacob's arms. "Don't you love your wife? Your son?"

Jacob's lip wobbled, and he nodded.

"I do," he whispered. "But when I lost my job, she cried. She asked me how we were going to live! Da had always told me that a wife's duty was to never question her husband, but to obey."

"How can a wife support her husband if she's never allowed to voice her opinion?" Alice asked. "A wife is there to be a helpmate, to share the responsibility for the family."

"I know... I – I'm sorry!"

"Do you love her?"

The woman sitting at the table cradling her son, stilled and looked up. Jacob raised his head and met her gaze. She gave him a gentle smile, and a tear bloomed on Jacob's cheek.

"Mary, my love," he whispered. "Forgive me."

She nodded, and he let out a low cry. "What have I done!"

"Jacob," Alice said softly. "Give me the knife." She held out her hand, and with a gesture of defeat, he lowered his arm and handed it to her.

Ross exhaled, only now realizing he'd been holding his breath.

"Come here, Alice," he said.

"Not yet, Ross."

"Do as I say, Alice, please."

"No," she said. "Jacob wouldn't harm me, would you Jacob?"

The man crumpled to the floor, shaking his head. "I'm sorry!" he wailed. "I shouldn't have listened to my da. I've failed you, Mary! Just like I failed Fanny!"

Mary crossed the kitchen, then knelt beside him and placed a hand on his shoulder. His body shuddered.

"Don't touch me, Mary," he cried. "I don't deserve you."

"Let me help you, Jacob," she said.

"How can you help me?" he asked. "I've no job. I can't protect you or provide for you."

The pitiful tone of Jacob's voice tore at Ross's heart. Most likely, the young man had been beaten all his life by a brutish parent and was now on the brink of losing his wits over deeds he had committed in the name of others.

He reminded Ross of another crumpled figure from two years ago—a woman bent over the body of her husband, driven to insanity from having been demonized by him. Ross had done nothing for Alice, but at least he could do something for this heartbroken young man.

"Perhaps I can help you, Jacob," he said. "Do you have any skills?"

"He worked with horses," Mary said, her voice timid. "He is—was—an ostler at the Saracen's Head in Holborn. But he lost his job when he had to tend once too often to his father, who'd been drinking. His father thought Jake's employment entitled him to free ale, but it came out of his wages. Jake gave half his wages to his sister, but his father took that from her, too. We often quarreled about it." She lowered her gaze before lifting it once more. "I'm sorry I was so hard on you, Jacob!" she cried. "I just wanted you to prosper. Your father caused nothing but trouble for you. I knew he'd take the money you gave Fanny. I only wanted what was best for us."

"My steward is always looking for willing workers," Ross said. "If you promise to serve me faithfully, I'll send word to him to employ you as an under-groom at my estate in Cornwall, if you wish it."

"And Mary?" Jacob asked. "What of her?"

"Your wages to be sent to her here, in London."

"Can't she come with me?"

Mary looked up at Ross. Her eyes shone with hope for her husband, but he detected an undertone of fear in their color, which matched the bruise on her face.

Alice took the young man's hand. "You must first prove yourself worthy of her, Jacob, as I'm sure you will. You understand that, don't you?"

The young man nodded.

"I'm sure Mister Trelawney will permit you to visit her on occasion," Alice continued. "And perhaps, when your wife is reassured of your devotion to her and her own safety, you can be reunited." Her voice grew soft, though it took on a determined, steely tone. "I must warn you, however, Mary may never feel truly safe with you after what you did to her. If she is to join you, it must be her choice and hers alone. She may never wish it."

Jacob nodded miserably. "I understand."

Alice squeezed his hand. "Take heart, Jacob. I've seen enough of the world to know the difference between one who is irredeemable and a man, or woman, who wishes to atone for a foolish mistake."

"Oh Jake!" Mary took his hand, and the young man drew her into his arms, his body shaking. The child ran toward them, and Jacob drew him into his embrace, both parents enveloping their child in loving arms.

"I'll come with you, Jacob," Mary said. "You need me."

Alice placed a hand on Mary's shoulder. "No, Mary. Give him time."

"Aye, my love," Jacob said. "Let me prove myself worthy of you first."

"Come, now," Ross said. "I'll take you to my townhouse where you can stay until I arrange your passage to Cornwall. Say your goodbyes to your wife."

The young couple shared a brief kiss, then Jacob lifted his son into his arms, held him for a moment, then passed him to his wife.

"Look after your ma, young Adam," he said. "Show your da you're a better man than he."

He nodded to Ross. "I'm ready to go now, sir."

Alice placed the knife on the table. Now that she was out of danger, she looked pale and drawn, as if her resolve, which had come to the fore in her hour of need, had now retreated.

Ross held his hand out to her. "Lady Hartford, permit me to take you home."

"But Mary…"

"Is safe and well," he interrupted. "Mary, is there anyone else in the house?"

"Aye. Mrs. Taylor will be upstairs, resting."

"Seek her out," Ross said, "but lock the door behind us first, in case of any more unwelcome visitors."

Mary lowered her gaze. "It's my fault. I shouldn't have ventured out against Mrs. Taylor's rules."

"Then go find her now and promise never to disobey her again."

"Yes, sir."

"Good girl." Ross held his hand out to Alice, and his body tightened as her cold, little fingers curled around his.

"Come, Alice. Let's get you home."

WITH JACOB SAFELY settled outside next to the driver, Ross ushered Alice into the carriage, dropped a shilling into the palm of the boy he'd sent to summon Hartford's coachmen, then climbed in after her. Now alone, her resolve crumbled, and she slumped forward. He drew her to him, and she melted into his embrace. Her soft figure molded against his body as if she belonged there.

He closed his eyes, savoring the moment of holding the woman he loved in his arms. It was not only her courage which had struck him but her compassion toward the young man. She had every right to hate Jacob. But, instead, she had recognized him for what he was—a foolish, misguided youth who'd made a terrible mistake. Her compassionate heart had wanted to give him a chance to make amends, and her steel core had stood up to the threat of a knife at her throat.

No other creature on earth was so wholly attuned to Ross's beliefs. Her quiet courage was his undoing. She was the missing piece of his soul, without which he could never be whole.

Yet she belonged to another.

"Oh, Alice, my love…"

She stirred in his arms.

"Ross..."

She whispered his name, and her breath caressed his cheek, igniting his need for her. He cupped her chin and held her sweet face in his hands. Her lips parted with a sigh, and she opened her eyes.

The soft blue of her gaze deepened as her pupils dilated, darkening with passion. He dipped his head and brushed his lips against her mouth. She gave a low whimper, then buried her hands in his hair and pulled him close, her body vibrating with need.

"Oh, Alice!" he cried, "I don't know what I would have done had you come to harm!" If all he could have was a few stolen moments in a carriage, it was enough. What mattered was that she was safe. Here. In his arms. "Forgive me, Alice," he said, his voice strained. "I must return you to Hartford. He'll be anxious to know you're safe."

Her body stiffened, and she pulled free from his grasp, guilt and sorrow in her expression.

"Did George send you?"

"He wanted to come himself," he said, "but he was taken ill."

She drew her hands to her face and gave a strangled gasp. "Dear God! Why did you not tell me this?" Her stricken expression tore through his heart. "Ross—how could you? What have I done?"

She wrung her hands together, her face wet with tears. "Oh George—George! Forgive me! Take me home! Now!"

He reached for her hand to reassure her, but she snatched it away. Her loyalty to Hartford was to her credit, but to see the pain it caused her was more than Ross could bear.

And it was his fault.

He leaned out of the window and roared for the coachman to make haste. It was all he could do to ease her suffering.

Alice remained silent for the rest of the journey. When the carriage drew to a halt, she pushed open the door. Ignoring the footman's helping hand, she climbed out and rushed toward the door to Hartford's townhouse. It opened and, without a backward glance, she slipped inside.

Once again, Ross had thrown temptation in front of her. Her loyalty and goodness surpassed any feelings she might have for him. But the love he bore her, which he'd striven to conquer for seven years, had only strengthened.

But she belonged to another. All Ross was capable of doing was increasing her pain.

Perhaps it was time he conceded defeat and married another. Alice was not—and never would be—his. She deserved so much better.

CHAPTER TWENTY

"ARE YOU QUITE well, George?"

Alice leaned forward, trying to discern her husband's expression in the candlelight. But he merely waved her concerns aside and resumed his attention on his roast beef.

"Of course, my dear."

But she had long since learned that an over-enthusiastic tone of voice hid fears and doubts. The past week, George seemed much older, and he struggled to climb the stairs more than usual. But each time she inquired after his health, he brushed her aside. Not out of the contempt Roderick had always shown, but out of an indulgence, as if he wanted to protect her from the harsh realities of life.

In anyone else she might have found his protectiveness stifling. But it came from his fondness for her and a desire to give her peace.

He sipped his wine and set the glass aside. "My dear," he said, his tone overly bright. "Have you heard from that young man at all? What was his name—Jacob Whitworth?"

"Yes, I have," she said, slicing through a piece of beef. "A letter arrived for his wife only yesterday. He had to commission Mister Trelawney's steward to write it for him, but I understand he's been learning his letters and hopes to write his own letter to Mary soon."

"Was Mary able to read it?"

"I read it for her," Alice said. "She wanted to wait until I visited her rather than ask Mrs. Taylor to read it. I think she's ashamed of giving

Jacob another chance."

"Those of us guilty of mere folly will always deserve a second chance, my dear," George said. "Perhaps in time, I can forgive the young ruffian for placing you in danger."

"I've experienced much worse, George."

His eyes narrowed and he nodded. "I know," he said. "Forgive an old man his indulgences in wanting to ensure you never have to suffer again. When I think of what you've gone through, I don't think I shall ever..." He caught his breath and leaned forward.

"George?"

"It's nothing," he said, rubbing his chest. "Merely a little indigestion. This beef is so excellent, I often forget myself and eat it too quickly.

He reached for his wine, and Alice resumed her attention on her dinner. A clatter of steel on porcelain made her look up and her chest tightened at the sight before her. Hartford leaned back in his chair, his hands clutching the tablecloth, knuckles whitened with the effort. Mouth open, he gasped as if fighting for breath.

She pushed aside her plate and leapt from her chair. "Help me!"

The two footmen in attendance rushed forward. "My lady?"

"You..." She pointed to the younger of the two. "Fetch the doctor!"

"At this hour? He'll be dining."

"I don't care, your master is ill! Get him!" She gestured to the other. "Help me with Lord Hartford."

She reached for George's necktie and loosened it, but he still gasped for breath.

"Alice..." he choked. "Alice, my love. It's my time. Let me go."

"No!" She took his hand and linked her fingers through his. He tried to squeeze her hand, but his fingers trembled, the flesh cold, the skin dry and thin as paper.

"Water..." he whispered. She picked up a glass and held it to his mouth.

He focused his gaze on Alice. Love glimmered in his expression, but it was overshadowed by another emotion.

Resignation. Acceptance.

A cold hand circled her heart. The pain of loss threatened to overwhelm her, but she fought it, striving to keep her voice steady. For him.

"That's it, my love." She caressed his cheek. "You'll feel better soon. Very soon. And I'm here with you."

His eyes crinkled into a smile. "My dear wife," he said. "I count myself the most fortunate of men to have you by my side at the end."

"Please," she said, "you mustn't say such things." She gestured to the footman. "Help me get him upstairs, then you must fetch Master Dominic."

"He'll be at Whites at this hour, my lady."

"I don't care where he is," she cried. "Send for him immediately. There's not an instant to lose."

George shook his head. "After the manner in which he spoke to you, I cannot allow him back."

She caressed his forehead and brushed her lips against his skin. "No, my love," she said. "It matters not what he's said. He's your son, and you love him. He must be by your side. I would not have it any other way."

"You truly are the best of women," he said, his voice tight. "We may not have had as long together as I would have liked, but these have been the happiest days of my twilight years. I never thought I would smile again after my beloved Cassandra passed away. But you, my dearest Alice, have made me whole again."

Hot tears stung behind her eyelids, and her body shook with grief. A calm hand curled around her shoulder. She looked up and recognized the butler.

"Let us take him upstairs, my lady."

"Of course, Fossett. Please, take the greatest care of him."

"I always do, my lady," the butler said, "as do you."

He lifted George to his feet, and Alice winced at the sound of her husband's breathing. Fighting back tears, she followed them upstairs and into his chamber. A chambermaid was already poking at a fire, fanning the flames which curled around the coals and licked through the logs.

Not long after they had placed him in his bed, she heard the main doors open and slam shut, and a sense of relief rippled through her.

The doctor.

But when the chamber door opened, Dominic stood in the doorway, hair unkempt, surrounded by a faint aroma of liquor and cheap perfume.

"Why have you disturbed my evening?" he asked. "I've been spending it in far pleasanter company."

Alice pointed toward the bed. His face paled as he caught sight of his father. Hartford's skin looked gray in the candlelight, his lips a dark blue, his mouth open as he fought for breath.

"What have you done to my father?"

Hartford lifted his hand and beckoned to his son. "She's looked after me and given me a new life, Dominic. But now my life is over, and she'll need someone to look after her."

Dominic barked with laughter. "You're not suggesting I *marry* her?"

"No!" Alice protested. The thought of being beholden to Dominic Hartford sent a ripple of fear through her. "I need no such protection, George. What I need is for you to be well. Do not give up hope while you have life."

"That life is fading, my love."

"Please, no!" she cried. "Don't say it, I can't bear it!"

"My dear child," he said, his tone taking on that of an overindulgent parent, "I've accepted my fate. I accepted it a long time ago when

Doctor Beckford first diagnosed me. I count myself fortunate to have outlived his expectations and that I have had you by my side at the end."

She bit her lip to fight the grief threatening to consume her.

"Please don't leave me, George."

"Everyone has their time," he said. "Surely you understand that?"

"Yes, I do," she said, "but that doesn't mean your time is now. Don't you want to live?"

"Aye, I do," he said, "and I have. I've lived a full and happy life." He smiled and closed his eyes as if reliving a memory. "I have been fortunate to be born into a world where I wanted for nothing. I had a wonderful wife who I loved, who bore me a son, and I thought my life was over when she was taken from me. But I have been so blessed to have found happiness again, my dearest Alice. With you."

"What will I do without you, George?" Alice whispered.

"I'll always be with you, dear one." He lifted his hand, and she took it and pressed it to her heart.

"You are a good woman," he said. "I'll remain in your heart forever, watching over you. But you must promise me one thing."

"Anything, my love."

He gave her a knowing smile. "Promise me you'll follow your heart, Alice. Find a man who will make you happy, who will give you everything I was unable to. A home, a future, children of your own. I shall rest far easier if I know you'll be happy with someone who loves you."

"George..."

He placed a finger on her lips to silence her protest.

"Indulge a dying man his last wish. It's what your dear mama would have wanted for you also."

She kissed him on the forehead. Hot tears splashed onto his face, and she wiped them away.

"I would rather have your smiles as I depart this earth than your tears, my dear."

"Dear George!" She forced a smile and caressed his forehead. His lips curled into a grin which shone in his eyes, tainted by the undercurrent of pain.

"That's better! Now, let my son hear my words. Dominic, come to me."

The bed shifted as Dominic sat beside his father. Alice stepped back to let father and son say their final goodbyes.

"Be a good man, Dominic," George said. "That's all I ever wanted for you. And be happy. You now have everything you wanted. The title, the estates…"

Dominic shook his head, moisture glistening in his eyes.

"Forgive me, Father, for disappointing you."

"You were never a disappointment, Dominic. From the day you were born, you were my pride and joy—and your dear mother's. Do not mourn me, for I shall be joining her, and I can tell her what a fine man her son has become."

Dominic bent his head, and his shoulders trembled. "Father…"

"No, let me finish, Dominic," George said. "I have one thing to ask of you. You must look after Alice for me."

"No, George," Alice said. "Don't ask it of him. Don't ask it of me."

Hartford shook his head. "I don't mean marry her, Dominic, for you'll never make her happy."

Dominic stole a glance at Alice, his eyes narrowing for a moment before he resumed his attention on his father.

"What must I do?"

"Under the terms of the entailment, I'm unable to secure a permanent annuity on Alice after I'm gone," George said. "I must therefore rely on you to direct the trustees and ensure she receives an income. I promised her independence and would ask that you fulfil that promise. I would not have her left destitute."

Dominic remained still, but Alice noticed a tic in his jaw as if he fought demons of his own.

"Promise me, my son," George said. "Grant your dying father this one wish."

Dominic dipped his head and placed a light kiss on his father's cheek. The old man sighed and lifted his lips into a smile. For a moment, Alice thought the color of his lips had turned pink and a ray of hope ignited within her. But it was the flare of a candle which, on reaching the end of the wick, released one final gasp of light before it extinguished forever.

George sank back against the pillows and sighed one last time. When Alice moved toward him, he showed no spark of life. The man who had delivered her from evil and given her a brief period of happiness, was gone.

She took Dominic's hand and gave it a gentle squeeze. Deep down, he loved his father. At the end, the two of them were united in their grief at the passing of the kindest man to walk upon the earth.

Dominic stiffened and pulled his hand free.

"Forgive me, Father," he said. "I didn't quite catch what you said."

CHAPTER TWENTY-ONE

ROSS SETTLED INTO his seat near the front of the chapel. He looked around the congregation, but there was no sign of the widow. Where was she? Society whispered that she was already looking for a third husband after sending her second into an early grave.

But society was wrong. The old viscount had been living on borrowed time. The fact that his heart had lasted so long was a miracle. And it was unfair to think so uncharitably of her. The shame in her eyes when they'd almost kissed spoke of her love for Hartford.

The music began, and the congregation rose as the chief mourners walked down the aisle carrying the coffin. Dominic led the party, his expression grim, mouth set in a hard line. Westbury walked on Dominic's right. The other mourners included Rupert Oakville and Hawthorne Stiles.

Ross turned and spotted a solitary figure near the back of the church. Dressed in black, a thin veil covered her face, but he'd recognize her anywhere.

Alice.

A hand nudged his shoulder. "Move over, old chap."

"Dominic." Ross wrinkled his nose at the odor of brandy and moved aside to make room. Another aroma pricked his senses. "Can I do anything for you?"

Perfume. An unmistakable scent which came from Paris and had cost Ross a small fortune. It was Kitty's favorite, and she'd promised not to wear it for any man but the one she loved the most.

Is there nothing a woman wouldn't do to further her own ends?

"I doubt it, my friend," Dominic said as he settled into his seat next to Ross. "But at least I was able to stop her before she drained Father's estate."

"Who?"

"That gold-digging harlot."

"What—Kitty?"

A spark of recognition crossed Dominic's expression before he smiled coldly and shook his head.

"No, I meant the *grieving widow*. Why she has the effrontery to plague me today, I don't know."

"Couldn't you prevent her coming if you find her presence so repugnant?"

"Believe me, I tried," Dominic said, "but she insisted. I even threatened to close down her pathetic little shelter. In the end, I granted her permission to stay until the funeral, on condition that she leaves immediately after."

"Where will she go?" Ross asked.

"Her father is taking her back. I hear he plans to marry her off as soon as possible. Assuming someone can bear to have her."

Before Ross could answer, the music struck up and the congregation stood to sing the first hymn.

⟫⟩⟨⟪

THE CEREMONY OVER, the party left the chapel and walked in single file back to the main house. Though he looked around him, Ross could no longer see her. Hawthorne fell into step with him, curtailing his long strides to maintain the same pace.

"Are you well, my friend?" Ross asked. "And your wife? I didn't see her in the chapel."

Hawthorne sighed, his breath forming a cloud in the frosty air.

"Frederica is suffering from sickness, or she would have been here to pay her respects."

"I'm sorry to hear that. Is she unwell?"

"Doctor McIver says it's due to her pregnancy. She was the same with our second child. It's nothing a month of rest cannot cure."

"A month of rest? Frederica?" Ross smiled. "I wish you well in your endeavors to keep her in check. I swear your lady wife's spirit has been cut from diamond it's so impenetrable."

"She'll do anything I ask," Hawthorne said, "if it's for the benefit of those she loves."

Ross sighed. Hawthorne knew his good fortune.

"Come on, Ross," Hawthorne said, his voice turning serious. "I fear the new Viscount Hartford might disgrace himself if he continues to make friends with his father's drink cabinet."

"I thought I smelled brandy on him."

"He finished the bottle before we left the house," Hawthorne said. "I didn't think his father's death would hit him so hard."

"What about the viscountess?"

"Don't tell me you're still smitten with her," Hawthorne said. "Besides, you're wasting your time."

"What do you mean?"

"Her father's promised her to de Blanchard."

A twitch of nausea coiled in Ross's gut. "That old lecher? How did you hear that?"

"De Blanchard was boasting about it in Whites yesterday. Apparently, Lady de Grecy has already paid him a visit to make the proposal. I can't imagine any woman being so anxious to have him for a son-in-law."

"Or a husband," Ross said.

A spattering of rain began to fall, and the party increased their pace. Hawthorne dug his hands into his coat pockets, shrugging his shoulders against the cold. But the cold could not penetrate Ross's skin. Fire and fury heated him from within. Fury at de Grecy for forcing her into another marriage and fury at de Blanchard for being the one to have her.

"Are you all right my friend?"

Ross looked up. Hawthorne's mahogany gaze was directed straight at him.

"I'm cold, that's all."

Hawthorne exhaled sharply through his nose.

"The marriage won't take place for some time unless de Blanchard secures a special license."

"Is that likely?"

"Hardly." Hawthorne continued to stare at Ross. "He needs the ear of the archbishop—or a good friend to speak on his behalf."

"And does he not possess either?"

"Charles is very particular about his friends," Hawthorne said. "There are too many men who view the clergy as an institution which exists to serve them, rather than the other way 'round."

"Charles? With such a familiar mode of address, I presume you know the archbishop well."

"He was up at Cambridge the same time as my father."

"And he views you as a friend?"

Hawthorne smiled. "A bishop and a magistrate have much in common. A bishop is in charge of the spiritual and moral wellbeing of the world. A magistrate ensures the bishop's wishes are manifested in the execution of justice. Ah! Here we are." He pulled his hands out of his pockets. "Let's see if we can get to the brandy before Dominic drinks his cellar dry."

Belfield Hall had taken on a gloomy demeanor, as if the building mourned the loss of its owner. And well it might. Even though the estate was under trust, it still needed a responsible lord to maintain it. The aristocracy might look down on men such as Ross who had earned their fortune through business, but their relative lack of business sense was to the detriment of their capital. In order to survive, even the oldest families needed to drag themselves into the nineteenth century.

The conversation in the morning room had degenerated into an amorphous buzz of vacuous comments and meaningless condolences. The sunlight cast a ray across the room in which dust motes danced and swirled. It illuminated a pair of pale blue eyes in a face which looked deathly white against the black lace of the veil which had been pulled back. Though she looked straight at him, he couldn't detect a flicker of recognition, but her fingers curled around the stem of her glass, and her knuckles whitened.

She blinked and broke eye contact, and the glass slipped from her hand and fell to the floor. Dominic stood beside her, a frown on his face. His hand curled round her arm. He leaned over her, his lips moving, but Ross couldn't make out the words.

Eventually, she nodded, and he released her arm. She bent to retrieve her glass, but Dominic grasped her shoulder and shook his head. She turned and slipped out of the room.

Ross ought to ignore her—let her return to her father and marry another title. But the pain in her eyes compelled him to follow her.

By the time he had made his excuses and left the house, the sun had fallen below the horizon. A large trunk sat near the main entrance, and two footmen carried another outside to where the Hartford carriage stood, waiting.

Ross hailed the footman beside the door.

"Is your mistress leaving today?"

"As soon as she returns from the chapel, sir."

"Thank you."

Ross set off toward the chapel.

By the time he reached the small, stone building, the rain was falling more heavily. Beside the chapel, a low fence enclosed the cemetery, carved, marble stones marking the generations of Hartfords who had been buried there during the four hundred years since the title had been bestowed on the first viscount by Henry V.

One headstone stood out among the rest. Pure white, it had yet to be muddied and weathered by the forces of nature. The stonemasons had done their work quickly.

A lone figure knelt by the gravestone. As Ross approached, she tensed.

"Alice," he spoke softly.

Her chest rose and fell in a sigh. "Leave me alone, Ross."

"What are you doing here?"

She gave a bitter laugh. "You think I'm here for my benefit, or..." she gestured toward the main house, "...or theirs?"

"Then, why?"

"Just go, Ross, you wouldn't understand."

He knelt beside her. "Explain it to me, Alice."

"I'm here for him," she said quietly. "For George. The only man to give me what I needed." She turned to face him, her eyes showing cold resolve, as if daring him to doubt her. "I don't mean money or a title, but affection, security, and peace. For a brief moment he taught me to trust again."

"As his widow you can't want for money," he said.

"I inherited nothing."

"That must be a disappointment." He cringed as he uttered the words, urged on by the demon sitting on his shoulder which battled his conscience.

She grasped his wrist, the motion unusually swift and strong for such a fragile-looking woman. Her body vibrated with raw anger.

"Enough!" she cried. "You have no right to speak so! I expected nothing from him. He pledged me an annuity, but the trustees denied it."

"Why would they do that?"

"Dominic can be very persuasive." A cloud of fear passed over her expression, and she resumed her attention on the gravestone.

"But you were Hartford's wife. Can't you petition the trustees?"

She shook her head. "An unconsummated marriage can be declared null and void. I have no wish to waste time pleading my case, which will only make me even more of a harlot in the eyes of men such as yourself."

The hurt in her eyes mirrored the shame in his heart. He moved closer. "Alice, I..."

"Leave me," she said. "Let me say goodbye to him in peace. If nothing else, you owe me that."

"Surely you can visit the grave again?"

"The new viscount has made it clear I'll not be welcome. After I leave today, I won't be coming back."

"Where will you go?"

"I will return to Papa."

"How could you contemplate such a thing?"

"Oh, it's easy for you, isn't it?" she scoffed. "You can earn your living. You're free. But I have nothing. Now that I've been turned out of Belfield."

"What will you do?"

"What can I do, Ross?" She reached out to the gravestone and caressed it, then rose to her feet, refusing his offer of help.

"I have two choices," she said. "While I still have some freedom, I must take the least abhorrent." She let out a sigh. "I'm tired, Ross, so tired. I have learned that battling against the tide of fate is a futile endeavor. I must learn to bend to the will of others, for if I remain resistant, I'll only break."

She turned to face him, her mouth set in a firm line. "And I vowed a long time ago, I shall *never* break again."

He reached for her hand, but she pushed him away,

"Leave me alone! Don't try to follow me."

She turned her back and disappeared toward the house. Shortly after, he heard the sound of the carriage leaving.

He sighed and addressed the grave. "I always thought you were one lucky bastard, Hartford. I only wish I could be as deserving of her as you were."

Before he left, he spotted a splash of color at the foot of the gravestone. A reminder of all the battles she had fought and lost.

Four red roses.

⤞⟫⟪⟨

As Ross approached the main house, he gestured to the waiting footman.

"Have my horse saddled while I take my leave of his lordship."

"Very good, sir."

Ross looked around the hallway. The trunk was gone.

"Ah, there you are, Ross," a voice said. "About bloody time."

A dark silhouette stood in the doorway to the morning room, a glass in his hand. He lifted it to his lips and tipped it up.

"Dominic, it's time I went home."

"Nonsense, old boy. You may not be cut from the same cloth as the rest of us, but you can at least join us in one final toast to father."

Ignoring the insult directed at his birth, Ross followed Dominic into the morning room. The guests had left except for three men. Westbury sat beside the hearth, a cigar in one hand, a half-full glass in the other. Oakville sat on his left, a sour look on his face. Hawthorne Stiles stood by the window, arms folded, seemingly transfixed by the view of the main drive. Ever the stoic magistrate, Hawthorne displayed little emotion save a slight frown on his face.

Dominic thrust a glass into Ross's hand and tipped a decanter over it, filling it almost to the brim. Ross jerked back as the liquid splashed onto his hand.

"Steady on, old chap," Ross said.

"Would you refuse my hospitality?"

"I need a clear head for the ride back to London."

Dominic waved his hand around the room. "Stay the night. The chaps are going to."

Westbury coughed. "I promised Jeanette…"

"Oakville's staying, aren't you?"

Oakville nodded, though he didn't smile.

"And you, Hawthorne?" Dominic asked. "Don't tell me you're ruled by your wife as well?"

Hawthorne remained silent.

Dominic snorted. "That's why I've no intention of taking a wife. Marriage leads to emasculation. I can't imagine anything more degrading than to be ruled by a woman."

Ross set his glass aside. "Degrading?"

"It's no different to having your balls cut off," Dominic said. "You only have to look at my father."

Anger flared within Ross, and he fisted his hands to suppress it.

"Not drinking, my friend?" Dominic asked. "Is my brandy not to your taste?"

"The liquor is good enough," Ross said. "But I cannot say the same for the company. You're drunk."

"I'm entitled to drink to my father's passing."

"You needn't be so triumphant about it."

"Why not?" Dominic asked. "Father was duped into wasting his money on that harridan. At least in death he's been spared her needling. Death is the only means of escape a man has from his wife."

"How dare you!" Ross cried. Westbury leapt to his feet and took Ross's arm. "Leave it, Trelawney. Dom's drunk. Don't dishonor the late viscount by quarrelling about his widow."

Ross shook Westbury's arm off. "I take issue with Dominic's remarks about money. You see, I heard rather differently."

"Oh, did you?" Dominic puffed out his chest in the manner of a stag challenging another. "Remember the last time you tried to best me? You ended up with a sword in your thigh."

"I don't want to fight you, Dominic, but I won't have you disrespect your father or the woman he married. You'd have her painted as an extravagant seductress, but I heard differently."

"Oh, did you?"

"Do you deny that the trustees of your father's estate…"

"You'll find it's *my* estate, now," Dominic interrupted.

"…that the trustees, on your orders, denied your stepmother the stipend your father had pledged?"

Dominic lowered his gaze as if a flicker of shame threatened to prick at him, then he laughed. "I don't deny it. I'm proud of it! That woman drove my father into an early grave. She deserves no special consideration from any of us, least of all you, Ross, the man she spurned for a title. I applaud myself for saving the small fortune an annuity would have cost the estate. I can imagine that woman living forever just to spite me."

"How dare you speak so!"

"Oh come, Ross!" Dominic laughed. "Everyone knows she made a fool out of my father."

"Your father struck me as no fool," Hawthorne said, a serious undertone in his deep voice. He turned and looked at Dominic. His features bore the expression of a magistrate trying to discern whether the witness in his courtroom was telling the truth. "Why do *you* think he married her?"

Dominic shrugged. "I suppose he wanted a nurse." A cruel smile spread across his face. "It certainly wasn't for the fucking."

"I say, steady on, old chap!" Oakville said. "There's no place for that kind of talk."

"It's true!" Dominic said. "And even if he'd wanted her for bed-sport, he wouldn't have had any luck. The mere thought of it terrified the life out of her!"

"How the devil do you know that?" Hawthorne asked.

Dominic looked away but not before he cast a sidelong glance at Ross.

Ross's stomach twisted at the sight of Dominic's face which bore the traces of his years of experience as a rake, the expression in his eyes which spoke of base, carnal knowledge.

Ross battled to fight the tide of acid welling in his stomach. "How *do* you know, Dominic?"

Dominic shook his head. "A man knows."

"Did you try to seduce her? Is that why your father turned you out—and why you took your revenge on her today, of all days, by turning her out?"

"Of course not." Dominic's answer came a little too quickly.

Hawthorne glanced at Ross and shook his head in warning. Now was not the time to challenge Dominic, not while his father was barely cold in his grave.

Oakville rose to his feet. "I think, perhaps, it's time you took your leave, gentlemen. I'll take care of Dom."

He strode across the room and took Dominic's arm. Dom pulled his arm free and lost his balance, falling against his friend. He directed a lopsided smile at Ross.

"I suppose she told you everything? Spread sordid tales of seduction?"

"She's said nothing about it."

"Well, she'd better learn to enjoy the activities of the bedchamber," Dominic slurred. "If de Blanchard has his way, she'll end up chained to his bed. That man's appetite is insatiable. He spends a bloody fortune on doxies in London and will want his money's worth from a wife."

Ross swallowed to fight the nausea which almost exploded in his gut at the thought of Alice in that man's possession. What had she told him only that afternoon? That she would have to bend so she didn't break?

"Come on, Westbury, Trelawney," Hawthorne said. "We've outstayed our welcome. The sooner we leave, the sooner Oakville can sober him up. Dom, we'll see ourselves out."

Hawthorne crossed the floor, and Ross followed him outside.

When the door closed behind them, Hawthorne sighed. "Bloody hell, I've not seen Dom that bad. His father's death has hit him hard."

"He seemed in more of a celebratory mood to me," Ross said.

Hawthorne placed a hand on his shoulder. "Don't worry about him."

Ross sighed. "I'm worried about *her*." He closed his eyes, trying to erase the memory of her tear-filled expression, the resignation in her eyes as she left the gravestone and walked in the rain toward her fate. Bile rose in his throat at the thought of her with de Blanchard, his fat, sweaty hands claiming her helpless body…

He drew a sharp breath. If she was unable or unwilling to fight the tide of fate, then someone must fight it for her. Perhaps it was time for Ross to prove his worth.

"Hawthorne, I need you to do a favor for me."

"A favor?"

"You're on good terms with the archbishop, yes? How quickly can you send a message to him?"

"Why?" Hawthorne raised his eyebrows, then his expression turned from bemusement to astonishment.

"You don't mean…"

Ross nodded. "I do."

"I'd advise against it, Ross. The path to that woman's hand leads to misery and betrayal. You've trodden it before."

"I know," Ross said.

Hawthorne sighed. "I could refuse to help you."

"I'm asking anyway."

"Will you two stop talking in riddles," Westbury said. "What are you asking Stiles to do?"

"He's asking me to help him make the biggest mistake of his life," Hawthorne said. "Again."

"It's my mistake to make," Ross said. "If you grant me this, I'll never ask you for anything again."

"Very well," Hawthorne replied. "As long as you're prepared to face the consequences, I'll do what I can to secure a special license for you. But I see little merit in wishing you joy. I never play a losing hand."

CHAPTER TWENTY-TWO

"I'M SO SORRY to hear you won't be able to visit us for much longer, my dear. You've been such a great help to us."

Alice lifted her teacup to her lips. "There's nothing more I'd like than to continue to come here, Mrs. Taylor, but it won't be possible."

"Perhaps after you're married?"

Alice shook her head and sipped her tea. The sweet taste did little to neutralize the bitter taste in her throat at the thought of her next marriage. De Blanchard had already called twice, his fleshy face leering at her over his multiple chins, his puffy fingers curling round the tip of the cane he was rumored to use on his servants with relish.

"I don't think my future husband would permit it."

"I shall miss you," Mrs. Taylor said.

"And I, you." Alice sighed. "Rest assured, I've done all that I can to secure you an income now the annuity from Lord Hartford has come to an end. Papa has promised to leave you alone if I do as he wishes."

Mrs. Taylor leaned forward and squeezed Alice's fingers. "We'll always be grateful for the money, Alice. But your company has meant more to me than money ever could. You've been such a help, and you gave hope to the lost souls here."

"I've done so little."

"No, my dear." The older women reached up to brush a stray lock of hair from Alice's forehead. "My dear, sweet, child, you have suffered more than these women can imagine. Yet, you have always shown such resolve, such kindness, and love and a dedication to help others. Where so many of us would use our suffering as an excuse to lie down and give up, you have used yours for good. We have been fortunate to have you in our lives."

"I'm so sorry I'm unable to do more."

"Perhaps in time, you will be permitted to visit us again."

Alice rose to her feet, using the action to disguise the tears which pooled in her eyes. Mrs. Taylor pulled her into an embrace, taking care not to look directly at her. She possessed the innate understanding that when one was suffering from despair, it's not cruelty which brings tears, but kindness and compassion.

"I'll be able to visit you for a little while longer, Mrs. Taylor," she said. "I'll not be married for a while yet. The engagement has not been announced, and the banns have yet to be posted."

"Then we must make the most of you while you're still able to join us."

The parlor door burst open and an elegantly dressed young man entered, his face aglow with youthful exuberance.

"Are you ready for me to escort you home, Lady Alice?"

"Of course, Edward."

She pulled on her gloves, fingering the wedding band on her left hand from Hartford. The thin metal band, a symbol of protection, would soon be replaced by the engagement ring de Blanchard had boasted of. According to Papa and Kathleen, it was one of the largest sapphires in London. But to Alice, it would never be anything other than a shackle to tie her to a life of servitude and misery. But she would weather her enslavement if it meant Mrs. Taylor was left undisturbed.

And if, as Papa had threatened, it prevented him from returning her to Bedlam.

They crossed the hallway, and Edward opened the front door.

"Oh look!" he said. "There's a carriage outside."

"Tell them to go away," Mrs. Taylor said. "They'll attract attention. We had enough of that when that young man Jacob Whitworth came barging in. Reporters and Lord knows what on my doorstep."

"I'll tell them to move," Alice said. "Come on, Edward, time to go. Mrs. Taylor, close the door behind us."

The carriage looked out of place in the shabby street with the footmen wearing smart livery and the horses' metal bits shining in the afternoon light. There was no crest on the side, so it was neither Papa's nor de Blanchard's. She strode up to it and rapped on the window.

The door opened, and her stomach jolted at the sight of the familiar face, the sharp planes of his features even more prominent in the shadows.

He held out his hand.

"Get in."

His voice vibrated through her body which yearned to obey, and she moved forward.

"Ross…"

Edward appeared at her side. "Mister Trelawney! What are you doing here?"

"Leave us, Edward," Ross growled and leaned forward, his eyes hard with resolve. "Take my hand, Alice, and get in. Now. Or I'll haul you in myself."

"Mr. Trelawney, sir," Edward said. "I can't permit you to do that. The lady is under my protection."

"I said, leave us, boy!"

Body vibrating with anger, he climbed out of the carriage, his body seeming to grow in the evening light, his shadow stretching across the ground.

"Leave, young whelp!" he roared. "Or I'll have you horsewhipped throughout this damn town!"

A couple strolling along the other side of the street stopped and stared at them. The woman began to move closer, but her companion held her back with a warning shout, then approached the carriage.

"Ross, you must leave," Alice pleaded. "You're attracting attention. You know how Mrs. Taylor values secrecy."

"Do you think I care for propriety?"

"I'm talking about the safety of the women in her care," she said. "You know how quickly word spreads. If their fathers or husbands discover their whereabouts, we'll have every thug in London beating on the doors."

He hesitated, doubt creeping into his expression, then he took her wrist and pulled her close.

"Then, you'd better get in," he said, "for I'm not moving this carriage until you do."

"Unhand the lady!" Edward cried.

"You think a tattling adolescent can stop me?" Ross asked.

Edward curled his hands into fists. "Fight me like a man!"

Ross threw back his head and laughed. "A young whelp is no match for a Cambridge boxing blue." He tightened his grip on Alice's wrist. "I suggest you leave, *boy*, before you do something you'll regret."

Edward looked to Alice, and she waved him away. "Go home, Edward. I am safe enough." She sighed in surrender and climbed into the carriage. "At least tell me where you're taking me."

"It's not far."

"That's not an answer."

"It's all you're getting."

She sat back and folded her arms. "Ross, I meant what I said the other day. I'm tired. I've had enough. Just let me go."

"So you'll give up, just like that?" His eyes flashed. "You'll hand yourself over body and soul to another monster to appease your father?"

Though his voice held a note of pain, rather than contempt, his words still cut her deep at the knowledge that society would, once again, label her a fortune-hunter.

"Think what you like of me, Ross. I no longer care."

He took her hand, cradling it as delicately as if he were holding a priceless treasure. He caressed the skin of her wrist with his thumb, and her skin came alive, sending a ripple of sensation through her body.

"You have no idea what I think of you, Alice," he whispered.

Fighting the instinct to pull him close, she withdrew her hand. "You've voiced your opinion of me often enough, Ross."

He leaned back and closed his eyes. "If I recall, I once told you that you were the one woman in the world I was capable of loving, that you had ensnared my heart forever, and that I would love you until the day my body turned to dust."

Her heart gave a jolt at the memory of his proposal, and for a moment, she was transported back to the day he'd made her the happiest of women. On that day, her future had stretched ahead of her, bright, warm, and loving.

But the harsh realities of her fate had destroyed the hopeful, young debutante she'd once been.

She dug her fingernails into her palm, then opened it again. Small, half-moon marks formed a line across her skin. But she felt nothing. Her body had long since grown numb to physical pain. She rubbed the tip of her thumb across the marks on her palm until they began to fade, then she looked up at the man next to her.

"That was a long time ago, Ross," she said. "We're different people now."

"Are we?" he replied. "I've always believed that the soul, one's very essence, remains unchanged. What we do, say, and think may change over the years. But what we believe, deep down, will always remain the same."

How little he knew her! Her faith had been destroyed countless times, reformed in the ashes of her destruction at Roderick's hands. All that remained was a tiny corner of her soul which she had kept hidden—her unwavering love for him. But if she succumbed to it, her destruction would be complete.

"What do *you* believe in, Ross?"

He opened his mouth to reply, but the carriage drew to a halt and a voice hailed from outside.

"We've arrived at the church, sir."

Ross rolled up the blind and lowered the window. "Very good," he said. "Make sure they're ready, will you?"

"Aye, sir."

"What's happening?" Alice asked. "Why are we at a church?"

"We're getting married."

"No!" she cried. "We can't."

"Why not?"

"Papa's going to announce my engagement."

"To that lecher?" Ross exhaled sharply through his nose.

"He's waiting at home for me now, Ross."

"I know," he replied. "Young Edward is most obligingly free with his information."

"Edward?"

A look of discomfort crossed his brow. "He didn't know why I asked him. I trust you'll forgive him his loose tongue."

"I can more easily forgive him than I can forgive you. Take me home, Ross. I don't know why you persist in torturing me."

He pulled her against his body. The memory of another pair of hands pushed into her consciousness, refueling the tide of fear, and she cried out, giving voice to the terror of Roderick's ghost, which still haunted her.

He relaxed his grip. "Dear God, Alice, you fear me?"

"Let me go, Ross."

"Only if you agree to be my wife."

"I can't!" she cried. "Don't torture me, please! Papa would never allow it."

"And you do everything your father dictates?"

"What else can I do? As soon as my engagement to De Blanchard is announced, there's nothing I can do. The banns will be read on Sunday. What can you hope to do?"

"You should ask me what I have already done, Alice. Once we're married, there's nothing your father can do. In a matter of an hour, you'll be free of him."

"I don't understand."

"I've secured a special license. Stiles is a friend of the archbishop."

"I don't know…"

A warm hand took hers. If she closed her eyes, she could almost believe love flowed through the fingers that circled around her wrist. But she could not bring herself to hope. Not again.

"Alice, it's all arranged. Come with me now, and we'll be man and wife. By the time your father finds out, it will be too late for him to prevent it."

"You sound as if you've already made up your mind."

"Yes, I have," he said. "I'm determined nobody will prevent me this time."

The brutal resolve in his voice held echoes of Roderick. The voice of ownership, that of a man intent on having his own way, ignoring the wishes of others.

"Do I not have a choice, Ross? Or will you take me by force?"

"I will *never* take you by force!" he cried. She cringed at the fury in his eyes which disappeared almost as soon as it had formed. He lowered his voice and shook his head, wrinkling his nose in disgust. "You'd rather bed that flabby viscount?"

"No, I…"

"Listen," he said. "Your choice is between coming under my protection or shackling yourself to the most notorious lecher in the whole of society. Which is it to be?"

She lowered her gaze, fighting the tears.

"No," he said. "Look at me." A fingertip pressed against her chin and tipped her face up. "Open your eyes so I might know the truth in your words."

Blinking away the fog of moisture, she focused on his gaze, which seemed to penetrate her soul.

"I give you a choice now, Alice," he said. "Come with me now and become my wife, and I promise to honor and protect you. I will leave you alone if that is your wish, to come and go as you please, to spend every waking hour at that damned shelter if you want to. But if you wish to marry de Blanchard instead, then say the word. If you reject me, I'll take you home. I'll wish you joy as Viscountess de Blanchard and promise you'll never be plagued by my presence again."

He traced a line around her mouth, stopping at the corner where he caressed her skin with his thumb.

"Make your choice, Alice. Will you marry me? Yes or no?"

"Ross, I..."

"No," he said. "One word. Yes. Or No."

She had never been free. All her life she had been the property of others, to be handed from man to man.

Ross, the man she loved, believed he gave her a choice. Freedom was not an option. Papa had made it abundantly clear that if she were not married within a month, he'd have her committed indefinitely to Bedlam.

She opened her mouth, but the word stuck in her throat and she swallowed and blinked again. The action released a tear which rolled unchecked down her cheek, followed by another.

In a tender gesture, he wiped her cheek with his thumb. "I don't want your tears, Alice."

"Yes," she whispered.

"Believe me," he said. "I don't. Your pain is my pain, Alice. It always has been."

She shook her head. "You misunderstand me, Ross. My answer is yes."

He closed his eyes, and his body trembled as if he struggled to maintain composure. Before he could respond, a footman opened the carriage door.

"They're ready, sir."

He took her hand and climbed out of the carriage, pulling her behind him. His grip strengthened as they followed the path into the church.

With urgency in his voice, he encouraged the waiting clergyman to proceed with all due haste. The witnesses, two men Alice didn't recognize, cast furtive glances at her belly, seeking a reason for the hurried, clandestine wedding.

Though the prospect of giving herself to De Blanchard had sickened her to the core, she could not view her third marriage, to the man she had loved beyond all measure, as anything other than the lesser of two evils.

CHAPTER TWENTY-THREE

ROSS HELPED HIS new bride out of the carriage.

A small party of servants lined up by the front door of his townhouse. Without a word, he led her toward them. The fear in her expression needled at his sense of honor. He'd delivered her from the clutches of that beast-of-a-viscount, yet her melancholy had only increased.

It might take years before Alice learned to trust him. That day might never come to pass.

The more he tried to convince her with words, the less convinced she would be. He would have to show he could be trusted by his actions.

The servants issued bright smiles and bowed and curtseyed in unison as he walked past them. When they reached the main doors, they opened from the inside to reveal the butler who issued a stiff bow.

"Welcome home, Mrs. Trelawney."

She tensed and looked around her, as if she were preparing to bolt.

Ross placed a light hand against the small of her back.

"Thank you, Mycroft," he said. "My wife and I wish to take tea, if you would be so kind as to arrange it."

"The arrangements have already been made, sir," the butler said. "Everything as you requested."

The butler gave a sharp order to the servants who scurried into the house and disappeared.

Ross took his wife's arm and led her toward the front parlor.

"Forgive me, Alice," he said. "My house is somewhat small. It's not as grand as you're used to."

She flinched.

"I–I'm sorry, my dear" he said. "I only meant that I hope it will be comfortable enough for you." He lifted a hand and touched her cheek. She stiffened and closed her eyes but did not move away. Emboldened, he caressed her skin until she opened her eyes again. Fear still filled them.

He had a difficult task ahead, repairing the damage which life had inflicted on her. But at least, today, he'd made a start.

"Come, Alice," he said. "I have a surprise for you, two, in fact, which I trust you'll find to your liking."

He pushed the parlor door open.

"Go and see."

She turned her head and a small cry of joy burst from her lips as she rushed forward.

"Monty! Lizzie!"

She picked up the creature Ross had used such subterfuge to acquire. The maid stood beside the basket, a smile of joy on her face.

A small spark of jealousy pricked at his conscience as he watched Alice cradle the pug in her arms, her body relaxed and open, showing her capacity for love. It was almost as if a different woman stood in the room compared to the tense, frightened creature he'd led up the aisle an hour earlier.

"Oh ma'am, I'm so glad to see you!"

"What are you doing here, Lizzie?"

"I'm in the master's employ."

"Papa?"

"No," the girl said, "Master Ross."

Alice turned to face him, her eyes wide and fearful.

"What manner of trickery is this?" she asked. "Lizzie was with me only this morning."

"I know," Ross said. "With Mycroft's help, I took the liberty of arranging for her to be brought here. Together with your dog, of course."

"I don't understand. How could you have known I'd come?"

"I planned it, Alice. I've been making preparations since Hartford's funeral."

She colored and looked away.

"Oh, ma'am!" The maid placed a hand on her mistress's arm.

Alice let out a cry and shook her head.

"Aren't you happy to see me, ma'am? And your dog?"

"Of course, I am," Alice said, "but to hear it was all planned, that my future was set out by another! Am I never to be free to decide my own fate?"

Before he could respond, a roar erupted from outside, and Mycroft's voice raised in protest.

"Sir, I beg you! You can't come in!"

"Out of my way, you bloody servant! Where's my daughter?"

Alice paled and clutched the dog to her breast as if her life depended on it. The fear in her eyes returned so strong that Ross could almost taste it.

"Stay in here," he said.

"But..."

"You're my wife now, Alice. Your father has no rights over you."

She flinched at his words but remained where she was. He slipped out of the parlor, closing the door behind him, and turned to face the newcomer.

"De Grecy. What are you doing here?"

"Don't play me for a fool, you upstart!" De Grecy said, his voice thick with hatred. "I'm here to reacquire what's mine. You took my daughter, and now you'll give her back before I set the runners on you."

"Your daughter," Ross said, keeping his voice light. "Do you mean my *wife*, perchance?"

"You can't possibly have married her," de Grecy said, "and I won't have her disgracing my name further as your harlot. Alice! Alice! Come out, you ungrateful chit!"

Ross fisted his hands. "What do you know of disgrace, De Grecy! You've treated your daughter as a commodity all her life, selling her to the highest bidder. But not this time."

"What makes you think you can have her, Trelawney? I'd never let a commoner court her when I can give her to a viscount."

"Perhaps not," Ross said, "but when that commoner is friends with an earl who's close to the archbishop, then courting is no longer necessary."

De Grecy's eyes narrowed, then comprehension flickered in his expression and his face fell. "You lie. There's no way *you* could have secured a special license."

"That's where you're wrong," Ross said. "I would invite you to verify the facts with Earl Stiles who's currently in town." He gave the viscount a lopsided smile. "My wife and I are attending his ball next week. The earl is extremely particular in his choice of acquaintance, but I would be happy to introduce you, as a favor."

The older man's jaw twitched, and he shook with poorly suppressed anger.

"A marriage license is merely a sheet of paper, Trelawney. And while a marriage remains unconsummated, it can still be annulled." He stepped closer to Ross, a cold smile on his lips. "Has the mare been rutted yet?"

"I fail to see that's any of your business."

"Alice! Come out here!" de Grecy cried.

"Leave my wife alone."

The parlor door opened, and a cruel smile crept across de Grecy's face. "As you see, Trelawney, my daughter knows where her loyalties lie."

"What do you want, Papa?"

She looked even more fragile than usual, as if her father's presence had drained her resolve. A lifetime of a loveless parent's disapproval had taken its toll.

De Grecy nodded toward Ross. "Have you spread your legs for him yet?"

She looked away, her body vibrating with distress, but not before Ross caught the shame in her eyes.

"Papa, please..." she whispered.

"It's a simple enough question, child. Has your marriage been consummated?"

She closed her eyes and clutched the dog in her arms.

"Yes or no, Alice!"

She flinched at her father's voice. Her pain was so tangible, Ross could almost taste it. What had she said that day at the shelter when young Jake had held her hostage? It didn't matter whether one was born into the lowest or highest part of society. A father still had fists which he could use to cow his children into submission.

She shook her head, her voice almost inaudible. "No, Papa."

"Then you must come with me now. Do as I say."

She moved forward, as if the force of her father's determination compelled her. Then she glanced at Ross and stopped and stood firm, her back a little straighter.

"Papa, I'm not a cow to be fought over at auction. If I wish to remain with my husband, I shall do so."

"Foolish child!" De Grecy snarled. "A cow is exactly what you are. It's what you've always been. And a bloody disappointing cow you've proven to be."

Ross moved in front of her, shielding her body, as if to protect her from her father's cruelty.

"Now you've had your answer, de Grecy," he said. "I must insist that you leave."

"Why you…"

"Now." Ross moved closer to his father-in-law until they almost touched. "I believe you're an advocate of using force to eject unwelcome visitors. Reluctant as I am to follow your specific brand of thuggery, I will do everything in my power to protect my wife from marauders. Alice is no longer your concern, and until she invites you into her home, you are not welcome. Is that clear?"

Ross held his gaze, not breaking eye contact. Like all bullies he'd encountered in his schooldays, the bully standing before him now widened his eyes at the challenge.

De Grecy moved back, a cruel smile on his face.

"I'll leave you now, Trelawney, but mark my words, I'll return with enough of my men to have that child dragged out of this slum if necessary. You may have friends, but don't think for one moment I'm entirely without allies."

He moved toward the front door and shouldered the waiting footman aside.

"Get out of my way!"

The footman shut the door behind him. "Shall I lock it, sir?"

"Yes," Ross said. "Please do. My wife and I are not admitting visitors for the rest of the day."

"R-ross…" Her voice shook with fear. "What can we do? He'll be back, with others."

"I can protect you."

"Can you?" she asked. "He doesn't like to lose. He'll do everything he can to get what he wants. Perhaps I should go."

"No, my love," he said. "I'll think of something."

She closed her eyes, her body trembling. When she opened them again, resolve had darkened their color.

"There is one thing we must do," she said.

"Which is?"

"We must consummate our marriage."

MONTY WHINED IN Alice's arms as she tightened her grip on him, seeking comfort from his gentle nature and soft fur.

"Alice, are you sure?" Ross asked.

She nodded.

"I dislike the notion of having to do this so—quickly," he said, "but perhaps it's the only way. Hand the dog to your maid and come with me." He nodded toward Lizzie. "Come here, girl."

A slim hand touched her shoulder. "Go with him, ma'am," Lizzie said. "I'll look after Montague."

The young maid smiled in sympathy and understanding as Alice lifted Monty into her arms. The footman and the butler stood by the door, discomfort in their stance as their attempts to render themselves invisible only served to emphasize their presence. Her husband's clear, gray eyes looked unwaveringly at her, drawing her in with their intensity.

She took his proffered hand and let him lead her upstairs.

"We'll go to your chamber," he said as they reached the top of the stairs, "unless you'd prefer to accomplish the deed in mine."

"As you wish, Ross."

"Very well." They reached a thick, oak-paneled door.

Shame burned within her, shame at the urgency in his voice and at the tension among the servants. The household was about to witness an act which, though supposed to represent a union of love between a man and a woman, would be a purely functional deed. From the moment she had accepted his proposal, so many years ago, she had longed for the day when he might make love to her. But not like this—not in daylight as if she were a doxy bent on earning a little extra cash before nightfall.

He led her into the chamber and toward the large bed in the far corner.

Strong hands took her waist, their solidity giving her comfort. Gently, but firmly, he spun her round until she faced him.

"Are you ready?"

"Yes," she whispered.

She sat on the edge of the bed and lay back. The canopy hung above her, rich red with a faint pattern of swirls. She focused on the circular marks, her eyes following the lines to divert her attention from the reality of what was about to happen. As her gaze moved across the pattern, she slowed her breathing, picturing an image, as she inhaled, of the air filling her lungs.

He climbed onto the bed beside her, and a warm hand caressed her face, coaxing her toward him until their eyes met.

"Do you want me, Alice?"

"Yes," she said. "I want you."

He caressed her skin, his fingers tracing a line across the front of her dress before he moved his hand lower and cupped her breast. She drew in a sharp breath and let out a little mewling cry as her nipple hardened to a painful little point and strained against the material of her dress, eager for his touch.

He fumbled at the buttons of her jacket, undoing them one by one. Her breasts ached at the rush of cold air, and a nugget of longing pulsed between her thighs. She whispered his name—the name which had entered her dreams so many times when she'd lain, battered and broken, in the Markham residence. The name of the man she had prayed would deliver her from her nightmares.

She cried out as a warm, wet mouth came down on her breast, drawing it in as his tongue circled the tip.

"Lord save me," he rasped. "How long have I dreamed of this moment! When I could claim you, at last, as mine."

A rush of cold air rippled up the skin of her legs, and he nudged her thighs apart. She closed her eyes, clenching her teeth to dispel the memory of Roderick.

The bed shifted as his weight came on top of her, spreading her thighs further apart. Hard flesh nudged against her, thick and insistent. She bit her lip, waiting for the pain, and a whimper burst from her throat.

Almost immediately, he drew back, his weight falling away.

"Alice."

The voice was not that of her tormentor. Rather than possessing the refined timbre of London society, a gentle Cornish burr softened its tone.

He caressed her cheek. "Open your eyes, Alice."

She complied, and the eyes which stared back at her were a clear gray, not the glacial blue which had always tightened her body with fear.

"Forgive me, Alice," he said, sadness thickening his voice. "I cannot take you unwilling."

Unwilling...

The memory of Papa's words formed in her mind.

De Blanchard will have you, Alice, willing or unwilling, I care not. And if you refuse him, I'll have you locked away forever.

She shifted her legs further apart. "I am willing, Ross. But you must be quick."

He shook his head. "I won't do that to you, Alice."

She reached up and grasped his hand. Even now, Papa might be outside. Her heart hammered, rushing through her head to a rhythmic beat. How long would it be before it was joined by the sound of Papa and his men beating down the door to drag her away?

"Please, Ross!"

Doubt crossed his expression, and he looked over his shoulder, as if his conscience stood behind him.

She pulled him close and he fell on top of her, then she shifted her legs as wide apart as she could and lifted her hips upward in desperation. With a grunt of effort, he thrust forward and plunged himself inside her.

"Oh, Ross! Yes!" she cried.

He withdrew and plunged in again, his breath hot and hard against her cheek. As he formed a steady rhythm, his movements grew stronger, his breath coming out in harsh gasps, until they culminated in a final cry. She closed her eyes, and the image of another man assaulted her consciousness.

She cried out, striking out with her hands, clawing wildly as she uttered Roderick's name, fearing she would be beaten for not pleasing her husband.

"Alice?" Ross touched his face, blood staining his fingers.

"I-I'm sorry…"

"You think me like that devil?"

Before she could reply, a shout echoed through the house.

Ross flew to the door and opened it, and the shouting increased.

"Curse your bloody father!"

She pushed herself upright, and he held his hand up.

"Stay here. I'll deal with him."

"No," she said. "I'm done with being told what to do."

He sighed, buttoned his breeches, then slipped out of the chamber. She could hear the shouting from the hall.

"Get out, de Grecy, before I send for the runners! You're not welcome here, and you can't threaten me, no matter how many thugs you've brought with you."

She exited the chamber and crossed the floor to the top of the stairs. Papa stood at the bottom flanked by two men. Ross stood halfway down the staircase, facing him.

"I've claimed her as mine, de Grecy, in the only way you understand."

"You mean you've actually bedded her?"

"The marriage is consummated, yes."

"You lie."

Alice moved onto the top step and Papa looked up at her.

"He speaks the truth," she said.

"Come closer so I may inspect you."

"I'm not an animal."

"That remains to be seen."

She descended the stairs but stopped as Ross held his hand up, issuing a soft command to remain still. Papa's lips curled into a smile of amusement.

"Well, well, well," he said, a sneer in his voice. "I underestimated you, Trelawney. Looking at the state of her, it seems that you have the makings of a man after all."

"I'm glad you think so, de Grecy," Ross said, hatred in his voice. "Perhaps now you're satisfied I'm capable of controlling my wife, you'll leave me to continue tutoring her in the arts of obedience."

Papa folded his arms and smiled coldly. "From the marks on your face, I'd say you're in need of lessons yourself, Trelawney. Take my advice and beat that behavior out of her until she learns who her master is. It wouldn't take much to have her readmitted to Bedlam. The evidence of her insanity adorns your face. Take care she's obedient, or I'd advise you to lock her up. A word from me and she could still be incarcerated."

"Thank you, de Grecy. I shall remember your advice."

Ross set his mouth into a hard line and his cheek pulsed, red liquid glistening where she'd struck him. It was exactly where Dominic Hartford had sustained his injury at her hands, evidence, he'd said, of her insanity.

One word. That was all it would take.

Papa sneered. "You're welcome to her, Trelawney," he said. "She's been nothing but a disgrace from the moment she drew breath. Don't expect a dowry."

Barking an order to the men beside him, he turned on his heels and marched out of the house.

Alice let out a sigh. "Will he return?"

"I doubt it," Ross said. "I believe I've emerged victorious. Your father has admitted defeat. He can no longer threaten you with Bedlam now that you no longer belong to him."

He gave a bitter laugh of contempt, and Alice swallowed, fighting the nausea churning within her. When put to the test, Ross had shown himself to be a match for Papa, not only in fending him off, but in affirming his ownership of her. The decision whether or not to incarcerate her now lay with him.

He turned to face her.

"We'd better get you cleaned up. I must show you around town before your father has second thoughts about accepting you're mine."

"No."

"Forgive me, but it must be done."

"Haven't you given me enough orders for one day?" she asked. "Do you wish to strip me of my free will?"

"I'll never deny you freedom, Alice, but I ask you to trust me. Go to your room and I'll send your maid to dress you."

"No," she said. "Let me exert my freedom by remaining here."

He drew her close and brushed his lips against hers.

She stiffened and pushed him back. "Leave me alone," she said, her voice cold. "If you wish for gratification, I suggest you find yourself a doxy."

He jerked back as if she'd slapped him, the expression in his eyes mirroring the pain of long ago when she had first rejected him.

But she couldn't yield. The shock in his eyes after he'd finally taken her, had been her undoing. He would have seen the marks on her body, the evidence of her insanity. Was he already beginning to regret having shackled himself to her?

"Very well," he said. "I'll leave you here, but I find myself in need of fresh air."

He descended the rest of the staircase and called the butler over. "Mycroft, I shall be out for the rest of the afternoon. My daughter does not return until next week, so while I am gone, nobody is to be admitted into, or to leave, this house."

He turned and looked up at her, determination in his expression.

"Nobody. Is that understood?

He crossed the hallway and disappeared through the main doors.

CHAPTER TWENTY-FOUR

"AH, THERE YOU are, Trelawney. I wondered if we'd see you today. You look like you've been in a dogfight."

Hawthorne reclined in his usual chair at Whites, a brandy glass in hand, Westbury next to him. He lifted his glass as Ross approached them.

"Are we to congratulate you, Trelawney?" Westbury asked.

"I doubt it," Hawthorne said with a short, bitter laugh. "Why would a man wish to spend the hours immediately following his wedding in this damned place?"

Ross remained where he stood. A footman approached him with a brandy bottle, and he shook his head.

"There, Westbury, what did I say?" Hawthorne drained his glass and waved the footman over. "Either the mare has bolted, or our friend has come to his senses." He held his glass out as the footman refilled it, then took a gulp. "Either way, Trelawney, I'd have expected to see you in a more celebratory mood."

Ross sighed and sat next to his friend, gesturing toward the footman.

"Over here!"

"Changed your mind, Ross?"

"Only in respect of the brandy."

Hawthorne's face creased with disapproval. "So, you went through with it?"

Ross sipped his drink. In one thing at least, Hawthorne was right. Today was no cause for celebration. He might have secured his heart's desire, the hand of the woman he'd always loved, but at what cost? For years he'd dreamed of their first time together, a union between two souls who were meant for each other despite the obstacles of society, propriety, and her cruel father. But the reality…

He choked as the liquor stung the back of his throat.

"You don't seem to be celebrating," Westbury said.

"Shut up and let me drink."

"What would your wife think of you?"

"At least *I'm* not ruled by my wife, Westbury," Ross growled. "All the world knows she wears the breeches in your household."

Westbury's eyes narrowed. "I'll let that one slide, Trelawney, since you look to be in need of commiseration. But I'd like to know why you took such pains to persuade our friend here to secure a special license to marry the woman if the marriage state has had such an immediate detrimental effect on your optimism."

"The devil take you, Westbury."

"Why did you marry her?" Westbury asked. "We always thought you were the sensible one of our set, the least likely to be played by a fortune hunter."

"Leave her alone," Ross growled. "She's done nothing to merit your disdain."

"You've said as much yourself, Ross. In this very room if I recall."

He flinched against the bare truth. "Aye, I have. And my conscience reminds me of it daily. But you of all men, Westbury, and you, Hawthorne, should understand that a man often seeks to hurt that which he loves the most. And a woman is capable of wearing armor fashioned out of stone in order to disguise and protect the tender heart within."

"What nonsense!" Westbury snorted.

Hawthorne frowned. "You mean to say our Lady Alice is not all she seems?"

Ross nodded. "She never has been. I believe there to be three people in the world who truly knew and understood her. And two of them—her mother and Hartford—are dead."

"So, if you're the one remaining survivor of her devotees, why aren't you with her?" Westbury smirked. "Suffering a guilty conscience? Don't tell me you've been with another woman!"

"How bloody dare you!" Ross leapt to his feet. A volley of frenzied tutting echoed round the clubroom, and one or two members rustled their newspapers to signal disapproval.

"Sit down, Trelawney," Hawthorne said sharply. "Westbury's only jesting. Though I do wonder whether he struck a nerve?"

"No," Ross said. "Since I terminated my *arrangement* with Kitty, I've not looked at another woman." He tipped his head back and drained his glass. "I couldn't do that to Alice, not even when she advises me to seek a whore out."

"She *what*?"

Guilt tore at Ross, thrusting the image of her tear-stained face into his consciousness. The self-loathing and disgust at what he'd done to accomplish her hand irrevocably tore at his heart. He told himself he'd done it for her, to keep her safe, and any sacrifice was worth that. But in order to achieve it, he'd sold his soul while she had offered herself like a sacrificial lamb. How many times had that monster Markham done the very same?

Hawthorne gestured toward Ross's face. "I take it those are battle scars. Did she fight you off?"

Heat warmed his face, and he averted his gaze from his friends.

Hawthorne's voice grew quiet and even, the voice he often used on witnesses in the courtroom. He gazed at Ross, his eyes darkening with intensity. "What have you done, Trelawney?"

"I've saved her from her father. And de Blanchard."

Hawthorne was no fool. Or could he read Ross's mind, delve deep into his guilt to understand what he'd done to make Alice wholly his?

"Where's your daughter?"

Ross sighed. "I sent her to Cornwall. She returns to London next week. After your soiree."

"Does she know you're married?"

Ross shook his head. "No, but she's met Alice, and they liked each other."

"That's before you presented the woman as her new mother. Did you not think of Amelia in your determination to secure your bride?"

"I *did* think of her," Ross said. "Amelia needs a mother." He shook his head as if to shake off the guilt, but it remained, clinging to him like the odor of cigar smoke which could never be washed out of a jacket. "Do you not agree it would be better for my daughter if she had a mother who I actually loved?"

"But does your wife love you?" Westbury asked.

Alice may have loved Ross at one point, until her father and society had persuaded her otherwise. But now? After what she'd endured, was she capable of loving anyone? Or did her broken mind prevent it? The scars marking her body spoke of an ordeal he dared not inquire about, scars which had ignited a raw anger in him when he'd lifted her gown to claim her.

And what had he done? Fueled by shame, angered by her fear of him, and utterly disgusted at himself, he'd fled in an attempt to run away from his guilt. But the guilt had followed him, fueled by brandy while his friends looked on. Alice needed understanding and compassion, but he'd denied her by indulging in his guilt and abandoning her, alone, in a strange home.

He set his glass aside and rose to his feet. Rather than drinking with his friends to obliterate his guilt, it was time to be a man and make reparations with his wife. De Grecy may have impugned his manhood, but that old bastard had no notion of what it meant to be a man. The late Viscount Hartford, on the other hand, was more of a man than the rest of London combined. What had Hartford once said? A creature recovering from abuse needed to be coaxed back into the world. Rather than leading her with a firm hand, she needed tender care, gentle words of love and encouragement.

But most of all, Alice needed to be left to come to Ross on her own terms.

CHAPTER TWENTY-FIVE

"*I*T'S NOT A *large gathering, my dear, and we can leave as soon as you wish it.*"

Despite Ross's words, dread coursed through Alice as he led her into the ballroom. Though nobody seemed to take notice of her, she felt the air shift as she entered the room, the subtle change in tone as the ladies whispered to their husbands that the Deranged Duchess, having sent two husbands to their graves, now paraded herself around with a third.

"Alice?" a soft voice spoke in her ear, and a gentle hand cupped her elbow and steered her toward their hosts.

Earl and Countess Stiles made a formidable couple. Frederica towered over the women and some of the men. Her hair, fashioned into a simple style, shone in the candlelight with reds and golds reminiscent of an autumn sunset. Though unadorned by jewels, she outshone every creature in the room, living proof that natural beauty would always conquer the elegance of ladies who considered themselves of superior birth. Alice saw herself as insipid in comparison.

Standing by her husband, Frederica moved her hand closer to his. In an absent-minded gesture, Hawthorne linked the smallest finger of his hand with hers. A slow smile crept across Frederica's face, though he did not look at her, the innate understanding of a couple deeply in love.

But any tenderness living in the earl's heart was reserved solely for his wife. With his reputation for savage clear-sightedness, Hawthorne surveyed the room, his gaze moving from guest to guest until, finally, his focus settled on Alice herself. His body tensed, and his jaw set firm as she approached him, clinging to Ross's arm for support.

"Alice, we're so glad you could join us tonight."

The countess moved forward, arms outstretched.

"Frederica." The low growl from her husband's throat checked her enthusiasm, but she still took Alice's hand and kissed her on both cheeks.

"May I be among the first to congratulate you, Alice, on your marriage," she said. "We both wish you every happiness, don't we, Hawthorne?"

The earl narrowed his eyes, then nodded. "Of course."

"Come, my dear," Ross said. "Let me find you somewhere quiet to sit."

"There's a very comfortable chair beside the fireplace," Frederica said. "I've asked Watson to remain in attendance, and he's pledged to guard it with his life."

Ross exchanged a look with Frederica. A smile curled his lips, and he steered Alice across the floor toward the waiting footman. He bowed as they approached.

"May I bring you a glass of champagne, madam?"

Alice settled into the chair. "Please, don't trouble yourself."

"It's no trouble," he said. "The mistress has tasked me to take care of you."

"Very well," she said, and he bowed and left.

"There!" Ross said. "Didn't I promise you'd be well looked after? Our hostess is most gracious."

Jealousy surged within Alice. It was a poorly concealed secret that Ross had once declared his love for Frederica. He had even taken over Frederica's late father's wine business, supplying liquor to the best households in London, from which he paid Frederica a regular stipend.

Alice's skin prickled with tension, and she looked up to see Hawthorne Stiles staring at her, his expression grim. Clearly, she was not the only creature in the room who remembered the day Roderick Markham died. Perhaps he, like many others, thought her residence at Bedlam should have been permanent.

The music started up and he turned to address his wife, his expression softening into one of devotion. The two of them moved, arm in arm, into the center of the room. Another couple joined them, followed by others until a small line had formed.

"Would you care to dance?" Ross asked.

His hand covered hers, and she flinched involuntarily.

"Forgive me," he said, withdrawing his hand. "I see I have been too forward."

The footman returned, holding a glass, and Ross took it and handed it to her.

"Drink this, it will steady your nerves."

"Alice!" a high-pitched, female voice cried out, and a young woman rushed toward her.

"Jane!" Alice said. "What a pleasure!"

Jane pulled her into an embrace. "I'm so glad to see you," she said. "Normally, I wouldn't attend anything so dreadful as a ball, but Jeanie's confinement has prevented her from coming, and she insisted I accompany Henry to stop him from getting under her feet at home." She lowered her voice. "I missed you dreadfully while I was in the country. But I hear Mrs. Taylor has hardly noticed my absence while she's had you to take care of her charges."

Her smile disappeared, and she addressed Ross. "I trust you're taking care of my friend."

"Of course," he said.

"Alice, why didn't you invite me to your wedding?" Jane asked. "I've only just heard of it from Jeanie."

"Forgive me Jane, it was rather sudden."

"Well, I trust your husband at least indulged you by celebrating the occasion."

Discomfort warmed Alice's blood, pricking her skin at the memory of her wedding.

"Miss Claybone, are you not dancing?" Ross asked.

"I doubt I'll find my match on the dancefloor," Jane replied. "I find the company of single men rather tedious."

"How so?"

"In my opinion, single men attend a ball for one purpose only."

"Which is?"

"To hunt, Mr. Trelawney. At least if a man is married his desperation to exert dominance over the opposite sex is tempered by the presence of a wife."

Alice sipped her drink, the champagne bubbles catching in her throat. "In my experience, the marriage state can do little to pacify the beast within," she said. "In some cases, a man's savagery is accentuated by it."

"Of course," Jane said, coloring. "I'm sorry. I should have realized."

Ross looked away, his gaze following the couples as they moved across the floor. When he'd first courted Alice, they had danced well together, and she had fancied herself the envy of the ballrooms. But now they were man and wife, how he must regret shackling himself to her!

Hartford had been an old man, happy to resign himself to a life of quiet retirement. But Ross was a man in his prime. His body glowed with health and virility, his form-fitting breeches hinting at the perfectly formed muscles of his legs.

A man such as Ross needed to dance. He had a right to enjoy the comfort and release of physical intimacy which every other man in the room was able to indulge in. By marrying him, she had sentenced him to a lifetime of skirting 'round an infamous madwoman. A woman he could no longer bear to touch.

Since withdrawing from her on their wedding day, he had not touched her again. While he saw to it that she had everything a woman in her position needed—money, comfort, servants, even her liberty—he denied her the one thing her heart desired.

Love. True, honest love. The passion which had lingered just out of reach when they'd kissed during the hunt, and which had almost spilled over when he'd rescued her from that desperate young man at Mrs. Taylor's. Her body's reaction to him had thrilled and terrified her at the same time.

Hartford had taught her to love again and healed her heart, though Ross had no use for it. But at least she had someone else she could love. Amelia returned to London tomorrow, and Ross had written to his daughter to say she had a new mama ready to welcome her home. Alice might never have children of her own, but she would love Ross's child and treat her as if she were her own. And Amelia would return that love.

As for Ross, he was a man, and a man needed female company. For his sake, she must show him she would not stand in his way.

"Alice, are you all right?" She looked up to see both her husband and her friend staring down at her.

"Forgive me, I was lost in my thoughts," she said. "Aren't you dancing, Jane? I'm sure Ross would oblige if you needed a partner."

"What, steal a newlywed from under his wife's nose?" Jane asked. "I couldn't possibly."

"On this occasion, you have the wife's approval," Alice replied.

Ross leaned over her. "Do you not wish for company?" he asked quietly.

"No," she said. He flinched at her denial but said nothing.

"I insist you dance with my friend, Ross. You're both in need of it."

"As you wish," he said coldly and held his hand out. "Come, Miss Claybone. I'd be honored."

Jane took his hand, and they joined the dancers. His prowess more than compensated for hers as he led her through the dance. His body rippled with ease as he glided between the dancers, each step in perfect time to the music. The air in the ballroom vibrated with approval as the onlookers turned their attention on him. Sometimes Alice saw the occasional, furtive glance in her direction, as if the guests marveled at how she'd managed to secure such a perfect specimen for a husband.

At length, she heard laughter as Ross and Jane exchanged a joke. The dance increased in pace, and they moved past her, twirling round. Ross's face was aglow with happiness.

The music finally stopped, and the dancers dissipated throughout the room. Ross and his partner remained on the dance floor, engaged in conversation with Hawthorne and Frederica.

A male voice spoke. "I trust you're enjoying the ball, Lady Alice?"

She turned toward the newcomer. "Westbury. Your Grace. I trust your wife is well?"

"Perfectly so, I thank you. May I sit?"

"Please do."

He nodded to the footman. "Fetch me a brandy."

"Very good, sir." The footman bowed and disappeared.

Westbury sat beside her. "I suppose I must call you Mrs. Trelawney, now. Forgive me for my earlier error. I'm afraid I'm in danger of losing my way trying to navigate through the history of all your marriages."

Her cheeks warmed under his disapproval.

"I understand enough of you and your friends to know you'll continue to refer to me by whatever name you wish, regardless of what I say or do," she said. "You'll not have used a name I haven't heard before."

"Such as?"

"The Deranged Duchess," she said. "Mad Alice. Seductress. The woman who killed two husbands and is now working on a third!"

"Keep your voice down," he hissed. "Do you think I'd use such vulgar expressions?"

"Whether you voice them or not, I hear the sentiment in your voice and see it in your eyes," she said. "I've weathered far worse than your censure, believe me, and I have endured everything you could possibly think of, and more besides." She waved a dismissive hand at him. "But, of course, that's not a subject for discussion in polite society. Such words and deeds are more commonly found behind closed doors. So, if you're not here to highlight my manifest evils, I rather wonder at your reason for wasting your time talking to me at all."

He opened his mouth to reply, then stopped himself, doubt creasing his brow. "I'm come to congratulate you on your marriage," he said. "I pray you'll make your husband as happy as he deserves."

She sighed. "I doubt that."

"So do I," he said. "Forgive me for being concerned for my friend. He's suffered loss and heartbreak, and I wish to ensure history is not repeated. Does that make me a bad man, given you've confessed freely of your inability to make him happy?"

"Nobody could make Ross as happy as he deserves," she said. "But I shall try."

"What's all this?" Ross appeared, Jane at his side.

Jane addressed Westbury. "Brother, what are you doing?"

"Congratulating Mrs. Trelawney on her good fortune."

Ross glanced at Westbury, then at Alice, and his smile disappeared. "My dear, you look distressed. Do you wish to leave?"

"On the contrary," she said. "Miss Claybone is still in need of a dance partner."

Westbury rose from his seat. "I can oblige on that front. I'll leave your wife in your capable hands, Trelawney. Come on, Miss Claybone, what say we show them how it's done?"

Westbury led his sister-in-law to the dancefloor, and Ross sat beside Alice.

"Perhaps you wish to dance now, my dear?"

"No, Ross," she said. "I'm tired."

"Then I'll take you home."

"I'm content where I am," she said, "and I'd rather you enjoyed yourself tonight. I have no wish to see you inconvenienced on my account."

A warm hand covered hers, and he turned his gaze on her. "My dear wife, what is my vocation in life, if it's not to be inconvenienced on your account?"

"Nevertheless, I insist. I would be happier if we remained here."

"Then remain we shall."

As the evening wore on and the guests found more interesting topics to discuss than Alice's third marriage, she found comfort in her inconspicuousness. The air, which had been thick with the scrutiny of others, thinned until she found she could breathe once more.

Ross had taken her insistence to heart and spent the rest of the evening alternating between Frederica and Jane as dance partners. His joy of life shone in his eyes as he laughed at their witticisms. The laughter increased as he joined his friends at the card tables. Westbury and Stiles continued to cast disapproving glances in her direction but showed no such hostility toward Ross.

How long would it be before his friends' obvious dislike of her took its toll on their marriage and made Ross regret his choice?

CHAPTER TWENTY-SIX

AS ALICE ENTERED the breakfast room, she heard her husband's voice, accompanied by an excited, high-pitched voice.

Amelia had returned home. Father and daughter sat together, deep in conversation while the child attacked a plate of eggs in front of her.

"Ah, here she is!" Ross said. "I wondered if you were ever going to rise this morning. Forgive us for beginning our breakfast without you."

The child was just as pretty as Alice remembered, soft brown hair curled into ringlets, a perfect round mouth, and light gray eyes which mirrored her father's. Her demeanor was all sunshine and merriment. A small hand clutched at Alice's heart. Though hopes for a child of her own had faded, she knew she could love the exuberant little girl who had entered her life.

The child set her fork down and looked up at Alice, and the light in her eyes died.

"I'm so happy to see you, my dear," Alice said. "Perhaps you remember me from when we first met?"

"No."

"What about Monty?" she asked. "You must remember the little dog I showed you."

"I don't like dogs."

"But you ran up to me and met him. On the bench in the park. Your papa was with you, and he asked you to have a look at the swans."

"Amelia." Ross placed a hand on his daughter's head. "Aren't you going to say how-do-you-do?"

The child smiled at her father. "Of course, Papa." She resumed her attention on Alice, her smile disappearing. "How do you do."

"I'm very well, Amelia dear."

"Must she call me Amelia? Everyone else, save Miss Trinket, calls me Miss Amelia."

"That's for servants and strangers, my love," Ross said.

The child set her mouth into a stubborn line. "I want her to call me Miss Amelia," she said. "And what must I call *her?*"

Ross hesitated. "I suppose you could call her Mama."

"Mama is dead." A flicker of pain glimmered in the child's eyes, and she pushed her plate aside. "May I go to my room?"

"Amelia, my dear, Alice and I were hoping we could take you to the park today, to feed the swans."

"You used to say Mama liked the swans," Amelia said.

"I know, my love," Ross replied, "which is why we want to take you. Alice is your mother now."

"No she's not!" the child cried. "I have no mother. I don't want to go to the park with her! I want to go with Miss Trinket."

"Amelia, my love, Alice is your family, not Miss Trinket. And I know you like Alice. You said so when you met her."

"That was before."

"Before what?"

"Before you used her to take Mama's place!"

"Don't you want us to be a family again, Amelia?"

"You mean like Georgia? With a mama and papa, brothers and sisters?"

"Of course."

"Can *I* have a brother and sister?"

Ross hesitated, then he sighed and looked away.

Amelia turned her gaze on Alice once more.

"I'm afraid I might not be able to have children," Alice said.

"That's not fair!" the child cried. "Papa, you promised! Why can't I have a brother or sister? Why must I always be alone?"

"You're not alone, Amelia," Ross said.

"I am!" the child cried. "You're never here, and Mama..."

She burst into tears, and Ross lifted her into his arms. "Amelia, my love, there's nothing I want more than to be able to give you a brother or sister."

"But *she* says I can't have one!"

He bent his head and buried his face in the child's hair while her little body shook.

"Perhaps she's wrong."

Ross lifted his head, sorrow and regret in their expression. A footman drew back a chair for Alice to sit, but she waved him away.

"Ross," she said. "Ross—I'm sorry. Do you regret marrying me?"

"Papa..." the child in his arms whimpered.

His chest rose and fell in a sigh. "My daughter's distressed." he said. "Perhaps it's best if you leave us alone until she's calmed down."

"As you wish." Alice turned to the footman. "Would you be so kind as to have some tea brought to the morning room? I'll break my fast there."

"Very good, ma'am."

As Alice sat alone in the morning room, cradling Monty in her lap, she heard laughter outside. She rose and crossed the room to the window overlooking the street. A phaeton waited by the front door. Ross was lifting his daughter into it, accompanied by a young woman neatly dressed in a plain gray gown, her hair scraped into a tight bun.

Amelia's excited voice filtered up from the street.

"Have you got the bread for the swans, Miss Trinket?"

"Of course she has!" Ross laughed. Without a backward glance, they set off, the laughter fading as the phaeton turned a corner and drove out of sight.

Ross needed a wife as much as Amelia needed a mother, and they both made it plain that Alice was incapable of fulfilling their needs. To hear their laughter was balm to her soul, though it warred with the pain of knowing they excluded her from their merriment.

The man she loved found comfort in his daughter but not in her. A voice of hope had whispered in her mind that Ross had married her for love. But no, it had been out of pity. She'd had her chance at love eight years ago but, in her weakness, cast it aside and broke his heart. Only now, did she understand the enormity of what she had lost.

She settled Monty in his basket and rang the bell for the footman. Within a minute, he appeared.

"Have you finished your tea, ma'am?"

"Yes," she said. "Please tell Cook there's no need to set the table for luncheon. I shall be spending the day in town."

"What shall I tell the master when he returns?"

"That his wife has gone shopping."

Her words were not a complete falsehood. By definition, shopping involved a transaction where one purchased goods or services in exchange for cash. In Alice's case, she would be purchasing the happiness of the man she loved, even though it would break her heart.

Chapter Twenty-Seven

A S ALICE REACHED the front door of the building, she checked the address scratched on the piece of paper in her hand. The townhouse appeared empty, the door and window frames painted an unremarkable shade of gray. It stood in the uncomfortable areas between the slums and brothels, and the rented accommodation of governesses and businessmen who enjoyed only a moderate grade of success.

In fact, it displayed the same degree of inconspicuousness which Mrs. Taylor fought so hard to achieve with her shelter. Inconspicuousness in this case, however, stemmed from a very different need. Rather than being for the benefit of the residents, the relative invisibility of this establishment existed for the benefit of the patrons who visited it.

Alice lifted the brass door knocker and rapped on the door. A curtain twitched in a first-floor window and, not long after, a key rattled in the lock and the door swung open to reveal a pale face, creases lining the eyes. The features were so bland, Alice almost believed Edward had given her the wrong address, until the woman spoke.

"What do *you* want?"

Though the voice was coarser than the voice she used when taking the air with her patrons, Alice still recognized the harsh tones of Catherine Bonneville.

"Mrs. Bonneville, may I come in?"

"I don't take visitors."

"That's not what I heard," Alice said crisply. "Or do you only admit men?"

The woman sighed. "Say what you've come to say, then leave me be. I'm in no mood to speak to wives."

"Not even one with a business proposition? Surely you have no qualms about accepting a coin for your services, no matter who offers it."

The woman laughed. "A coin? I wouldn't get out of bed for less than ten pounds."

"From what I understand of your reputation," Alice said, "you prefer to stay *in* bed when conducting business."

The woman sighed. "I've no time for this. Go away." She moved to close the door, but Alice wedged her foot in it.

"Do you remember me?"

"The Deranged Duchess?" The woman laughed. "Not so deranged, were you? You snared yourself another nob. And for some inexplicable reason, after you saw him off, you managed to connive yourself into Ross Trelawney's bed. Oldest trick in the book, that is—claiming helplessness."

Alice thrust her hand into her purse and pulled out a sheaf of notes.

"Perhaps now we've exchanged insults we may conduct our business? I'm prepared to discuss it on your doorstep if you'll not admit me, but I assume you'd favor discretion over publicity."

The woman glanced at the notes. Hunger glittered in her expression, but Alice detected something more. The desperation of a woman alone. Perhaps the two of them were not very unalike. In a world where society derided them, Kitty Bonneville traded her body for a coin, where Alice had traded her body for the security of a marriage. But they shared the same objective.

Survival.

Kitty pulled the door fully open. "Come inside, quick."

Alice followed her into a parlor. Despite being almost noon, Kitty was dressed in a nightgown. She reached for a stole from the back of one of the chairs and drew it round her shoulders.

"Forgive me for not lighting the fire," she said. "Do you want tea?"

"No, thank you." Alice said.

"Then what do you want?"

"I want you to sleep with my husband."

"With Ross?"

"Yes," Alice said, rushing the words to get them out before she lost her resolve. "I can pay you fifty pounds now, then ten pounds each week for...for as long as my husband wishes the arrangement to continue."

Kitty shook her head. "Well!" she said. "I heard you had the qualities of a doormat, but I commend Ross on persuading his wife to purchase his mistress for him. Of course, he's an excellent negotiator, as I learned to my cost, but he's surpassed himself today. I must congratulate him when I see him."

"So you'll do it?"

"Why did he send you?"

"He didn't," Alice said. "He has no idea I'm here."

Kitty threw back her head and roared with laughter.

"I'm serious!" Alice cried.

"Forgive me," Kitty said, "but it's the first time a wife has sought out a courtesan with which to deceive her husband. You've been married barely a month. Has his appetite for you already waned?"

Alice lowered her head in shame. "My reasons I shall keep to myself. All I wish is for you to agree."

Kitty shook her head. "You must first tell me why. Ross is a virile man. I heard he raced across London to marry you and carried you up the aisle over his shoulder. Not the actions of a man indisposed to sleep with his wife."

Alice cringed and curled her fingers round the cash in her hand. Kitty stopped laughing and her expression sobered. She frowned and leaned forward.

"Perhaps you find the company of the opposite sex not to your taste? Or does Ross compare unfavorably with Roderick Markham?"

Alice drew in a sharp breath and jerked back. The nightmare of Roderick's image sprang from the dark recesses of her mind, and she lifted her arm to fend him off.

The woman opposite her leapt from her seat and took her hand. "Mrs. Trelawney!"

Alice pushed her away. "I see I've made a mistake in coming here. I just wanted Ross to be happy."

"And you think rutting is the key to happiness?" Kitty asked.

"Why else do you do what you do for a living, Mrs. Bonneville? Men have needs. Ross has needs. He has friends, a flourishing business, and a daughter he loves. But I have no idea why he married me. In doing so, he struck a poor bargain for himself."

Kitty's expression softened. "Are you sure?"

"I–I cannot satisfy him," Alice said, shame warming her cheeks. "Above anything else in the world, I want him to be happy. I cannot give him what he needs, and even if I could, he doesn't want it from me."

She rose to her feet. "Forgive me, Mrs. Bonneville, I'm inconveniencing you. I won't trouble you any longer." She peeled off a series of notes and placed them on a table beside her chair. "There's twenty pounds for your trouble. I'll see myself out."

Without a backward glance, Alice headed for the main door. Only when she'd crossed the street did she look over her shoulder. A pale face looked out of the parlor window. Its owner lifted a hand in acknowledgement, then closed the curtains.

CHAPTER TWENTY-EIGHT

"LADY ALICE, I didn't expect to see you again!"

Mrs. Taylor pulled her through the door, into a warm embrace of crisply starched linen and strong, matronly arms. "Of course," she said, her chest rumbling against Alice's body, "that doesn't mean you're not welcome, but I assumed you'd be busy with your new husband."

Or perhaps she'd assumed Ross wouldn't permit her to visit anymore? On the contrary, Ross had granted her request to resume her visits to Mrs. Taylor, though whether it was out of affection for her, or a desire to keep her away from Amelia, Alice didn't know.

Mrs. Taylor released Alice and held her at arm's length, looking her up and down, then gave a satisfied nod.

"I was relieved to hear you'd not married de Blanchard. I trust Mr. Trelawney treats you well?"

Alice nodded, and Mrs. Taylor smiled. "Of course, we expected nothing different. After all, for many months, now, he…"

"What would you like me to do today?" Alice asked, unwilling to linger on the subject of Ross.

"There's some mending in the parlor needing attention," Mrs. Taylor replied. "Fanny tries ever so hard, but her hands make it difficult, poor thing. She'll be glad of the help."

A lone woman, barely more than a girl, sat in the parlor, a torn sheet on her lap. She looked up from her work and her body stiffened as she saw Alice.

"Mrs. Taylor, I…" she curled her fingers into the sheet on her lap, her eyes narrowing as if she winced in pain.

"Fanny, my dear, there's nothing to fear," Mrs. Taylor said gently. "This is Mrs. Trelawney, come to help you."

"Oh!" the girl's face creased into a smile. "Begging your pardon, ma'am."

"Please don't get up on my account," Alice said. She moved toward the mending basket and pulled out a dress with a long rend in the skirt. "May I sit beside you?"

"Oh!" the girl said again, coloring. "I don't know."

"It's all right, Fanny," Mrs. Taylor said. "Mrs. Trelawney is not here in her capacity as your mistress. We're all friends here. Rank and class mean nothing. Sit down, Mrs. Trelawney. I'll fetch some tea."

Alice complied and, after selecting a matching thread, began stitching the tear in the dress. Companionable silence was always a better inducement to gaining trust than incessant questions, and she focused on her work.

After Mrs. Taylor had set the tea tray on a table and excused herself, Alice poured a cup and handed it to Fanny. Discomfort creased the girl's features.

"Don't you like tea?"

Fanny took the cup, and it slipped in her hands and fell to the floor. The contents splashed onto Alice's skirt.

"Oh, mercy, forgive me!" she cried and lifted her arms as if to protect herself.

"It was an accident, Fanny," Alice said. "No harm done, save a little soaking for Mrs. Taylor's carpet which, I believe, has seen better days."

Fanny bent down to pick up the cup and it slipped from her hands again.

"Here, let me help," Alice said.

The girl turned her head away and buried her hands in the sheet, as if to hide them, and hunched her shoulders as if to make herself appear smaller or even invisible.

The memory of her own need for invisibility tightened Alice's chest. She reached for the girl's hands. "Fanny, you're not to blame for what he did to you."

"How do you know what he did?"

"Someone hurt you," Alice replied. "I can see it in your eyes. Was it your husband? Or your father?"

The girl hesitated, then whispered. "My Da."

"And you had nobody to protect you?"

"My brother. But he left. Jake was frightened of Da and wanted me to go with him, but Da wouldn't let me. He said he'd make me work on the streets if I tried to leave him."

"Where's your father now?"

"Dead." The girl's face took on a shuttered expression, and she resumed stitching.

As Alice watched her, she noticed the stiffness in the girl's fingers as she fumbled with the needle. On closer inspection, both hands were adorned with purple marks, the deep color visible beneath the lace of her gloves. The fingers of her right hand were twisted and misshapen, as if they had been repeatedly broken.

Unwilling to intrude on the girl's pain, Alice busied herself with clearing the tea tray, wiping the carpet as best she could, and returning the crockery to Mrs. Taylor's kitchen. When she resumed her seat next to Fanny, she picked up her mending in silence as the girl continued to struggle with her work.

As the afternoon wore on, the two women worked through the basket. Fanny's posture relaxed a little, but Alice still waited, not wanting to force her into a conversation.

At length, the girl folded her sheet and placed it on the table.

"Finished?" Alice asked.

"Yes."

"You've done well, Fanny. Mrs. Taylor will be pleased."

Fanny sighed, and Alice could almost feel the girl's gaze upon her as she resumed her attention on her mending.

Eventually Fanny broke the silence. "I-I suppose I must thank you, your ladyship."

"How so?" Alice asked.

"For what you—and Master Ross, of course—did for Jake."

Alice set her sewing aside. "What do you mean, child?"

Fanny colored and looked down, but not before a flicker of shame crossed her expression. "For taking him on, after..." she gestured toward Alice "...after what he did to you."

"I don't understand."

"My name's Fanny Whitworth."

As Alice studied the girl's features, recognition slid into place—the same sandy-colored hair brown eyes of the desperate young man who'd stormed into Mrs. Taylor's house, the frightened youth Ross had offered employment at his country estate.

"You're Jacob's sister?"

A small smile of love and admiration crossed Fanny's features. "He's doing ever so well, your ladyship," she said. "Mary read me his note only last week. He wrote it all himself, too. He's been learning his letters."

"Is Mary here?"

"No. Master Ross found lodgings for Mary and Adam in St Austell. I'm to live with her when I'm better. The doctor says it should be soon." Pride and admiration shone through Fanny's voice. "If I may be so bold, the master's like the knight who slew the dragon. He's looking after Jake ever so well! Fifteen pounds a year! Would you believe it? I'll be going to Cornwall!"

"To Cornwall?"

"Yes, I'll get to see the sea! Master Ross says Jake's working so hard that when he's ready, he and Mary can have the head groom's cottage and an extra five pounds a year. And he's offered me a position. He must be the best master in the world!"

"Oh, Fanny, I'm so pleased Jake's doing well."

The girl leaned forward and took Alice's hand, wincing as she curled her fingers round Alice's wrist. "Please believe me, mistress, Jake's not a bad man. He's learned his lesson and is doing all he can to make up for what he did to Mary. Some men are born bad. Others do bad things. Jake's not like Da was. He knows he's done wrong and is sorry for it."

Love for her brother resonated in Fanny's voice and, on instinct, Alice drew the girl into an embrace. Beneath her dress, her little body was fragile enough to snap in two.

The door opened, and Mrs. Taylor stepped in.

"Fanny dear, it's time for your supper. Run along to the kitchen while I speak to Mrs. Trelawney."

The girl bobbed a curtsey, then slipped out of the room.

Mrs. Taylor took the seat she'd vacated. "What do you think of Fanny?"

"I like her," Alice said. "She's loyal and gentle. Yes, I like her very much."

Mrs. Taylor's face split into a smile. "I'm glad of it!"

"And her poor hand…"

Mrs. Taylor sighed. "I fear it will never mend completely," she said. "So, I'm glad your husband is willing to make allowances for it."

"Allowances?" Alice asked.

"There's few employers who'd take a young girl like Fanny into service, and even fewer men who'd pluck her off the streets. She owes Mr. Trelawney her life."

"What can you mean?"

"Has he not told you?" Mrs. Taylor gestured to the window. "It's a cruel and dark world out there. The women here would all testify to that. But, occasionally, a beacon of light shines through the darkness."

She took Alice's hands. "Shortly after he packed young Jacob off to Cornwall, your husband came looking for Fanny. The young man was terrified for his sister, of how his father would react when he learned Jake would no longer be giving him money."

"And my husband sought the girl out?"

"He did more than that." Mrs. Taylor shook her head. "I cannot comprehend the wonder of it, but he found her. Three days of searching, it took. The poor child feared she was to hang."

Alice shivered with horror. "To hang?"

"While he was beating her, Fanny's father slipped and fell. He hit his head and died on the spot."

"It was an accident, surely?"

"Aye, he was drunk. But can you imagine what the poor child thought? She'd fought to defend herself, and he fell down the stairs. Heavens above, Mrs. Trelawney, he broke every finger of her right hand. After a lifetime of subjugation and abuse, she feared the gallows awaited her, and she ran away. Your husband found her and brought her here."

"When was this?"

"Shortly before Christmas.

"Why have I never seen her here before?"

"She was sorely ill when he found her," Mrs. Taylor said. "They feared it was the putrid sore throat. He had his physician tend to her in separate lodgings so as not to infect any of us. I offered to take her in anyway, but he wouldn't hear of it until she was recovered. Once Mr. Trelawney believes Jacob has learned his lesson, Fanny will join her brother in Cornwall. She loves children, babies especially. She's ever so good with the tiny ones here. Only last week, he said Fanny would make an excellent nursemaid."

A nursemaid...

The nugget of hope which flared inside Alice on hearing of Ross's goodness, died at Mrs. Taylor's words.

Though he knew she could never give him one, Ross—the best of men—planned to have a child.

The ache for her lost babies resurrected, Alice rose to her feet, praying she did not betray her pain, and took her leave.

CHAPTER TWENTY-NINE

A SHRILL CRY cut through the night, and Alice jerked awake. The candle beside her bed had yet to burn out, and the flame flickered as she climbed out of her bed. Roderick's ghost had not visited her dreams tonight. Instead, the nightmares were plaguing another unfortunate soul.

Perhaps it was one of the servants.

Alice picked up the candle and stepped out of her chamber.

The cry rang out again. It came from Amelia's room. Alice hesitated. Her desire to comfort the child warred with her memory of the child's hostility. Despite Alice's efforts, Amelia's dislike of her had intensified, as if emboldened by Ross's inability or unwillingness to check her behavior.

It was obvious the child had not been given the opportunity to grieve properly for her mother. Ross's reluctance to speak of the matter prevented Alice from raising the subject. She longed to heal the wounds which scarred the child's soul, but the barrier of resentment of the woman Amelia viewed as having supplanted a beloved mother was too high for a child of eight years to scale.

She needed to wake Ross. Amelia had not yet permitted Alice to enter her chamber, and Ross had asked her to respect the child's wishes.

Her heart gave a lurch. Was Kitty with him? Might she open her husband's door and find her in his bed? By inviting Kitty's services,

Alice had willingly sacrificed her self-respect to ensure Ross's happiness.

Ross's heart had once beaten purely for her. Even a broken heart might weather a storm better than any ship, steering its course straight and true. But too much had happened since she'd broken his heart. The events which destroyed her body and mind had shattered his heart. And like the ship, a heart, when battered by one storm too many, surrenders to the deep and sinks without trace.

For some reason, Ross was reluctant to show his child the deep love which Alice knew he was capable of, preferring instead to shower the child with toys and gifts. Amelia clung to his meagre displays of affection, like a drowning man scrabbling at a thin twig floating in a stormy lake.

"Mama!" Another cry rang out, accompanied by a series of sobs which cleaved Alice's heart in two, and she rushed into the child's bedchamber.

She was met by a myriad of colors. An enormous rocking horse stood near the window, adorned with a bright red saddle. Toys filled the chamber, together with a dollhouse with intricate features, as if fashioned by the best architects of London.

The room was filled with everything a little girl could wish for. But the vibrant surroundings only served to diminish the vitality of the small figure lying on the bed in the center of the room. Clad in a white nightgown, Amelia looked frail and colorless in comparison. It was as if her father, subconsciously acknowledging his lack of outward empathy toward his daughter, had attempted to compensate it by surrounding her with material objects. But they only served to accentuate the lack of love in her life.

Overcome by the need to ease Amelia's heartache, Alice rushed toward the bed.

Amelia's eyes opened and she cried out. "Mama! Is it you?"

Alice pulled the child into her arms. "She's watching over you, sweet one." She rocked her to and fro, whispering words of comfort and stroked her hair.

The child stiffened in her arms.

"Why are you in my room?"

"I have bad dreams, too," Alice said, "and I don't want to see you suffering."

"What happens in your dreams?"

Alice closed her eyes against the memory of Roderick. But if it would ease this little girl's pain, she would willingly suffer his memory again.

"A bad man tries to hurt me," she said. "But I have learned to deny him in my dreams, and it's made me stronger."

She took the child's hand and interlinked their fingers. "Tell me about your dreams, Amelia," she whispered. "Together we can fight them."

Amelia looked up at Alice, and for a moment, the child's eyes flickered with the need to be cherished and understood. Then the moment passed, and she pushed Alice away.

"An angel visits me in my dreams," she said. "Mama comes to me."

"What does she do?" Alice asked.

"I don't want to tell you."

"But it might help."

"No!" the child cried. "It won't! You're the monster! That's why you have bad dreams, you deserve them. Mama was taken from me, and you've come to take Papa away, too."

"Amelia…"

Alice reached for her again, but she slapped her hand away and began to scream.

"Papa! I want Papa!"

The door burst open, and Ross flew into the room.

"Good heavens!" he cried. "What's happened?"

Alice backed away from the bed. "Your daughter needs you, Ross."

Brow furrowed in guilt, he nodded and crossed the room to his daughter who reached out for him. He hesitated, then lifted her into his arms.

"Mama!" she wailed. "I want Mama!"

"I know, baby," he said, "I miss her, too."

"Tell me about her, Papa."

"Why speak of her, Amelia, darling?" Ross asked. "It would pain you too much."

"A portrait, then? I never knew her! Didn't you love her?"

"Yes, I did," Ross whispered.

"What about *her*?" Amelia asked.

Ross turned his head and looked at Alice, his eyes full of guilt and fatigue. Then he closed his eyes and shook his head. "What matters is that I loved your mama, sweet one."

"Tell her to go."

"Amelia, I..."

"You said I could always have everything I wanted. To make up for not having a mama."

"Perhaps it's best if I go," Alice said.

Ross didn't reply but held his daughter more tightly while she continued to cry.

With nothing else to do, Alice returned to her chamber.

The candlelight cast a ray across the room, highlighting the edge of the flowers in the vase she'd placed beside her bed only that morning.

Four red roses.

She climbed into the bed and traced an outline of the flowers in the vase, fingering each petal while she whispered four names in her head.

Eventually, the sound of crying outside lessened and grew silent. A door closed in the distance, and footsteps approached. A shadow moved across the gap between the door and the floor.

She sat up, holding her breath, fighting the urge to hope he would come to her. The door handle seemed to turn a fraction, then the shadow moved and the footsteps receded, leaving her alone.

Love still resided within her husband's heart.

But not for her.

CHAPTER THIRTY

ROSS WATCHED HIS wife the next morning for signs of distress. But as she entered the breakfast room, she responded to his greeting with the cold civility of a society lady.

"I trust you're well this morning," he said.

She sat in her place and turned to him. "Why should I not be?"

"You were not too distressed last night, when you saw Amelia?"

"Of course not," she said. "Forgive me for intruding on her privacy. It won't happen again. But I'd urge you to overcome your shortcomings as a parent and take better care of your child."

"What would you know of being a parent?"

She slammed her glass on the table and rose to her feet. A footman rushed to her chair and pulled it back. She turned and issued him a quick, tight smile, then swept out of the room.

Shortly after Alice left, Miss Trinket appeared with Amelia.

Ross gestured toward a chair. "Sit down, Amelia. Miss Trinket, would you care to accompany us?"

"I've already breakfasted, sir."

"I insist."

At a nod, a footman set a place for the governess.

A door shut outside, and he rose and moved to the window overlooking the street. Alice stood on the doorstep, wisps of hair peeking out from beneath her bonnet. In her arms she cradled that ridiculous dog of hers. She bent her head and touched the back of the dog's head with her nose in a delicate, tender gesture, then she looked up. Ross's heart jolted at her expression. The blue of her eyes which barely ten minutes before he'd thought so cold, now reflected deep despair. She turned her head away, then descended the steps and disappeared out of sight.

By the time Ross finished his breakfast, Amelia had left for the schoolroom with Miss Trinket. The atmosphere had been thick with discomfort. Amelia's distress and Ross's guilt had only exacerbated the governess's obvious unease at sharing a meal with her employer. No doubt when she corresponded with the agency, she'd regale them with stories of how an employer with a background in trade enjoyed peculiar habits compared to a gentleman.

As he rose from his seat, the butler appeared at the door.

"What is it, Mycroft?"

"There's a..." he hesitated, "...a *lady* to see you, sir. I took the liberty of showing her into the parlor. I apologize if I acted out of turn."

"How so?"

"She refused to leave without seeing you, and you wouldn't want her sort loitering on the doorstep."

"Thank you, Mycroft," he said. "Perhaps you could bring us some tea?"

The butler bowed and disappeared.

The visitor stood by the parlor window, her face in profile, forming a silhouette against the light of the morning sun. As Ross entered the room, she turned to face him.

"I hadn't expected to see you again," he said.

"Is that how you greet an old friend?"

Dressed in a pale yellow silk gown, her honey-blonde hair shimmering in the sunlight, Kitty had not lost her beauty. Her mouth was redder than he remembered, rich, ruby lips which used to bring him to his knees. But she no longer held any power over him.

As if she understood, her smile disappeared. A seductress played her cards with caution, unwilling to use her resources when they promised insufficient return. Like any speculator in business, she looked him up and down as she had the first moment they'd met. But this time, she performed her calculations and found him wanting.

"What do you want, Kitty?"

"I'll come straight to business."

"I'd rather you didn't," he said. "I've no wish to trade in your particular commodity again."

She let out a snort. "You always were too obsessed with commerce to make love properly, Ross."

"Which is why I'm still solvent, Kitty. I've had enough experience to identify which transactions are loss-making."

"In the financial sense? Or in relation to matters of the heart?"

"I have no heart, Kitty. Surely you must have realized that by now?"

"Of course I do," she said. "You and I were forged in the same smithy. I was never naïve enough to believe you considered our business agreement to be anything other than temporary."

Footsteps approached, and after issuing two smart knocks, a maid appeared with a tray. On Ross's orders, she set the tray down, poured two cups, then scuttled out of the room.

Kitty wrinkled her nose. "Tea? Not a ritual I indulge in."

"No," Ross said, picking up his cup. "You always preferred drinks and clientele of a harder variety."

She sighed. "Now we've concluded the pleasantries, let me to tell you why I'm here. I assure you, it's not for the pleasure of your company."

"Then to what do I owe the honor?"

"Your wife."

"My *wife?*"

"She came to see me."

"For what purpose?"

"She asked me if I would resume my status as your mistress."

Porcelain clattered as his hand slipped, and he dropped his cup on the floor. It shattered on impact, and hot liquid splashed on his ankle.

"Yes," Kitty said. "I wondered if it had been all *her* idea. Thank you for confirming."

"You lie," he said. "She's too much of a lady to associate with you."

Kitty reached into her reticule and pulled out a sheaf of notes.

"Here's twenty pounds," she said. "Your wife offered me fifty at first, but I refused. She then gave me this for her troubles."

"To pay for your silence, I suppose?"

"Then why would I return it to you?"

"Because you're a meddler, Kitty, and because you can't bear to see a man happy if he's not with you."

"You're not happy, though" she said, hardening her voice, "and neither is she. But at least she's trying to do something about it."

"By giving money to you?"

Kitty snorted. "To think I considered you the most intelligent of my patrons! Society may view your wife as a madwoman, but she understands more about human nature than anyone. She possesses the insight required to truly understand a man's needs—even those he's unable to admit to others, or to himself."

Alice...

Kitty was wrong. Alice knew nothing of his needs.

"So, my wife doesn't love me," Ross said. "Have you come to bask in your triumph?"

Bitter laughter echoed around the room. "My dear, Ross," Kitty said. "When I heard of your marriage to Alice, I thought you'd made the biggest mistake of your life, because she didn't deserve you. But I now wonder if it's she who made the mistake, for you don't deserve her."

"What do you mean?"

"She came to see me out of desperation," Kitty said, "because she wants you to be happy, and is prepared to break her heart to do it. If that's not an act of love, I don't know what is."

"But you'd always said..."

"I know," Kitty interrupted. "I always thought her a vapid little creature. But, like the rest of the world, I was fooled by the façade of the soulless beauty. Your wife has spent her life carefully erecting a barrier to protect herself."

"You speak nonsense."

"You know I don't. Your wife must have endured much to craft such a disguise." She looked out of the window, her expression wistful.

"Shortly after he married Alice, Markham set up a friend of mine as his mistress," she said. "The temptation of a duke's patronage was too much for Bessie, young and foolish as she was. He had a reputation for being *ungentle* in bed. I tried to warn Bessie, but she wouldn't listen. She weathered it as best she could, until he beat her so badly, she could hardly walk. He tossed her out onto the street, and she survived a month."

A shudder rippled through Ross. "Why did you not say anything of this?" he asked. "Or tell the authorities?"

She gave a bitter laugh. "I believe society accepts it as a hazard of my occupation. In their eyes, a harlot deserves her fate. But a wife's fate is worse, for the law endorses abuse at her husband's hands, choosing to refer to it as *correction*. Think on that, Ross, when you try to understand why your wife might wish to pay another woman to satisfy you."

He shook his head. "You can't think I would treat he like that...that *monster*," he said. "It's because she doesn't want me."

"Has she shown no sign of affection at all?" Kitty asked. "Or is it easier for you to ignore it? Believe me, Ross, I know what a woman in love looks like. Your wife might be afraid, and well she might, but the answer is not to refuse to touch her. Alice didn't purchase my services because she does not want you. She did it because you do not want her."

"You're wrong," Ross said.

"Am I?" She rose and moved toward him until the tips of her slippers touched his boots.

"Don't get up." She placed a hand on his shoulder and leaned forward, displaying the front of her gown, the swell of her breasts and the valley between them where so often he'd buried his head. She parted her lips and warm, sweet breath caressed his cheek.

"Aren't you going to enjoy the services purchased?" she purred. "A man who has his wife's approval is a lucky man indeed."

He gritted his teeth and dug his fingers into the arms of the chair, his body tense as a coiled spring.

"Yes," she whispered. "I can feel it." A firm hand touched his knee and moved along his leg, until it reached the top of his thighs. Expert fingers fumbled at the buttons of his breeches.

"Do you want me, Ross?"

"Leave..." he said, his voice sticking in his throat.

"You want me, don't you," she said. "You want to bed me."

The spring snapped, and he leapt to his feet. "No!" He pushed her back so violently, she fell to the floor. "I don't want you! I only want her! I've only ever wanted her!"

"Why?"

"Because I love her!" he roared. "Not Caroline, not you, but her! It's always been her!"

He brought his hands to his face to cover his shame and stem the tears which stung his eyes.

"I've never loved anyone else," he said, giving voice to the pain and guilt which had plagued him since the day Alice had rejected him, while he'd watched others lay claim to her.

"I tried to love another," he said. "Oh, Caroline, God forgive me, I tried so hard to love that dear, sweet woman, but I failed. Each time I looked at her, I wished she were another. She died because of me. It was my punishment for not loving her. She deserved so much better than I."

The pain of his admission coursed through his veins as if voicing his love finally allowed it to break free.

"Alice…"

He lowered his hands, bracing himself for her scorn. But the woman at his feet watched him with understanding.

"I knew it," she said. "The truth, at last."

"Congratulations," he replied, bitterly. "Does it please you to know that a man can suffer from unrequited love as much as a woman?"

"You're a simpleton if you think Alice doesn't love you," Kitty said. "She set aside her happiness in order to secure yours. Few people are capable of such love."

Ross reached out a hand to help her up. "What do you know of love?"

Ignoring his hand, she rose to her feet. "Neither you nor I are deserving of love, Ross. And I refuse to regret something I can never aspire to. The only regret I'm in danger of experiencing is your inability to comprehend how much your wife loves you."

She moved to the window and patted her hair, looking at her reflection.

"If you want my advice, Ross, I'd speak to her. I believe I saw her walking toward Hyde Park."

"You've been watching her?"

"I respect her enough to deem it inappropriate to visit while she's at home."

He moved toward her, and she held up her hand.

"No, Ross, don't come any closer. Our business is concluded. I only hope I've served your wife properly, though perhaps not how she intended."

Before he could respond, she opened the door and disappeared. Voices echoed outside as Mycroft escorted her out of the building. As he adjusted his necktie, he noticed a sheaf of papers on the tea tray.

A pile of pound notes. He didn't have to count them to know how many there were.

CHAPTER THIRTY-ONE

THE AIR HAD turned colder. As Alice strolled along the path, a gust of wind blew a pile of leaves into a vortex which swirled in the air ahead of her, mirroring the discomfort in her mind. Cradling Monty in her arms, she hurried on, narrowing her eyes, which stung with tears brought about by the cold. The ground was firm beneath her feet, impassive and unyielding, but the sky was clear, the low sun casting sharp shadows across the grass. A leaf blew in her direction, and she caught it in her hand.

When Alice was a child, Mama had said that if she could catch a leaf from the sky, she could make a wish.

But that wish must be spent wisely, Alice. Only when you gain your heart's desire will you learn the price which must be paid.

Only now did Alice understand what Mama meant. She had, finally, gained her heart's desire, the hand of the man she had always loved. And now she was paying the price.

She turned the leaf over and studied the thin, protruding veins which spread out from the center, forming a pattern like cracks in glass. Less than a year ago, she had sat in this very park and studied just such a leaf. Everything around her was the same as it was then. Unchanged.

Except her. She had traveled as far as any human being could hope to. She could now weather the stares of the passers-by, because she no longer cared what they thought of her. What did reputation matter? It was a smokescreen, which society used to divert its attention from the injustices of the world.

Had she not married Roderick and weathered his blows, she would never have found her vocation in helping others. She'd have lived out her days as a contented society lady, unaware of the world around her save for a tight circle of gossip, embroidery, and tea.

But one regret remained. She had failed her husband. Guilt and grief still clung to him, forming an impenetrable wall through which she couldn't pass.

For the women at Mrs. Taylor's, Alice had something to give them—a quiet word, a gentle hand, or an understanding ear. But for Ross, her feeble attempt to ease his pain had only succeeded in widening the gap which stretched between them like a vast desert. How long would it be before that desert became impassable and Ross, and his child, were lost to her forever?

"Aunt Alice!"

A child's excited voice called out ahead. Alice looked up to see a familiar face. Framed by soft hair which curled at the ends, the child standing before her had grown in the past year. But there was no mistaking the deep-set, brown eyes which looked at her with such intensity.

"It *is* you!" she cried. "I knew it! I told Mama I saw you coming into the park."

"Georgia!" Alice said. "How you've grown! I swear you'll soon be as tall as your mama."

"Mama's here," the child said. "She brought me to London yesterday."

Alice's heart lifted at the news. The company of a dear friend such as Frederica would lift her spirits.

"Do you like London, Georgia?"

"Oh yes!" Georgia said. "Mama promised me I could see Amelia as soon as I arrived. And she said you're Amelia's mama, now. Is that true?"

Alice sighed. "I've married her father, Georgia, but I'm not her mama yet."

"Can you come for tea today?"

Alice shook her head. "I must wait until I'm invited, Georgia, dear."

"I shall demand you're invited," the child said. "Mama's always talking about you. Here she comes!"

A woman appeared at the end of the path, dressed in a deep red gown and dark brown jacket. Bright red curls peeked from the rim of her bonnet, as if, like their owner, they could not be tamed.

Alice quickened her pace, eager to see her friend again, but checked herself as a man approached Frederica and linked her arm with his. Together they approached Alice. Frederica's expression was open with affection and delight, but Hawthorne's, as usual, was more guarded.

He gave her a stiff bow. "Mrs. Trelawney."

"Lord Stiles." Alice dipped into a curtsey.

Frederica rushed forward, her enthusiasm and capacity for love shattering the formalities. Opening her arms, she pulled Alice into an embrace, her tall frame almost engulfing her.

"Alice, it's good to see you. You're looking more beautiful than ever, my dear. I swear the fresh air is working wonders for your health. And you've Monty with you, I see. As charming as ever!"

She held out an open palm to the little dog, and he gave a grunt of satisfaction as Frederica scratched him behind one ear. After a while, his body stiffened in Alice's arms, the signal he always gave when the attention became too much for him. Frederica withdrew her hand and smiled.

"I see young Montague has a discerning character, and rightly so. He understands that trust is a privilege which must be earned rather than a right to be exercised."

"May I pet him?" Georgia looked up at her mother, her eyes shining with eagerness. She reached out to Monty, and he gave a low growl.

"Forgive him, Georgia," Alice said. "He's nervous around people he doesn't know. He's more comfortable at home, if you'd like to visit him there."

"I'd love to!" Georgia said. "Can I, Papa?"

Alice focused her attention on the dog in her arms, ready to take comfort in him when Hawthorne's denial came. A large, firm hand touched her shoulder, and she looked up into a pair of brown eyes and the face of a man who bore responsibility for countless lives as he dispensed justice in the courtroom.

"What do you think, Mrs. Trelawney?" he asked. "Should I permit Master Montague to entertain my daughter when he growls at her?"

"I'm not in a position to pass judgement on his worthiness as a host," Alice replied. "Others must judge him for themselves. He may value my good opinion, but I fear the rest of the world would disagree with him."

The corner of his mouth twitched. "When cornered, an animal will use its teeth and voice to ward away predators. But if he, or she, is prey to the unscrupulous, how else can he protect himself and their loved ones?"

"Monty wouldn't harm Georgia, sir," Alice said, "if that's your concern."

"Hawthorne!" Frederica said. "Do you intend to torment my friend?"

"Of course not," he said, maintaining his focus on Alice.

No longer plagued by the discomfort she'd once felt at such close scrutiny, she met his gaze with equal steadfastness.

At length he smiled. "I'm sure Master Montague would never harm another creature other than out of a need to defend himself. Many creatures have the appearance of aggression, but are, in fact, merely misunderstood. While I always prided myself in possessing the insight necessary to dispense justice, I would like to think I am in possession of sufficient humility to accept where I may have committed a misjudgment. In my career, and in other matters, I have learned that while it's important to remain steadfast, it's even more important to admit when I might have been wrong."

He removed his hand from her shoulder and gave her a bow. "I believe I've made an error of judgement, Mrs. Trelawney. Montague, I understand, is of the very finest character, all the more admirable for concealing his true goodness within a form which society might have once referred to as *insipid*."

"His nature has always been gentle, sir," she said. "But he's careful to conceal it, for in revealing his soul, he exposes oneself to hurt."

Hawthorne was no longer talking about Monty.

"Let me be the first to apologize," he said, "to Montague, for my previous inability to discern his true quality."

He held out his hand. "Perhaps, if he's amenable to the notion, he may permit you to accept my apology on his behalf."

She took his hand and long, lean fingers curled around her own in the strong grip of a man who had, throughout his life, taken what he wanted. But now, he was asking her forgiveness. Freely and without agenda.

"I very much look forward to receiving your invitation to tea, Mrs. Trelawney," he said. "And, I trust you are well?"

"Yes," she said quietly. "I'm well.

Frederica placed a light hand on Alice's arm. "Are you sure, Alice, dear?"

Alice nodded. "I'm married to a good man."

"Yes, you are," Frederica said. "You deserve happiness after all you've endured. I know Hartford was a good man, a kind man. But Ross…" she hesitated, coloring. "Ross is the man you were destined for."

"Perhaps I'll pay him a visit this afternoon," Hawthorne said. "We can make arrangements for Georgia's visit then. I'm sure she's anxious to see Amelia again. Amelia must be so glad to have a mama at last."

Alice looked away in shame. Would Ross tell Hawthorne of her proposition? That she had offered to find him a whore to make up for her own inadequacies? Would he tell him that Amelia loathed her?

She withdrew her hand.

"Forgive me, Lord Stiles," she said, her voice stiff. "Monty needs his exercise, and I have no wish to detain you."

"You're not…"

"Hawthorne," Frederica interrupted him. "I believe my friend is in need of solitude. Is that not so, Alice?"

Echoes of pain glimmered in Frederica's eyes, a pain mirrored in Alice's memories. A shared pain of what they had endured at the Roderick's hands.

"Take care of yourself, Alice."

Alice dipped a curtsey, then continued along the path. Before she reached the end, she turned back. Frederica stood arm-in-arm with her husband, their daughter by their side. The perfect, happy family which Alice yearned for, but could never have.

CHAPTER THIRTY-TWO

*A**LICE, WHERE ARE you?*

Ross thrust his hands into his coat pockets and hunched his shoulders against the cold. He'd walked the length and breadth of Hyde Park, but she was nowhere to be seen. Surely she couldn't still be in the park? She'd catch a chill being outside for so long.

But his instincts had told him she was here, hidden among the secluded paths where she could find refuge from the company of others.

As the path veered toward the water's edge, he spotted a bench set back from the walkway, almost completely concealed among the bushes. A lone figure sat, cradling something in its arms. Body stiff and erect, she weathered the cold, as if she sought comfort from it. Did she really believe she was safer out here in the twilight, rather than with him at home?

She made no attempt to move as he approached. She might have been a statue save the slight tensing of her body. Her lips parted, and small puff of breath clouded in front of her.

He sat beside his wife, taking care not to touch her, as if physical contact would break the spell and cause her to flee. The dog lifted its head and stared at him, watching him reproachfully, as if in accusation for the wrongs its mistress had suffered. Monty snarled.

"Shh." A gloved hand caressed the animal's fur, and it grew quiet.

He waited for her to speak, but she remained still and silent, as if willing him to ignore her and pass her by.

But he could no longer ignore her. "Mrs. Bonneville paid me a visit," he said.

She drew in a sharp breath, and her fingers curled into the little dog's fur. She closed her eyes, and a tear rolled down her face.

He reached for her hand, and she flinched.

"Forgive me," he said. "I want to understand. But if it pains you too much, we need never speak of it again."

He sighed, wishing he could find the words to unlock the barriers she had erected around herself. But deeds, not words, were the key to gaining her trust.

"I-I'm sorry." A faint breeze rushed through the trees, almost completely obscuring her whispered words.

But he had always heard her. From the moment he'd first declared his love for her, when they were idealistic young people, blind to the prejudices of the world, and through the years of her abusive marriage and incarceration. How often had he lain awake at night, widowed and alone, trying to convince himself she deserved it, but ultimately, unable to ignore her voice in his mind, pleading for release.

"It is *I* who should be sorry," he said. "I thought only of myself when I forced you into marriage, when I..." he broke off, the memory of her tear-stained face searing through him "...when I took you like a harlot."

She turned her head away and bit her lip.

"You're cold, my love," he said, softly. "Let me take you home."

She shook her head. Did she still fear him?

"Alice, I promise never to hurt you," he said. "I only want to be a good husband, to take care of you. And I'll ask nothing in return, not even for you to trust me. Trust must be given freely, not taken or demanded by others."

He reached for her hand again, stopping midway.

"May I?"

She nodded, and her chest rose as she held her breath. He covered her hand with his, and she breathed out. A tear splashed onto the back of his hand.

"I may have forced you into marriage," he said, "but I stand by the vows I made. I shall love, honor, and cherish you until I breathe my last." He gave her hand a gentle squeeze. "Alice, a marriage is not only conducted in the marital chamber. I can't begin to think what Markham…"

She withdrew her hand, wincing as if she had taken a blow.

"Forgive me!" he cried.

"It's not you," she said. "It's the memories. I try to fight them, but sometimes they resurface, especially since we…"

"Consummated our marriage?"

She nodded.

"Oh Alice, I'm doubly ashamed of that day," he said. "I wanted to protect you, to keep you safe from your father, safe from your nightmares. But instead, I let them in. I took you unwilling."

"No," she said, "I was willing, Ross, so willing. But I couldn't fight the memories."

She shook her head. "I can't remember a single day when he did not beat me."

She buried her hands in the little dog's fur, the silent companion who demanded nothing from her. "I used to lie awake at night and pray that his mistress had satisfied him, so he'd not be angered by my failings."

"Surely you can't think that I…"

"I wish it were so. I want to…" she hesitated and colored. "With you, I want…" She shook her head. "Forgive me, Ross, but I'm afraid of what will happen if I yield. But I long to yield to you, to give myself to you." She turned her gaze on him, her eyes red-rimmed with pain. "But no matter how hard I fight it, I cannot conquer the memories."

She broke off, biting her lip as if she were willing her body into stillness. How many times must she have conquered her fears, driven them deep inside her where they festered in the dark corners of her mind, only to return and torment her in her madness?

"Lord Hartford helped me see that not all husbands beat their wives. But I can never be sure whether other men are like George, or like *him*."

The pain in her voice tore into Ross's heart. "Forgive me, Alice, it was cruel of me to expect you to speak of it. Let us say no more."

"No, let me tell you," she said. "I owe you that, at least. To explain why I sought out Mrs. Bonneville."

He took her hand again. Though she stiffened, she made no attempt to pull away. Perhaps, in time, she might begin to trust him.

"You owe me nothing, dearest Alice. It breaks my heart to think of what you must have endured to do it, to think you believed that to lie with another woman would make me happy!"

"But you…"

"I pledged to remain faithful only unto you," he said. "And I will never break that vow. There's only one woman in the world I wish to sleep with. If I can never have her, I will accept that. Above all else, I want you happy and safe. I have no wish to add to your scars."

She flinched and moved a hand to her stomach.

"How can you bear it, having a flawed wife?"

"Your scars are not of your own doing."

She fell silent, turning her head to gaze at the Serpentine where a swan glided silently along with the current, followed by a small party of cygnets. At length, she sighed.

"I was a poor wife to him," she said. "I broke my vows on our wedding night, when I tried to deny him. Even though I understood the futility of it, still I fought him. But it did no good. I came to learn that he relished the struggle. But I couldn't bring myself to surrender, not at first. Fool that I was, I convinced myself that if I continued to fight him, he'd eventually leave me alone."

She broke off and lowered her head, as if in prayer. "I realized my folly when he brought a knife into the bedroom."

Dear God…

Nausea tightened his throat. The scars on her body which he'd glimpsed the day they consummated their marriage—parallel lines stretching across her stomach and thighs.

"Alice. Dear sweet lord, Alice! To think that a man would…at knifepoint…" He shook his head. "I know not what to say."

"I understand," she said. "I've lived with the shame of it ever since. The marks of my failings will stay with me as a reminder."

"No!" he cried. "You've nothing to be ashamed of. No words I utter will ever be sufficient to convince you to trust another creature after your trust was betrayed so brutally. It is *I* who should be ashamed."

She turned her gaze on him. "Do I shame you?"

"No, my love," he said. "I am ashamed of my own actions, for not snatching you away seven years ago, for doing nothing while you endured so much evil at that man's hands. And now I want, so much, for you to be happy, and can only feel shame at my inadequacy as a husband." He moved to withdraw his hand, but she caught his wrist and curled her fingers around his. His heart swelled at the gesture.

"Come, Alice," he said. "Night is falling, and I would not want you to catch a chill. Will you come home?"

For several heartbeats she remained still, then she nodded.

"I won't ask you to trust me, Alice," he said. "But I promise to do my utmost to earn that trust."

"And you'll ask nothing in return?"

"No," he said. "For I deserve nothing. And I will never take any-thing from you that you aren't willing to give."

She rose to her feet. "I wonder…" she hesitated, "…would you care to carry Monty home?"

Her arms trembled as she held the little dog out. A small step, perhaps, but it was a step. An expression of trust.

He held out his arms, and she handed the pug to him. The animal let out a whine.

"Hush, Monty," she said. "He'll take care of you."

Cradling the dog under one arm, he held out his free arm, and she took it.

Her physical scars would mark her until the day she died. But, as for the hidden scars which lay deep within her, perhaps they might heal after all.

CHAPTER THIRTY-THREE

ROSS WATCHED HIS wife pour the tea from an armchair beside the fireplace. Across from her, Amelia sat on a two-seater sofa with Miss Trinket. His daughter's mouth was turned down in a scowl, but the best way to heal both his wife's and his daughter's wounds was to rebuild his family. He could never replace the lost souls they still grieved, but he could forge a new, and special, family all of its own.

Today's tea was the first step. While Amelia had spent the day on her lessons, Alice had taken the air in the park again and had returned with a healthy bloom on her cheeks.

"Did you enjoy your day, my dear?" he asked.

She looked up from pouring the tea. "Yes, thank you, Ross."

"Perhaps next time Amelia might join you. Would you like that, Amelia?"

Amelia turned her head away and stared out of the window.

"Would you like to take a walk with me, Amelia?" Alice asked, seemingly oblivious of the insult.

The child moved closer to her governess who gave her a nudge.

"Amelia, dear, your mama asked you a question."

The child mumbled something and shook her head.

"What did you say, child?" Ross asked, his voice sharp.

"Mama is dead."

Ross sighed. "Sweetheart, it does no good to speak of her."

"You never speak of her!" she cried. "It's like she never existed!"

Miss Trinket pulled her into an embrace.

"Amelia, my dear," Alice said. "I understand how you feel. I lost my mother, too, and I still miss her."

"Did your father miss her, too? Or did he forget her and replace her with another?"

"A man is permitted to marry again, Amelia," Ross said. "He cannot be expected to be alone all his life."

"You have *me*, Papa. Don't you love me anymore?"

"Of course, I do."

"Then why put me in danger..." Amelia pointed to Alice "...with *her?*"

Alice stiffened.

"I don't know what you mean, Amelia," Ross said.

"I overheard Betsy say it! She was laughing, with Simpson, about the Deranged Duchess, and how children are not safe around her."

A sharp intake of breath was the only indication Alice had heard as her body grew still. Ross leaned forward.

"What else did they say?"

"Ross," Alice said, "leave her alone."

"No," he said. "Amelia, continue."

Fear clouded Amelia's expression, and she glanced at Alice. "They said she'd kill you, like she'd killed all her husbands. And she'd kill me, too. They said, one more murder and she'd be carted off to the madhouse."

Ross gripped the arms of his chair, striving to conceal the anger vibrating through his body.

"What else did they say?"

"Ross, that's enough," Alice said.

"Alice, let me deal with this," he said. "Amelia, tell me what they said!"

His daughter glanced at Alice again and shook her head.

"Tell me, child!" he roared. "Tell me what they're saying!"

"No!" Alice cried. "Stop it, Ross! Can't you see you're frightening her? She's not to blame."

His anger drained at Alice's defense of his child.

Alice reached toward Amelia, but the child shrank back. She gave a sigh and rose to her feet.

"I should go," she said. "For her sake and yours."

She moved to the door and left. With a nod from Ross, the governess left the room, too.

But he'd seen the pain in his wife's eyes. He had promised to give her a home where she could be safe, yet in that home the staff were spreading malicious gossip about her.

But she had set aside her own pain and placed Amelia's happiness first.

***

BY THE TIME the sun had disappeared, the household had fallen quiet. Alice returned to the parlor, but Ross was nowhere to be seen.

Driven by a need to ease Amelia's pain, she ventured into the schoolroom. The child sat at a desk, alone, reading a book.

"May I join you?"

The child shrugged her shoulders, then resumed her attention on her book, idly flicking through the pages.

"Where's Miss Trinket?"

"She's taking her supper."

Hostility vibrated in the child's body. Unwilling to intrude on her privacy, Alice took a seat at the opposite end of the room.

Amelia closed the book and turned to look at Alice. "Has Papa dismissed Simpson and Betsy?"

"I believe so."

"Is it because of you? Are you deranged?" The child flinched as she uttered the words, as if anticipating a blow.

Alice sighed and looked away. What could she hope to do against the pain of a child unable to grieve for her mother, who sought to ease that pain by lashing out?

"I am whatever you think me to be, Amelia," she said.

"Miss Trinket punishes me if I say bad things," the child said. "Why don't you?"

"I have no right, Amelia. And until you have accepted me, I'll leave such matters to your Papa."

"I shan't stop," the child said. "What will you do then?"

Alice smiled and shook her head. "I've endured far worse and dare say I shall do so again. Believe it or not, I understand how you feel."

"How can you?"

"Because I understand your pain, Amelia. You're not a bad child. You're merely hurting."

Her body yearned to reach out and give comfort. But she fought her own needs.

"You lost your mama," she said, "and I understand that, for I lost my mother also. I was lucky enough to have known her for a brief time when I was young. You have never known your mother, and your loss is the greater for it."

Uncertainty crossed the child's expression.

"I loved my mother," Alice said, her voice catching. "She was the only person in the world who loved me without hope of reward. I harbor a special place in my heart for her which can never be occupied by another."

The child's eyes glistened, and she pushed the book aside.

"I have no wish to replace your dear mother," Alice said. "She should always be honored and remembered, for she brought you into the world."

She moved closer and placed a light hand on Amelia's shoulder. The child flinched but made no attempt to move.

"I only hope that, perhaps one day, you might begin to find a little room in your heart for someone else, someone who would love you, in her own way. If you would let her." Alice removed her hand. "But I have no right to expect it, Amelia."

"Mama..." The child closed her eyes. "Mama..."

"I know," Alice whispered. "I'm so sorry she's not here. But we can keep her memory alive. I'd love to see a portrait of her. She must have been very beautiful, for you're such a pretty child."

"I'm not permitted to speak of her."

"Why ever not?"

"Papa said so."

"Does Miss Trinket not speak of her?"

"She's forbidden." The child's chest rose and fell in a shuddering sigh. "I had a miniature of her." She let out a sob.

"Do you still have it?" Alice asked. "Perhaps it may give you comfort."

"I took it from Papa's study," the child cried. "When Miss Trinket found it, she told Papa, and he made me give it back."

"Your Papa was very wrong to do that," Alice said. "I'll make sure he gives it back."

The child looked up. For a moment, a sense of hope flickered in Amelia's eyes as if she wanted to reach out to her. Then she looked away.

Alice caressed her head.

"It's time your mother became a part of this house, whatever your Papa says. It's cruel to deny you." She turned toward the door and froze.

Ross stood in the doorway, body rigid, his mouth a dark slash. "What are you doing?"

No longer would she be cowed by a man's anger.

"What *you* should have done a long time ago, Ross," she said. "I'm letting your daughter remember her mother."

His eyes narrowed.

Undeterred, she continued. "Amelia must never be allowed to forget her mother. Why have you chosen to forget Caroline? Is it to ease your guilt?"

"That's enough," he growled. "Do not speak her name. It's not your right."

"Maybe not," she said. "But it's *your* duty."

"My duty?"

"Some duties must never be ignored."

He shook his head and lifted a hand to his face.

"Caroline..." he said. "I failed her. I can't bear the guilt."

"You must set aside your guilt, Ross," she said. "Do what's best for your daughter. Do you have any idea how fortunate you are, how many men and women exist who'd lay down their lives to have a child of their own?"

"Then what should I do?"

"Take care of Amelia," she said. "Be a father to your daughter. Give her what she needs, not what you believe she wants."

"Papa?" Amelia looked up at her father, hope and hurt in her eyes.

"I'm here, dear one."

She reached out to him, arms outstretched. "I want Mama!"

"I know, sweetheart," he said. "I miss her, too. But she would not want you unhappy."

"Can you not tell me what she was like? I want to know."

Ross hesitated and looked up at Alice.

"Speak of her," Alice said. "She has a place in your child's heart. Nurture it."

"And you?"

"What of me? You think there's anything I can do? You need to do this, Ross. Face up to it."

He lowered his head and curled his arms around Amelia.

"Forgive me, Amelia," he said. "I know you miss her."

"Then why do we not speak of her?"

"I was afraid, Amelia. But not anymore. Your mama would have loved you so much."

"Tell me about her."

He nodded and kissed her. "Of course, little one," he said. "I should have done this a long time ago. Would you like to see her portrait?"

Alice moved to the door, and he looked up at her. "Won't you stay?"

"No," she said. "Your daughter needs her father *and* mother. I am neither."

She left the nursery and returned to her bedchamber. A vase stood in the center of the room with four roses in it, and she fingered the delicate blooms. A ripple of nausea threaded through her, and she drew in a deep breath, savoring their soft scent.

CHAPTER THIRTY-FOUR

ROSS HELPED HIMSELF to eggs, then settled in his chair at the breakfast table. Amelia sat beside him, a full plate in front of her.

"Eat, Amelia," he said. "You don't have to ask."

She picked up a slice of ham and chewed it.

"It's good?"

She smiled and nodded.

Last night had only been the beginning, but Amelia had warmed to him as he spoke of Caroline, telling her how the two of them had met. At first, the guilt which had lingered in his mind drew forth, as if it were poison leaving a wound. But as he continued, it peeled away until the two of them grieved for Caroline together.

Afterward, he'd taken Amelia to his study where he'd hidden all the paintings of Caroline, the images which had been too painful for him to see until now, when he confronted his guilt for his daughter's sake.

It was a start. Amelia now wore a locket which contained Caroline's likeness. A portrait of Caroline now hung over the fireplace in the schoolroom, and a miniature hung on the wall in the breakfast room.

The door opened, and Alice walked in. She hesitated on seeing them, but he stood and held his hand out.

"Join us, Alice."

She looked around the room and her lips parted as her gaze settled on the portrait. But rather than display the jealousy he'd expected, her face lit up into a smile. Why was it that he continually underestimated her and assumed she had the same failings as he? Alice was, and always would be, a better person, driven by her need to ease the suffering of others.

Whereas he had always been driven by the need to ease his own suffering.

Amelia pointed across the room. "Do you see Mama's portrait on the wall?"

"I do," Alice said, "and I'm glad of it." She spooned scrambled eggs onto her plate, then moved toward her seat opposite him.

"Papa, may I ask you something?" Amelia asked. She cast a nervous glance at Alice. "Might Alice sit next to me for breakfast?"

"Of course," Alice said. "I would be delighted." She settled into a seat beside Amelia and began eating her breakfast. Though outwardly she displayed nonchalance, Ross couldn't help but notice her hands tremble as she ate.

"What do you think of Mama?" Amelia asked. "Is she not pretty?"

"Oh yes!" Alice said. "Didn't I say I knew she must have been beautiful?"

"Papa has given me another portrait of her. It's in the schoolroom. Would you like to see it?"

"I'd be honored. Perhaps you can tell me about her."

The child nodded, chewing on a mouthful of food. "Papa said she used to ride horses," she said. "He told me you're an excellent horsewoman."

"Your Papa is too kind."

"No, Alice," he said. "I'm not kind enough. Not to you."

Alice glanced at Ross, the gentle curve of a smile on her lips, and his body warmed at the tender expression in her eyes. A jolt of desire ran through him and his manhood hardened, straining against his breeches. After the disastrous consummation of their marriage, he'd avoided touching her, unwilling to see the terror in her eyes again. Instead, he had languished in his bedchamber, the relief he sought from his hand failing to quench his hunger for her.

The air crackled with unmet need.

Amelia rattled on, unaware of the tension. "Alice, w-would you teach me to ride?"

"If your Papa permits it."

"I'll permit anything you like," he said.

Alice colored and resumed her attention on her breakfast.

"You could teach me, too, Papa?" Amelia asked. "Can I then have a horse of my own? And Alice, too?"

Ross looked at the eager little girl's face. Unwilling to disappoint her, he sighed. "Yes, one day," he said, "when you're older. But now, how about I buy you a new doll instead? Or even two?"

Disappointment clouded Amelia's expression, but she nodded and resumed her attention on her breakfast. Her quiet acceptance of his denial cut him deeper than any childish tantrum she might have displayed.

Alice waved a footman over and whispered to him. He nodded and left the room.

"What have you asked for?" Amelia asked.

"You must be patient," Alice said, "then you'll see."

Moments later, he returned, carrying a bundle of fur.

"Ah! Here we are," Alice said. She took the pug into her arms. "While you wait for a horse of your own, Amelia, permit me to introduce you to someone very special."

Amelia reached for the dog. He gave a low growl, and Alice placed a hand on his back.

"Hush, Monty!" she said. "Would you make a bad impression on a young lady eager to make your acquaintance?"

Amelia drew her hand back. "Why does he growl?"

"He needs to be reassured that anyone new in his life means him no harm," Alice said.

"Does he bite?"

"No," Alice said, and she looked lovingly at the animal in her arms. "He'd only bite if he was in danger."

"Is he never in danger?"

"Not when he has me to protect him from those I deem untrustworthy," Alice replied.

"Why do you let me near him?"

"Because I know you can be trusted."

Ross held his breath as the woman he loved placed the little creature she cherished into his daughter's arms. He prayed Amelia would not betray Alice's trust.

He needn't have worried. His daughter's face split into a brilliant smile, and she sat still, as if she dared not breathe.

"There you go, Monty." Alice caressed the little dog's fur. "Didn't I tell you Miss Amelia was a friend?"

"Do you talk to him?" Amelia asked.

"Of course," Alice replied. "How else can he get to know me?"

"And you've told him about me?"

"Yes. He's anxious to make your acquaintance."

"Are you sure he'll not bite me?"

"Not if you're gentle. Show him your hand."

Amelia held her hand out, and Ross held his breath as the dog sniffed her fingers. A little pink tongue appeared and licked Amelia's fingers, and she giggled.

"It tickles!"

"It means he likes you, Amelia," Alice said. "Would you like to give him a tidbit? He's partial to a little ham, if you'd be obliging enough to share your breakfast."

"Oh yes!"

"Pick up a small piece," Alice said. "Slowly, so as not to alarm him."

Amelia held a piece of meat in front of the pug's nose. He sniffed it, then in a swift gesture, snatched it between his teeth, his tail wagging.

"There!" Alice said. "You've made a friend!"

Amelia looked up at Alice, her eyes shining with delight. "May I give him another?"

"Perhaps tomorrow." Alice replied. "We mustn't overindulge him. He appreciates a treat all the more for it being given on rare occasions. But from now on, if you like, Amelia, would you like to be the one to give him his treats?"

"Oh yes, please!"

A clock chimed in the distance, and Ross pulled out his pocket watch.

"Amelia, it's time for your lessons," he said. "Miss Trinket will be waiting."

The child's face fell.

"Monty could join you in the schoolroom," Alice said. "I can ask Lizzie to fetch his basket."

Amelia hesitated, stroking the dog's fur, then lifted her head, her expression shy.

"Could you come, too? Papa, may Alice join me today? If she wishes, of course."

Alice lifted her gaze to Ross and their eyes met.

"I think it an excellent idea," he said.

Alice smiled and rose from her seat. "Come along then, Amelia."

She swayed to one side. For a moment, he thought she was going to faint, then she clutched the back of her chair. Her eyes darkened with fear, in contrast to her pale face.

Ross leapt to his feet.

"Alice! Are you all right?"

ALICE CURLED HER hands round the back of her chair, willing the nausea to dissipate.

Her husband rose and moved toward her.

"I'm quite well," she said, forcing hardness into her voice. "Just a little dizzy, that's all. I stood too quickly."

"Does it happen often?"

She opened her mouth to lie, but she couldn't. Not to him.

He sighed. "How long have you been concealing an illness from me?"

"I'm not ill!" she said, fear sharpening her voice.

"I'll send for McIver, to be sure."

"Please, no!"

"If you wish."

She fled before he could change his mind.

Doctor McIver had been present when her insanity was diagnosed. He was the one man, save Ross, who had the power to have her incarcerated again.

CHAPTER THIRTY-FIVE

A S THE SUN slipped below the horizon and the shadows lengthened across the parlor floor, quick, determined footsteps echoed
outside the door. It opened, and Alice looked up. Ross stood in the
doorway, concern and guilt etched into his expression. A man stood
beside him.

Doctor McIver. The man who'd declared her insane and committed her to Bedlam.

His scrutiny unsettled her now as it had terrified her then.

Panic coursed through her, and she leapt to her feet, looking
around the room for an escape route.

The instinct to flee gripped her, and she bolted toward the window. Two strong arms wrapped around her.

"Alice!"

"No! Ross!" she cried. "You promised!"

"You told me you had her consent," the doctor said. "Mrs.
Trelawney, you have my word I'll do nothing without your permission." He frowned at Ross. "Misguided though your husband's actions
are, he asked me here out of concern for your health. Nothing more."

He gestured to a seat. "May I?"

"Of course," Ross said.

The doctor held up his hand. "It is not for *you* to grant permission,
Mr. Trelawney," he said. "Leave us."

"But I sent for you."

"You're not my patient," McIver said. "Permit me to ascertain whether your wife wishes to be. Now, go."

Ross opened his mouth, then nodded and disappeared, closing the door after him.

The doctor gestured to a chair.

"Will you sit with me?"

"I assure you, I'm quite well," she said.

He raised his hands, palms open in a gesture of appeasement. "I'm not here to hurt you."

"What has my husband said?"

"That you fainted this morning." He set his medical bag on the table. "I understand your reluctance to let me examine you."

She said nothing, and he waited. Apprehension swelled within her, and she broke the silence to dissipate it. "I apologize if you've taken the trouble to come here. My husband, I'm sure, believes..."

"What your husband believes is of no matter," the doctor said. "Whatever passes between us today will not leave this room, unless you wish it."

"But, my husband..."

"Wishes you nothing but good, I assure you." He leaned forward and lowered his voice. "Permit me to break a confidence, but I believe I can be forgiven. Three years ago, your husband came to see me shortly after your—your..."

"My incarceration?"

McIver sighed. "He begged me to overturn my diagnosis. He even secured the services of a solicitor to challenge it. But there was nothing he could do once you were admitted. I regret sending you there, my dear, for I can see you're perfectly sane. But I thought it was the best course of action for you, and for your safety, to remove you from society. I am not here to affect an incarceration, Mrs. Trelawney, and neither is your husband. Permit us both to atone for past mistakes."

"Ross pleaded my case?"

McIver nodded. "Will that sway your decision to agree to speak to me?"

"No," she said. "I'm sorry, but I'd rather you didn't examine me."

"Very well," he said. "May I ask you a few questions instead? Or, perhaps you could describe your symptoms."

"I felt a little sick, that is all."

"Are you eating well?"

"Yes. My husband tells me…"

She broke off, unwilling to reveal too much.

The doctor smiled. "Does he say that you are in need of good food?" His smile broadened. "I guessed as much, my dear. Your husband cares a great deal about you. You're much less thin now than you were back then. Perhaps your sickness is merely due to a richer diet."

"Perhaps."

"Is there anything else you can tell me?" he asked.

She turned her head away. The silence lengthened, and eventually he sighed.

"I'll prepare a tonic for you. Other than that, I'd recommend drinking more water and less wine. And plenty of fresh air."

He rose from his seat and picked up his bag. "Forgive me for taking up so much of your time. With your permission, I'll tell your husband that you're suffering from a minor stomach ailment which should clear up in a week or two…" He lowered his voice "… but if you continue to feel unwell, I would hope you'd trust me enough to send for me again. Believe me when I say I want nothing more than to see you well and happy."

She looked into his eyes, kind eyes which showed understanding and compassion.

"Very well," she said. "I'll send for you if I'm still unwell."

"Thank you, Mrs. Trelawney. I'll bid you good day."

After he excused himself, Ross entered the chamber. But her fears of him probing her with questions were unfounded. Silently, he drew her into his arms and placed a light kiss on the top of her head.

"I'm glad my wife is well."

CHAPTER THIRTY-SIX

"A TOAST, TO good friends!"

Ross raised his glass and addressed the room.

The prospect of a dinner party had terrified Alice, but after her husband had respected her wish not to reveal what had passed between her and Doctor McIver, she owed it to him to agree.

He smiled at her, and her heart fluttered at the desire in his eyes. But he had been true to his word and not touched her since they had spoken in the park. Occasionally, when she moved to take his hand, raw need showed on his face. But then he withdrew, as if he were terrified of breaking her.

Had she revealed too much that day? Did he now view her as broken beyond repair?

"Your husband seems in good spirits." The sofa shifted as a woman sat beside her, holding a glass of water.

Alice nodded to her. "Duchess."

The woman rolled her eyes, expressive emeralds which flashed in the candlelight, "It's Jeanette," she said. "How many times have I told you not to stand on ceremony with a good friend?" She drained her glass and set it aside.

Alice nodded to the empty glass. "Would you like a glass of brandy?"

"Good heavens no, I can't abide the stuff at the moment. Henry teases me about it, but he's not the one who has to nurse our daughter."

She straightened her posture and patted her stomach. "What do you think, Alice? Has my figure returned?"

"Of course it has, and well you know it," a new voice said. Alice looked up into the eyes of her old friend.

With one hand on her stomach, where her pregnancy was already showing, Frederica sat on Alice's other side. "You have the body of a goddess, Jeanette," she said. "I swear you become more goddess-like with the birth of each of your children. If you have any more, we'll have to ask Henry to erect a temple in your honor."

"How is the baby, Jeanette?" Alice asked.

"My Henrietta is a delight," Jeanette said. "The easiest confinement I've ever experienced, hardly any pains at all. All I had to do was sneeze, and she slid out."

Alice choked on her brandy which stung in her nose.

"Jeanette!" Frederica chided.

Jeanette laughed. "I always forget my manners when among my best friends. Forgive me, Alice, I hope you'll take that as the compliment it's meant to be. I love my sons to distraction, but I swear boys give their mothers more trouble in the womb than girls."

"What do you wish for, Alice, when your time comes?" Frederica asked. "A boy or a girl?"

"I–I haven't really considered it," Alice said.

"Ross will want a son," Jeanette said. "In much the same way a duke needs an heir, a businessman wants sons to follow him. My poor papa was cursed with three daughters and taught us to learn the skills of the boardroom rather than those of the parlor." She gave Alice a mischievous smile. "As a consequence, none of us grew up to be ladies. Henry despairs of my behavior to this day."

"Henry wouldn't have you any other way," Frederica laughed. She took Alice's hand. "You'll make a wonderful mother when your time comes."

"You flatter me."

"It's not flattery if it's the truth," Jeanette said. "My sister Jane is forever singing your praises, saying how the children at Mrs. Taylor's cling to your skirts whenever you visit them."

"They're just children, Jeanette," Alice said. "They know nothing."

"On the contrary, they know everything. Children possess remarkable insight, which is eroded as they enter adulthood. From what Jane says, you were born to be a mother. I look forward to the day when you present us with your child, be it a son or a daughter.

Alice smiled and swallowed back the tears which threatened to form. Choice of gender was a luxury she could not afford when she spent each night alone in a cold bed.

CHAPTER THIRTY-SEVEN

ROSS STROLLED ALONGSIDE the Serpentine, his wife on his arm. As usual, she cradled her dog in her free arm. He'd once thought the animal ridiculous and inane, but he now saw Monty for what he was, a companion who would never hurt her, never betray her.

She had another, if only she could learn to trust him.

Amelia clutched his free hand, a spring in her footsteps as they drew closer to the water's edge.

"Will we see swans today, Papa?"

"No..." Alice whispered. But she wasn't looking at Amelia. She stared straight ahead at a couple walking toward them.

A man and a woman, arm in arm. They bore the stiff demeanor of a society couple who ventured into the park to be seen, rather than to enjoy their surroundings. They directed their gaze over Ross's head, noses in the air as if they assumed anyone they encountered was unworthy of their notice.

"Ross..."

Alice's voice betrayed her anguish on seeing her father.

The couple stopped before them, and Ross gave a stiff bow.

"Lord de Grecy."

The viscount wrinkled his nose and glanced at his daughter.

"What's this?" he asked, "a family outing?"

At all costs, he must preserve his wife from her father's scorn. "Alice, go and look for the swans," he said. "Take Amelia with you."

She hesitated, and he pushed her toward the water.

"Do as I say, Alice."

De Grecy's face wrinkled into a sneer. "Still having trouble disciplining her, Trelawney? You should take a firm hand to her. If you're man enough."

"That's your daughter you're speaking of, de Grecy," Ross said. "You should have more respect."

"Respect!" de Grecy scoffed. "I've never heard of anything so preposterous. A woman is the property of her husband, not the other way 'round."

"I'll not force my wife to do anything she doesn't wish to," Ross said. "Can you say the same, de Grecy, or do you prefer a biddable slave for a wife?"

The woman on de Grecy's arm drew in a sharp breath. "Well, really!"

A passing couple stopped, doubtless eager to watch the entertainment. Another couple joined them, and Ross recognized Dominic Hartford with Kitty on his arm.

"You've insulted me and my wife," de Grecy sneered, "but I never thought you were a real man."

"What, because I'll not take my wife unwilling?" Ross asked. "That makes me more of a man than you'll ever be. A man's strength is not determined by brute force. He must use his strength wisely and should never treat a human being, a wife, servant, or employee, as a possession. Alice is not a possession. She's a brave, formidable woman. You'll never understand or appreciate her, and for that, you have my pity."

"How dare you!" De Grecy raised his cane.

"Papa!" Amelia let out a cry, and Alice pulled the child behind her as if to protect her from de Grecy's hatred.

De Grecy swung his cane, but Ross caught it with his hand and gripped it.

"Give it back," de Grecy hissed. "Give it back, or I swear to God,

I'll strike you!"

"After you insulted my wife?"

"What, that worthless creature?"

"Worthless?" Ross cried, anger boiling in his gut. "She's worth a thousand of you!"

"Then you're a damned fool, and she's a madwoman!"

Ross fisted his hand and smashed it in de Grecy's face. De Grecy staggered back with a roar of anger, holding his nose.

"I'll have you shot for that, Trelawney!"

"Try it," Ross said, raising his fists. "I'd take much pleasure from teaching you a lesson in respect."

"Ross, no!" Alice's voice sliced through the fog of anger clouding his mind, and he pulled back.

"Why stop, Trelawney? Are you a coward?" de Grecy sneered.

Ross shook his head. "Never. You deserve a good pummeling, de Grecy, but I'll leave you alone. Not because it's what you deserve, but it's because my wife has asked it of me."

"I'll have you arrested! I'll have you thrown out of Whites!"

Ross let out a laugh. "You think I care for membership of a gentlemen's club over my wife? You cannot hurt what I value, de Grecy."

"What about your business?" de Grecy asked. "In a society where reputation is everything, a word or two in the wrong ear could destroy your livelihood."

"You're a fool and a coward!" Ross cried. "I care not what you do. If all you're capable of damaging is my income and position in society, then you cannot touch me. If I have to live as a pauper, I'd be a happy man as long as I have the one thing I value. My family. You're a fool for not realizing that in your daughter you had the greatest treasure in the world."

De Grecy cast a glance at Alice, who still clutched her dog under one arm and held Amelia tightly with the other.

"My daughter is nothing," de Grecy said. "A disgrace to my name."

"You're wrong," Ross said. "She's a better person than you could ever be. She's weathered battles and atrocities which would have felled the strongest man and emerged from it without a shred of bitterness. In my view, that makes her the strongest person I know."

He took a step closer to de Grecy, and the older man shrank back, fear in his eyes.

"And I will devote my life to her," Ross said. "I shall give her the safety and security she's been denied all her life. I will be strong for her, as she is strong for me. And I'll never force or compel her to do anything she has no wish to. I will never ask her to relinquish control over her destiny."

"You can do nothing if I have you arrested," de Grecy snarled.

A laugh erupted from behind de Grecy as Dominic moved closer.

"Viscount Hartford," de Grecy said. He glanced at Kitty and curled his lip in distaste.

"What seems to be the problem?" Dominic asked.

"You must have seen this—this ruffian strike me!"

"On the contrary," Dominic said. "I saw a man defend himself against an unprovoked attack. If anyone deserves to be arrested, it's you. But I can seek a second opinion. If you wish it. My excellent friend, Earl Stiles, is a magistrate, and he'd consider it a privilege to look into the matter. Perhaps we might call on him to discuss it?"

Dominic winked at Ross. Defeated, de Grecy muttered a curse, took his wife's arm, and strode past them.

"I suppose I should thank you, Hartford," Ross said.

Dominic shook his head. "It was nothing. I believe I owe you—and your wife—much." He nodded to Alice. "Your servant, ma'am."

Alice glanced at Ross. "May we resume our walk now?"

"Of course, my love," Ross said. "We've still to find those swans."

She lifted her lips into a smile, and they continued their walk after bidding Dominic good day. Amelia's laughter warmed the air as she spotted two swans gliding along the water, and she grasped Alice's hand, begging her to accompany her. After handing Monty to Ross, Alice followed the child, laughing at her enthusiasm. As she glanced back at Ross, he could swear he saw a glimmer of trust in her eyes.

CHAPTER THIRTY-EIGHT

"Did you enjoy the ragout, Alice?"

Alice looked up as the footman removed her empty plate. Her husband sat across the table, watching her carefully, his eyes pale in the candlelight.

"It was delicious, thank you," she said. "My favorite."

He leaned back and smiled. She reached for her glass and sipped her wine.

The footman reappeared and placed a tall glass in front of her.

"Your sorbet ma'am."

She leaned forward, and an exotic scent filled her nostrils.

"Orange."

"If I recall, you were rather partial to an orange, once." The rich timbre of his voice resonated in her soul and brought forth a memory of happier times.

It was the memory of an eager suitor presenting a young debutante with an offering with which to woo her. An orange, fresh from Spain, its rich, tangy aroma had warmed her blood and softened her heart. It had set him apart from the other young men with eager eyes on her fortune, who'd tried to court her with jewels and adornments, mere bait to hook her with in order to secure her dowry.

But one young man had stood apart from the rest. Ridiculed by Papa for having secured his fortune through trade, for having no name of consequence, yet he was the only one who had not viewed her as a business acquisition.

In the end, it was his simple offering of a fresh orange which had secured her heart. The next day, she'd accepted his offer of marriage and they had enjoyed four days' blissful courtship.

Until Papa had forced her to reject him and set her on the path to destruction.

"Do you like it?" His voice returned her to the present. The contempt she'd seen in his eyes the day she rejected him had been replaced by the tenderness which had captured her heart.

She dipped her spoon in and lifted it to her mouth, relishing the taste which burst on her tongue. "Delicious."

He smiled. "I've not indulged in an orange since we last ate it together. Perhaps my enjoyment is all the greater for such a long abstention."

Her body responded to him, and a pulse of longing rippled through her.

He set his spoon down and pushed his empty glass away. "Have you finished, my dear?"

She nodded and rose from her seat.

"Then I shall retire to my port and bid you goodnight."

He held his hand out, and she moved toward him, propelled by longing. She took his hand and warm, strong fingers curled around her wrist.

What had he said? That he'd never take anything which she was unwilling to give. She tipped her face up to him and offered her lips, a gesture of her free will, however small.

He cupped her face and caressed her skin with his thumb. His lips brushed against her forehead, and she closed her eyes, her body humming in anticipation of the blissful release to come…

But he moved away. "I trust you'll sleep well, my love," he said. "I shall see you in the morning."

He issued a stiff bow, then retreated out of the room, leaving her alone.

⋙✦⋘

AFTER DISMISSING HER maid, Alice slipped into her bed. The candle flame flickered as the air moved, casting shadows across the chamber. As per her instructions, Lizzie had left her door ajar. She drew her knees to her chest and waited.

What other reason would he have had for ensuring tonight's supper consisted of all her favorites? Though fear still threatened to paralyze her, she could conquer it in the knowledge that the reward would be all the sweeter, the thrill of his touch, the sweet sensations in her body...

As footsteps approached, she held her breath. He could not fail to notice her open door—an invitation, however small.

A shadow appeared near the doorframe. The candlelight reflecting off the door handle glimmered as the handle moved. Her body tightened in anticipation, palms slick with sweat, the only sounds the ticking of a distant clock, almost completely obscured by the heartbeat in her ears.

The handle moved again, then the door closed with a click and the light disappeared. The footsteps faded into the distance.

He didn't want her.

He'd promised not to take her unwilling. Had he, in fact, meant that he had no wish to take her at all?

She climbed out of bed, fighting the demons in her mind which taunted her, whispering of the flaws which rendered her undesirable. Picking up the candle, she crossed the floor and slipped out into the corridor. At the far end, a thin shaft of light stretched across the floor, the beam occasionally broken by shadows as he moved about in his chamber.

Though she could withstand physical pain, the heartbreak of rejection threatened to cow her. But she gritted her teeth to maintain her resolve, approached the door, and knocked.

It opened to reveal her husband half-dressed, shirt open to the waist. Gray eyes widened in surprise. "Alice, have you been taken ill?"

"No."

"Then why have you come?"

She met his gaze, laying her soul bare to him. Understanding flashed in his eyes, and he shook his head.

"Alice, I can't…"

She lowered her gaze. "Have I been rendered so foul that you can never touch me, Ross? Do I disgust you that much?"

She closed her eyes to shut out his revulsion. "Forgive me for troubling you. Goodnight."

"Stay."

She froze at the soft command. A hand cupped her chin and gently, but firmly, coaxed her head up.

"Look at me, Alice."

Unable to conquer the shame, she shook her head.

"Open your eyes."

He pulled her to him, and she opened her eyes and looked up into a deep gray ocean. A silver flame shone from within, pulsing to a rhythm of desire and pure need.

"Alice, I want nothing more than to make love to you," he said, his voice hoarse, "but I cannot risk your peace of mind by taking what I want."

"What if *I* were to risk it?" she asked. "If I were to give myself freely to you?"

"Do you know what you're asking?"

"I do."

"Are you not afraid?"

"Yes," she said. "I'm sorely afraid. But true happiness cannot be achieved without facing one's fears. And I am willing, Ross, so willing."

"But the last time, we..." He broke off, pain and guilt in his expression.

She lifted her hand to his lips to silence him. "The last time was in haste," she said, "a necessity. But I have no wish for that to be the only memory I have of our union. I want to understand the pleasures a man and woman can share. I want you to teach me, Ross, so that I forget my past. Help me to become whole again."

Without another word, he took her hand and pulled her into his chamber.

CHAPTER THIRTY-NINE

ALICE LOOKED AROUND her husband's chamber. Everywhere she saw dark, masculine colors, no evidence of femininity, as if a confirmed bachelor resided here.

It was a room fashioned for a lonely man.

A generous bed almost filled the room. Four carved posts supported a large canopy, draped in dark green material. Wooden panels adorned the walls, broken by the occasional tapestry depicting hunting scenes in dark shades of blue and green punctuated by the occasional thread of gold. Thick, dark curtains hung from floor to ceiling, obliterating the night outside. To one side a fireplace stretched almost the entire width of the room. A fire rippled and glowed, bathing the room in a warm light, silhouetting the body of the man before her.

He took her hand and pulled her further into the room. A shiver rippled through her as if cold fingers brushed against her skin. She tensed, as if Roderick's ghost threatened to leap from the flames at any moment.

"Are you frightened, Alice?"

Unable to hide the truth from him, she nodded and looked down.

"No, Alice." His voice, soft but firm, seemed to vibrate through her bones, willing her body to obey.

"Eyes on me."

She looked up.

"That's better." He reached behind him until he found what he sought—a vase of flowers on a table beside the fireplace. Then he held out his offering to her.

A single rose.

"Take it," he whispered.

She curled her fingers round the stem and lifted the bloom to her lips, breathing in the faint perfume.

"The rose is you, Alice."

"I don't understand."

He traced the outline of the bloom, running a fingertip around the edge of a petal.

"Each petal represents a token of your faith in me," he said. "I won't take anything that you are not willing to give freely. With each step I take tonight, you must give me your consent in the form of a petal. If you wish me to stop, you can simply cease to give me any more petals."

"And when there are no petals left to give?"

He caressed the rose, his nostrils flared as he worshipped the curved forms of the flower. A shiver rippled over her skin as if she could feel his fingertips on her, and she drew in a sharp breath as desire pulsed deep within her.

Though his eyes darkened, the fire in them seemed to glow more brightly, pulsing to a rhythm in unison with the tremors in her body.

"Then, and only then, will you be wholly mine."

The soft aroma of the rose mingled with another scent, the spicy, musky scent of man. His chest rose and fell in a soft sigh, and his eyes shimmered with raw, male desire.

"Shall we begin?"

"Yes," she whispered.

"May I unlace your gown?"

She nodded. With his gaze fixed on her, he remained motionless, as if he waited for her to emerge from the shadows. She plucked a petal and held it out to him, her hand trembling. His mouth curled into a smile as he took it, and her breath quickened as he brushed his fingers against her own.

He caressed her chin, then followed a path down her neck to the top of her nightgown where he traced the outline until he reached the laces. Deftly, he pulled them free, caressing her skin with his knuckles until her gown lay open at the front. He lowered his gaze to her breasts, and his lips parted as he drew in a sharp breath, and the petal fluttered to the floor.

"My God, Alice," he whispered, his voice hoarse. "You're beautiful."

Her nipples puckered under his scrutiny, but despite the hunger blazing in his eyes, he made no move. At length, he sighed, lifting his gaze slowly, as if reluctant to look away from her breasts.

"May I kiss you?"

She plucked another petal. He took it and brushed his lips against hers. She parted her lips to invite him in, but he drew back.

"Ross…" she whispered.

"My love?"

"Kiss me."

He lowered his mouth to hers again, and soft, firm lips claimed her. His tongue probed against the seam of her lips and willingly, she welcomed him in, surrendering to the taste of him.

A low sigh rumbled in his chest, and he deepened the kiss. She pulled him closer, burying her hands in his thick, silken hair as he devoured her mouth. With a low growl, he nipped her lips, then followed a path along her chin, leaving a trail of open-mouthed kisses, until he nuzzled her ear and whispered hoarsely. "May I undress you?"

His voice reverberated in her mind, sending a thrill through her body. She closed her eyes and took a deep breath to dissipate the fog of need, then pulled off another petal. A hand closed around hers and claimed the petal before letting it fall to the floor. Eager, tender fingers tugged at the fastenings of her gown, opening it fully. A burning need swelled within her, and she moved toward him until her nipples brushed against his open shirt.

"Alice..." He sighed in desperation. "God save me, Alice, I want you so much I could die from it!"

He reached for her breast, then curled his fingers into a fist and drew back. A whimper bubbled in his throat, and his body shook as if he fought to control a savage beast within him.

Slowly, he held his hand out to her.

"Will you join me in my bed?"

A thrill rippled through her at the deep notes of need in his voice, and she pulled her nightgown fully open and let it fall to the floor. He closed his eyes and let out a low groan. She plucked another petal and placed it in his palm. He closed his fingers around it.

He opened his eyes once more and let the petal float to the floor, releasing a sweet aroma.

She took his hand, and he laced his fingers in hers and drew her to the bed. He sat on the edge and pulled her onto his lap, turning her gently round until she faced outward, her back to him.

"Ross..." A shiver of fear rippled through her.

"No, my love." His hot breath tickled her neck. "Listen to my voice, Alice. I'm here with you."

His words anchored her to the present, and she relaxed against him. His voice rumbled in her ear. "You have no idea how long I've dreamed of this moment, Alice. To have you naked in my arms."

Her longing only increased.

His chest expanded against her as he drew in a long, lingering breath. "Ah." His voice tickled against the sensitive skin at the base of her neck. "I can smell your need." He circled an arm around her waist and held her close. "Do you ache for me as much as I ache for you?"

She tightened her grip on the rose and winced as a thorn pricked her fingers. With his free hand, he caressed the skin of her neck, peppering nibbling kisses behind her ear. Soft whispered words of desire coursed through her mind as he nuzzled her skin. He traced a path along her body, across her belly, his fingers taking light, dancing steps toward her thighs. Then they stopped, and he rested his palm on her thigh, tantalizingly out of reach of the secret place where her body ached the most for him.

He remained still, his heartbeat thudding against her body. The tide of need grew within her, and she parted her thighs to ease the longing where the heat threatened to explode into a flame.

"May I touch you, Alice?"

She ripped another petal free. He held it between his fingers, making no move until a cry of need escaped her lips. His mouth curled into a smile against her skin, and he traced a circle on her thigh with the petal. The delicate touch sent a shiver through her. Her breath grew ragged as she squirmed, her body begging him to ease the agony which burned in her core.

"Ross…"

"You must learn to be patient, my love." His voice sent a wicked thrill through her. "Remember what I said. Your consent must be given freely."

He traced the petal across her belly. "You must be willing…"

He moved higher, toward her breasts which ached for his touch.

"Without fear…"

Her skin tingled as the edge of the petal traced the outline of her breasts.

"Eager…"

A mewing cry burst from her lips as the petal brushed against the tip of her nipple.

"Ready…."

The petal slipped from his grasp.

"And mine…"

A warm hand claimed her breast, squeezing, caressing. She let out a low cry at the surge of moisture between her legs.

"You have the most beautiful breasts," he whispered. "Soft and shapely. Fashioned perfectly to fit my hands." He ran his thumb across her breast, teasing the pleasures from her.

"May I claim your breasts as mine, Alice?"

She nodded.

"Ah..." he sighed, "...if only I could keep you here, naked, in my bed for eternity." He drew in a deep breath and the source of his own need pulsed, hot and hard, against her back. "If only I could have you here waiting for me day and night. I would never have need of anything mortal again."

He moved his hand away, and she arched her back, offering her breasts to him.

"What do you want, Alice?"

Her voice caught in her throat, and she let a tiny gasp.

"Tell me what you want."

"I want..."

"Tell me, Alice," he whispered. "There's nothing so arousing for a man to hear what his woman needs from her own lips."

"I–I want you to touch me."

He placed his hand on her belly.

"Like this?"

She parted her thighs, willing him to touch her where the need burned.

"Or perhaps this?" He moved his hand to her hip.

"No!" She shifted her legs further apart. "Ross, please! I cannot bear it!"

He inched his hand lower. She reached out and clawed at his arm, and the rose slipped from her hand. "Ross!"

"Tell me what you want," he whispered. "Ask, and it shall be yours."

"Touch me, Ross."

"Tell me again."

"Please!" Pure need overcame her shame, and she writhed against his body. The sensation of pleasure increased as she moved against his restraining arm, the thrill of placing herself at his mercy.

He let out a low growl, then dipped his hand between her thighs. Her body jerked as the flame pulsed through her and she arched her back, chasing the pleasure which increased with each slick movement of his expert fingers. For a moment, he stilled, and she lifted her hips, offering herself, pleading with her body. Then he plunged his finger inside her, and her body shattered.

She threw back her head and cried out, releasing the raw need which had swelled within her, a need borne of years of waiting, years of suffering while she had thought she'd cast away the man she loved. The pleasure she had only dreamed of became a reality—devouring her, consuming her.

At last, the wave of pleasure receded, and she fell back against him, taking comfort from the solidity of his body.

Soft words of love caressed her mind while she clung to him. She shifted position, and he let out a strangled groan, his body hard and ready.

He was her husband. His very bones vibrated with need, a need no living man could conquer.

Yet, he remained still. He was waiting for her invitation.

She tugged at his arm, and he released his grip on her. When she turned to face him, his eyes were closed, the tendons in his neck bulging as if he struggled to fight a battle in his mind.

"May I touch you, Ross?"

His breath caught in his throat, and he opened his eyes, the pupils dilated so they looked black in the firelight. He lowered his gaze to her body, and she tipped her head forward, letting her hair tumble over her stomach to hide the scars.

"No, Alice." He swept her hair aside. "Never hide yourself from me. Every part of you is beautiful. To me, you are perfect."

He lifted a lock of her hair to his face and breathed in, then he let out a low growl of agony. The source of his pain bulged in his breeches, and he gritted his teeth. The desire to ease his pain overcame her fear of rejection, and she took his hand.

"Ross," she whispered. "May I touch you?"

He sighed and said nothing.

Then she understood… She touched his forehead with the rose, tracing the outline of his face.

"Ahh…"

His lips parted as she followed a path down his neck to his chest, tracing the outline of his muscles. His knuckles whitened as he fisted the sheets in his hands, his body shaking.

"Alice," he said through gritted teeth. "How you torment me!"

"What do you wish, husband?"

"I cannot hold on…"

She sat back, and he let out a groan of frustration.

She kissed the rose, then held it out to him.

His eyes widened, and he lifted his eyebrows in question.

"Take it," she said. "It's yours."

He shook his head.

"It's not mine to take, Alice."

"But it's mine to give." Her hand trembled. "And I give it to you here and now, freely and completely."

He curled his hand around hers.

"I will cherish your gift."

"I know."

He plucked the rose out of her hand and placed it on the bedsheet. She lay back on the bed, offering him her body and her trust.

He unbuttoned his breeches, and his manhood sprang free, hard and ready. The muscles of his chest rippled with each movement as he crawled toward her.

A spike of fear surged within her, and she closed her eyes.

"No," he growled, his voice a deep rumble, willing her body to obey. "Eyes on me."

They locked gazes as he moved closer until he covered her body with his.

With his knee, he nudged her thighs apart, then lowered his head and captured her mouth.

"Alice…" he groaned. "My Alice, I always knew you would be my undoing."

His hardness pulsed against her thigh. She parted her legs, and he brushed against her center. She tensed, a distant memory of pain seeping into her consciousness.

"No, my love," he whispered. "You're ready for me. There will be no pain. Only pleasure."

He thrust into her, and a ripple of ecstasy coursed through her. He withdrew, then plunged in again, and she let out a gasp as the exquisite pleasure increased, pulsing deep within her.

"Ross…"

"Yes, my love," he said, his voice a hoarse whisper. "Say my name again." He withdrew once more then pumped his hips.

"Ross!"

"Yes," he growled. "Yes, my love. Tonight you shall scream my name so none shall ever doubt again that you were meant to be mine."

With a final thrust, he roared her name, his voice breaking, and he collapsed onto her, his body spent. He buried his face in her neck, nuzzling against her skin, whispering her name. Exquisite aftershocks rippled through her until eventually they grew still, their bodies molded together.

"My Alice…"

With the crackle of the fire and the deep ticking of the clock in her ears, she drifted into a contented sleep.

CHAPTER FORTY

A LICE CLASPED HER hands together to temper the apprehension shivering through her. She had expelled her breakfast again, and Ross had sent for Doctor McIver, pleading with her to indulge him this one time. Now, after an examination, she had given Ross permission to speak to the doctor, and her heart hammered at the prospect of her diagnosis.

As her gaze settled on the fireplace, the memory of her husband's body elicited a smile. That morning he had crossed the floor naked to tend to the fire, the muscles in his legs rippling with each step. Her gaze had followed the line of his back as it curved gently toward the base where two dimples cast tiny shadows in his flesh just above his firm buttocks.

Footsteps approached, and Ross opened the door, a broad smile on his face, one hand behind his back.

"Where's the doctor?"

"I've sent him home."

"Why? Is there something wrong?"

"On the contrary, my love. There's nothing wrong at all."

He brought his hand to the front. In it, he held a single white rose.

"I don't understand."

He glanced toward the vase beside her bed where she had placed four red roses the day before.

"You're with child."

"Pregnant?"

"Yes," he said, "and you very likely were pregnant when McIver first came to see you."

"But, I can't be. Not after Roderick…"

He knelt at her feet and handed the flower to her. "Let us not speak of the past. The good doctor has assured me your body is sound and that there's every chance you'll carry your child to full term." He took her hand and kissed it. "But I have asked him to indulge my insistence that you rest."

He took her hands, his eyes soft and pleading. "I will ask that you grant me this request, which I do out of love."

The initial joy at the prospect of a child surrendered to the fear and she turned away.

"No, Alice," the tender overtones of his voice resonated through her heart. "You must never turn from me. I know you're frightened. I can feel it. But I will do everything in my power to keep you and our child safe."

He moved closer until his soft breath caressed her skin.

"Let me banish your fears forever, my love. Let me collect the pieces of your soul and bind them with mine. Let me fulfill my destiny, Alice, and mend your broken heart."

"Ross…"

He drew her into his arms, and his body shuddered as he held her close.

"I am also afraid," he whispered, "though only now do I understand where my true fear lies."

"What does a man have to be afraid of, Ross?"

"My sex does not render me immune from fear or weakness," he said. "I rather think it makes me more susceptible to it. A man can fear many things, though he'll refuse to admit it, even to himself."

He placed a light kiss on her forehead. "But if I am to ask honesty from you, my love, then I must also give it freely. My greatest fear is failure. But over the years, I've come to understand that some failures are easier to bear than others."

He brushed his knuckles along her chin.

"When I was growing up, I defined failure as not measuring up to my father's standards, not succeeding in my business. But I now know that only one thing could ever signify failure to me. Shall I tell you what that is, Alice?"

She lifted her hand and placed it over his. His skin was cold, and she ran her thumb over the back of his hand. His eyes narrowed, and he drew in a shuddering breath and then moved closer until their lips almost touched.

"The biggest fear I harbor, dearest Alice, is that I will fail in my endeavors to deserve you."

"Ross..." Her quiet whisper granted him the permission he sought, and he brushed his lips against hers.

His gentleness was her undoing, and hot tears spilled onto her cheeks. He broke the kiss, and a sense of loss tightened her skin, but he clasped her hand and held it to his heart.

"Weak soul that I am, I tried to love my first wife. She claimed a piece of my heart, and I loved her with my body. But my heart, my soul, have only ever belonged to you, dearest Alice. I pledged in that church, before witnesses, before God, that I would cherish and protect you. And I do so again, I pledge myself to you, Alice, to love you until I draw my last breath."

She lifted his hand to her lips.

"Oh, my Alice," he breathed. "Let me spend the rest of my life striving to earn your love."

"You already have it, Ross."

"Then I am, without doubt, the luckiest man in the world."

EPILOGUE

Six months later...

R OSS SHIVERED AS a shrill cry tore through the air.
"Alice!"

A strong hand clasped his shoulder. "Stay where you are, Ross."

"I should be with her, Hawthorne."

"It's not a man's place," Hawthorne said. "Jane's with her."

"She needs her husband, not that hellion!" Ross snarled. "Can't you hear her screams?"

"All confinements come with a good dose of noise, my friend," Hawthorne said. "Women give birth every day."

"Women die every day." Fear churned in his gut like acid.

"You can't think about what happened to Caroline," Hawthorne said. "Think of my Frederica. Three births, the first in difficult circumstances, and she came through wonderfully. Alice is stronger than she looks."

"You heard what McIver said," Ross growled. "The bastard gave me a choice between her and the child! Would he do that if she were not at risk?"

"Doctors ask that question all the time."

Footsteps approached, and Jane Claybone appeared at the door, hair unkempt, tears glistening in her eyes.

"Dear God!" Ross leapt to his feet.

"You have a son."

"What of my wife!"

She nodded. "A little tired, but she's well."

He sprinted past her and, taking the stairs two at a time, ran to his wife's chamber and burst through the door.

Alice lay on the bed, face pale, the toll of bringing their child in the world evident in the dark rings under her eyelids. Her chest rose and fell in a sigh, and she opened her eyes, and recognition sparkled in their depths. "Ross."

She held her arms out, and he lifted her into a sitting position.

"My love, are you well?"

"Yes, but first, you must meet your son." She nodded toward the corner of the room.

Doctor McIver stood, holding a bundle in his arms, a broad smile on his face.

"What did I promise you? A healthy wife and a lusty bairn. Here, take him."

Before Ross could protest, the doctor dropped the child into his arms—the small being which had been the source of so much pain to his beloved wife.

But also, the great happiness. Alice's face glowed with joy. The baby opened his eyes, and Ross placed a kiss on his forehead.

"Our son." He met Alice's gaze. "And my wonderful wife. I have a gift for you in the garden. When you are well, I'll show you."

Alice glanced at the doctor. "May I get up now?"

The doctor shook his head. "You've had a difficult birth, Mrs. Trelawney. I'd advise you to rest."

"Please!" Fear glimmered in her eyes. It was the fear which, though she had conquered, still visited her at night in her dreams. The fear of incarceration. She had conquered it, but during the latter stages of her confinement, when she'd been kept in her chamber for days, the fear had returned.

"I need air and light," she said.

"Not outside."

"The orangery, then?" Ross asked.

"Very well," the doctor said, "but you must take the greatest care of her."

"I intend to," Ross said. "For the rest of my days."

He handed the baby to his mother, and she cradled him, the purest love and devotion in her expression, then he placed a blanket round her shoulders, scooped her into his arms, and carried her into the orangey and placed her in a wicker chair facing the garden.

"Amelia is anxious to see you," he said, "but I want to share this moment with you first."

"What moment?"

"Look out the window."

The orangery overlooked the garden. The front half contained a shrubbery. Lavender bushes formed a neat, regimented row, leading to a birdbath in the center in which a group of starlings chattered at each other, throwing up droplets of water with their wings. Behind it, a trimmed box hedge led to the back of the garden where a tall row of trees obscured the houses beyond.

"What am I looking for?" she asked.

"See that box hedge near the back? I had it fashioned into the shape of a swan to remind you of the swans in the park. While you're resting at home, I have brought the park to you."

"Thank you."

"Do you know why else I had my gardener shape it into a swan?" he asked. "It's because swans mate for life. The swan is me, for I have only ever had one true mate, only ever loved one woman."

He knelt beside her and took her hand, caressing her fingers.

"I have one more gift for you, my love, if you'll permit me the indulgence."

He pointed out of the windows. In front of the birdbath stood four shrubs. The ground beneath them had been freshly dug, a deep, rich brown standing out against the grass. The shrubs themselves looked quite unremarkable, but the glossy dark green leaves were unmistakable. They concealed stems with sharp thorns intended to protect the fragile blooms which would brighten the garden with color and sweeten the air with their fragrant aroma.

"They're roses," Alice said.

"Four of them," Ross replied. "One for each of your lost children. You have no need to carry four roses with you. Your children have a home here, a memorial which will reside in the garden forever."

"Oh, Ross!"

He lifted her hand to his lips and kissed it. "I cannot take all the credit," he said. "Amelia helped me. She wanted her brothers and sisters to be a part of our family. She'll always remember Caroline, but she told me that *you're* her mama, now. She has been so anxious to see you. May I permit her to?"

"Of course!"

He called out and issued an order to the footman who arrived. Shortly afterward, he returned with Amelia who held Monty in her arms.

The child moved forward, uncertainty clouding her features.

Alice reached out a hand to her and smiled. "I see Montague has found himself a protector."

"Oh, yes!" Amelia said. "I've been feeding him sweetmeats just like you showed me." A ripple of uncertainty crossed her face. "Have I done wrong? You said I should not give him too many."

"Sometimes one is deserving of a few extra treats, Amelia," she said. "I'll wager Monty and you have earned more than a few."

Amelia's expression showed uncertainty. "I'm sorry I said all those horrible things to you."

Alice nodded. "It doesn't matter, Amelia. I understand."

"Promise me you'll never leave?"

"You have my word."

"Am I…" The child hesitated and colored before glancing at Ross. Still kneeling at Alice's feet, he smiled and nodded his encouragement. "Am I your daughter?"

Alice's took her hand. "You always have been," she said, "and you have a brother now, just like you've always wanted."

"I wanted a brother or sister so badly, but I didn't want to lose you, Mama Alice, neither did Papa. He said so."

Amelia looked up at him. "Tell her, Papa," she said, pride in her voice. "Tell her what you said to the doctor."

He rose to his feet and sighed.

"Well, if you won't, I shall! Papa said he'd put a bullet through the doctor's heart if you came to harm."

"Ross!" Alice clutched the baby to her breast.

He took her hand. "Do you doubt it, my love? You are my world, and I am lost without you. You and Amelia make me complete. And now, you have given me a son. I would never have dreamed I could be so happy."

Ross kissed his wife. They watched the perfect sunset together as a true family. It marked the end of today, but the beginning of all the days to come.

The End

About the Author

Emily Royal grew up in Sussex, England, and has devoured romantic novels for as long as she can remember. A mathematician at heart, Emily has worked in financial services for over twenty years. She indulged in her love of writing after she moved to Scotland, where she lives with her husband, teenage daughters and menagerie of rescue pets including Twinkle, an attention-seeking boa constrictor.

She has a passion for both reading and writing romance with a weakness for Regency rakes, Highland heroes, and Medieval knights. Persuasion is one of her all-time favorite novels which she reads several times each year and she is fortunate enough to live within sight of a Medieval palace.

When not writing, Emily enjoys playing the piano, hiking, and painting landscapes, particularly the Highlands. One of her ambitions is to paint, as well as climb, every mountain in Scotland.

Follow Emily Royal:

Website: www.emroyal.com
Facebook: facebook.com/eroyalauthor
Twitter: twitter.com/eroyalauthor
Newsletter signup: mailchi.mp/e5806720bfe0/emilyroyalauthor
Goodreads: goodreads.com/author/show/14834886.Emily_Royal

Made in the USA
Middletown, DE
07 March 2020